Angela Thirkell

Angela Thirkell, granddaughter of Edward Burne-Jones, was born in London in 1890. At the age of twenty-eight she moved to Melbourne, Australia where she became involved in broadcasting and was a frequent contributor to the British periodicals. Mrs. Thirkell did not begin writing novels until her return to Britain in 1930; then, for the rest of her life, she produced a new book almost every year. Her stylish prose and deft portrayal of the human comedy in the imaginary county of Barsetshire have amused readers for decades. She died in 1961, just before her seventy-first birthday.

Mrs. Thirkell . . . has a great flair for lampooning, in the deftest possible way, social customs and certain types of people . . . [Her] brilliant, easy, conversational . . . style carries the reader along in a glow of pleasure.

—*Saturday Review of Literature*

The charm is in the light touch, the delicate probing of character and sparkle of wit.

—*New York Herald Tribune*

There's no stopping after just one novel.

—*Publishers Weekly*

ANKLE DEEP

By the Same Author

Other books by Angela Thirkell

August Folly
Before Lunch
The Brandons
Cheerfulness Breaks In
Close Quarters
Coronation Summer
County Chronicle
The Demon in the House
A Double Affair
Duke's Daughter
Enter Sir Robert
The Grateful Sparrow
Growing Up
Happy Returns
The Headmistress
High Rising
Jutland Cottage
Love Among the Ruins
Love at All Ages
Marling Hall
Miss Bunting
Never Too Late
Northbridge Rectory
The Old Bank House
Peace Breaks Out
Pomfret Towers
Private Enterprise
Summer Half
O, These Men, These Men
Three Houses
Three Score and Ten
What Did It Mean?
Wild Strawberries

ANKLE DEEP

A Novel by

Angela Thirkell

MOYER BELL

Wakefield, Rhode Island & London

Published by Moyer Bell
This Edition 1996

**LIBRARY OF CONGRESS
CATALOGING-IN-PUBLICATION DATA**

Thirkell, Angela Mackail   Ankle deep

1. Barsetshire (England : Imaginary place)—Fiction.
2. Married people—England—Fiction I. Title.

PR6039.H43A82 1996 96-46714
823'.912—dc20 CIP

ISBN 1-55921-158-X

Cover illustration: *The Brook* by John Singer Sargent

Printed in the United States of America
Distributed in North America by Publishers Group West, P.O. Box 8843, Emeryville CA 94662, 800-788-3123 (in California 510-658-3453).

To
My Father and Mother
from
their loving Angela

CHAPTER I

To find oneself connected with a wrong number on the automatic exchange is so inevitable as not to be at all funny. So, lightly passing over the anger and the politeness of the two subscribers with whom the exchange chose to connect her, and equally passing over the few blasting words which passed between Fanny Turner and the operator whom she had summoned to her assistance, we shall choose to cut in at the moment when Mrs. Howard's parlormaid had gone to tell Mrs. Howard, in a form of speech of which her mistress found it impossible to cure her, that Mrs. Arthur Turner wanted her on the phone.

"Is that you, Fanny?" said a nice voice.

"Yes, dear Mrs. Howard," said Fanny in a nonbutter-melting voice.

Butter would have melted in Fanny's mouth, just as certainly as ginger was hot in it, but Fanny talking to Mrs. Howard, who was old enough to be her mother, was very different from Fanny talking to one of her numerous young men who were perhaps not quite young, but still unmarried, which somehow in itself constitutes youth for a man, though not so markedly for a woman.

"What is it, dear?" asked Mrs. Howard.

"Do you think you and Mr. Howard could come down to us for a week end on the nineteenth?"

"I think so, Fanny. I must ask Will when he comes in and if we can't come I'll let you know."

"That will be lovely. Then I'll expect you both on the nineteenth unless I hear from you."

"That's it, Fanny, we'll come unless I let you know. I'll ring up tonight if we can't come."

"That's splendid. Then I'll expect you if I don't hear."

"Very well, dear. Goodbye for the present, then."

"Goodbye, Mrs. Howard. Oh—Mrs. Howard—"

"Yes, dear?"

"I'll let you know which train if you do come."

"Thanks, dear. I suppose you'll have the children with you as it's holidays?"

It was extraordinary that Mrs. Howard didn't know Fanny better than this. It wasn't that Fanny didn't love her boys, but though she felt sentimental when they went back to their preparatory school—or rather to their preparatory schools, for having a healthy mind in a healthy body apiece, they quarreled so awfully that the harassed head master of their first school had implored Arthur to remove some of them, preferably the twins, and Fanny had taken a short cut to avoid trouble by choosing a separate school for each—she would have felt sentiment of an infuriated kind if their excellent schools had had to close for mumps, or break up a week earlier for measles. Fanny's extremely busy life, which included too many lunches, dinners and theaters to leave her time to give that attention to her family which she would otherwise have wished to give, hardly allowed for resident children, and if Vanna, which was what they all called Arthur's mother since an outburst of caravanning some years before, liked to have her grandchildren during the holidays, who was Fanny that she should presume to interfere? Of course the excessively annoying part, to other wives and mothers, was that Fanny's boys continued to be healthy in body and mind and adored their mother, while her neglected household ran itself with smoothness and economy. This is one of the phenomena that discourage one from pursuing the domestic virtues. The Fannys always get the best of it both ways, just as the painted, brow-plucked, cocktail-swigging young minxes settle down quite as well as their less behaviorist sisters. It is all most annoying.

In any case, Mrs. Howard quite realized Fanny's attitude towards the offspring, and it would be inquiring too much to ask whether she had honestly forgotten for the moment, or was deliberately exercising a slight sarcasm which always came oddly from her. She looked so good, and was such a darling, and so patient and understanding with Mr. Howard who, although also an angel, could be relied upon to be fiendishly trying at times; and yet Fanny, who would brazen it out equally with a duchess or a taxidriver, feared Mrs. Howard as she feared nothing else on earth except the rare moments when Arthur asserted himself. So it was with an apologetic tone which she would certainly never have used to anyone else that she said:

"Well, you see, Mrs. Howard, Vanna hasn't had the children really to herself for ages—"

"Not since last holidays, I suppose," Mrs. Howard's voice put in.

"No, not since last holidays," said Fanny. She infused into this statement a pathos that spoke of an aging grandmother deprived by blindness, deafness, distance and poverty of the sight of adored grandchildren. Though, as a matter of fact, Mrs. Howard knew (and was well aware that Fanny knew that she knew) that the boys spent most of their holidays with Vanna, not to speak of odd Whitsuns, Ascension Days, and other religious school outbreaks, and that Vanna was quite capable of going to the Pole or the Equator at any moment, being quite well off and as full of vitality as her daughter-in-law. So she allowed a moment's chilly silence to reign. Silence on a telephone is even more nervous than in conversation, so Fanny repeated, though without the pathos which she now quite justly felt was wasted:

"No, not since last holidays. Besides, I thought it would be quieter and more amusing for you not to have them at Waterside."

"It was very nice of you to think of me, Fanny," said Mrs. Howard. "Then that's settled: we come unless you hear from me. Goodbye."

Mrs. Howard was evidently afraid of a repetition of their last prolonged sentences about coming unless one heard, for she hung up abruptly.

Fanny lighted another cigarette and rang up the Essex and Southend Bank's head office in the City.

"E. and S. Bank speaking," said a competent female voice.

"Mr. Ensor, please," said Fanny.

"I don't know if he is free," said the competent female voice. "I think he is in conference."

"Not for me," said Fanny truculently. "Tell him it's Mrs. Turner. And look here—you might give us a line where everyone can't listen in. I heard half your typists giggling last time I rang him up."

The competent female voice appeared to see some sense in this, for it effaced itself in favor of a series of whirrs and clicks, which were followed by a male voice. It is now, thanks to the efforts of our lady novelists, next to impossible to describe a man's voice as either deep or attractive without rousing feelings of rage and nausea in every breast, but if there were any manner of conveying these qualities without mentioning them, or even hinting at them, this would be the place to do it.

"Hello," said the male voice.

"Hello," said Fanny.

The male voice, featuring impatience, replied, "Who is it?"

"Me, of course," said Fanny.

"But *who*?" said the male voice.

"Oh, blast you—" began Fanny, and the words seemed to touch a chord, for Mr. Ensor's voice immediately became more human.

"Oh, Fanny," he remarked.

"Yes, Fanny," replied Mrs. Turner, adding with some acerbity, "I know they're all ringing you up all day long, but you might know my voice by now, and anyway I'm married and they're not, so it's all aboveboard."

"Well, lots of them are married too," said Mr. Ensor with some spirit.

"Forward beasts," said Fanny. "Look here, Val, I want you to come down on the nineteenth for the weekend. The Howards are coming and I'll get a charmer for you."

"I'd love to, Fanny," said Mr. Ensor. "But probably I can't get down till late. I've a conference."

"I don't know why you and your telephone girl can't think of different excuses," said Fanny coldly. "She said 'conference,' and I said "Don't be a fool", and she put me on to you at once. People don't have conferences on Saturday afternoons. What is it? Tea and a cinema?"

Mr. Ensor laughed. "Something of that kind, Fanny. Can I make it the 9.15?"

"You can take my invitation or leave it," replied Fanny. "Don't be surprised, though, if the village has gone to bed and you can't get a car. We shan't turn out for you in the middle of the night."

"That'll be all right," said Mr. Ensor.

"Far from right," said Fanny, "if you have to carry your suitcase two miles and wake us up at midnight. I'll tell the village Ford to sit up for you and bring you out."

"Thanks, awfully," said Mr. Ensor.

"Not at all," said Fanny. "Goodbye. Oh—Val—"

"Yes," said Mr. Ensor's voice.

"Do you mind who the charmer is?"

"Not a bit," said Mr. Ensor.

"I'll try to get a good one with heaps of money," said Fanny kindly.

"Trust you to show tact," said Mr. Ensor's pleasant voice and he hung up the receiver.

Fanny hung up her receiver too and giggled. One of her favorite meddlings was to provide a succession of possible brides for Valentine Ensor. It is true that he had already had a singularly unsuccessful marriage and was in no position, even if he had had the wish, to marry again, as he was paying a large allowance to a technically guiltless wife. But it took more than that to keep Fanny from matchmaking. To Valentine's alternate fury and amusement she brought up one young woman after another who seemed to her a suitable person to mend a broken income and a rather less broken heart, but the net result appeared to be a distinct increase in expenditure for the future bridegroom, owing to the number of dinners and dances in which Fanny's well meant efforts landed him. Meanwhile it suited Fanny excellently to have him on her list of young men.

It was now nearly thirty years since Valentine Ensor and Arthur

Turner had met at their public school. Even then Arthur had been a tall, fair, silent boy, absorbed in his one ambition to be a successful surgeon. To this there had been family opposition, as there was a family business which he was expected to carry on, but he went his own way, working fiercely and doggedly, asking for no help. The war he took in his stride, making a considerable reputation for himself. His father had died during the war, leaving him just enough money to live on. Then he met Fanny, who was in full career as a heart breaker, first hated her, then loved her, and finally married her amid universal disapproval which did not in the least affect either of them. Since then he had risen to Harley Street eminence as a surgeon, encouraged by Fanny, who said that it was so much more distinguished to marry a surgeon than a doctor because then he was called Mr.—a chain of reasoning peculiarly her own—and insisted upon Arthur being a specialist even before they could afford it, because one really could not live in a house where the front door bell or the telephone might ring at any moment of the night. Her ambition for Arthur had, however, been thoroughly justified, and by the time we meet him he was high in his profession, and earning enough to gratify every caprice of his adored Fanny.

His mother, having been sufficiently brought to heel, was ready to be taken on again as a valued and useful friend. Fanny's attitude to her mother-in-law was perfect. She adored her, laughed at her escapades, made excellent copy out of them for her lunch parties, found for her the name Vanna which all the grandchildren used, and made use of her in every possible way. Vanna saw through Fanny, was grateful for her affection, and loved having the boys, who had not yet reached the emancipatory stage, to play with.

When Arthur was married Valentine should, according to a long-standing promise, have been his best man, but this was not possible. His family were connected with an old banking business which assured a career for him. He entered it soon after leaving Oxford, and his place was kept for him during the war. His friendship with Arthur appeared to be based on contrasts. He had no near relations who required keeping in their places. His tastes were for people, and many friends, and most decidedly for what Fanny called charmers. So much so, in fact, that Arthur had spent a good deal of time in pulling him out of the various scrapes in which he involved himself. Finally he married, towards the end of the war, a charmer who had every virtue, every grace except that of fidelity. Arthur found the role of confidant to the complaints of both sides more and more difficult, and was much relieved when the bank sent Valentine abroad on their affairs for some years. Abroad, domestic relations became more and more embroiled. Valentine came back with the news that his wife had transferred herself permanently to another man. Against Arthur's strongly-worded advice he let her divorce him, and then paid her an allowance which cramped him considerably. These misfortunes had not, however, in the least affected his taste for charmers, and he danced, flirted and weekended more assiduously than ever, and was surprisingly good at his work. He used Arthur's and Fanny's house in London as a cross between a club and a confessional, and spent with them at Waterside the few weekends which were not dedicated to the houses of the various charmers' parents. On the whole, life was not unkind to him, especially as he was one of the happy people to whom debt is a natural condition.

Fanny reached for her address book and began looking through it for possible charmers. Having turned down one who was pretty but poor, and another who was pretty and rich, but had views about gentlemen with pasts, she was just contemplating an American widow of wealth and charm recently acquired by her, when the telephone bell rang.

"Hello," said Fanny.

"Oh—Fanny—"said Mrs. Howard's voice.

"Oh, Mrs. Howard," said Fanny, "it's not to say you aren't coming?"

"No, not that, but rather worse. Aurea is staying with us."

"Aurea?" asked Fanny.

"My married daughter, you know."

"Oh, *Aurea*," said Fanny, as if that made it quite different. "Arthur's old flame."

"Not in the best taste, Fanny," remarked Mrs. Howard's voice.

"Sorry, Mrs. Howard," said Fanny, "but Arthur did have a tremendous passion for her years ago, didn't he?"

"Before he met you, anyway, Fanny," replied Mrs. Howard. "But what I wanted to say is that Aurea is going back to Canada in May, and Will hates leaving her for the weekend. So I was going to suggest either that we come down later, or that you would let me bring her with us."

Fanny made the mental calculations of a drowning man and answered with enthusiasm:

"I'd love you to bring her, Mrs. Howard. The more the merrier, and I was just looking out for a charmer for Val, and if he falls for Aurea then Arthur will be greenly envious. It ought to be a perfect weekend."

Mrs. Howard laughed very agreeably down the telephone.

"You expect too much, Fanny," said her nice voice. "Aurea is a charmer to her father and me, but after all her children are as old as yours."

"Val likes them at *any* age," Fanny hastened to reassure her.

Mrs. Howard appeared from her silence to be considering this statement.

"Don't take any notice of me, Mrs. Howard," pleaded Fanny. "We'd love to have Aurea, and I want to meet her. I've heard so much about her from Arthur and Vanna. Come down early on the nineteenth—to lunch if you can."

"Very well, dear," said Mrs. Howard, "and thank you very much. Goodbye."

Fanny hung up the receiver and giggled again. She foresaw a delightful opportunity of annoying Valentine. He, according to her plan, was to form a rapid attachment for Aurea, but when he expected to take her out for a walk, or other occupation for two, she was to be given to Arthur, when Valentine would obviously have to flirt with Fanny. As they both had excellent technique, it would be fun for Fanny, and if Valentine were annoyed, his position as guest would forbid him to show it, at any rate before the Howards. As for Arthur, whom Fanny genuinely adored in spite of the way she kept her hand in with her cavaliers, it would be delightful to give him the pleasure of conversation with the love of his youth. His technique was poor, but at least he should have the opportunity.

Filled with these pleasant thoughts Fanny took up the telephone again and found her mother-in-law at home.

"Good morning, Vanna darling," she began. "I suppose it's all right about the boys coming to you on Thursday."

"Of course it is," answered Vanna's voice—not at all the voice of a mother-in-law. "Are you and Arthur very busy these holidays?"

"Frightfully busy, darling," said Fanny, "and full up every weekend. Oh, Vanna, I wanted to ask you something. Mr. and Mrs. Howard are coming on the nineteenth and they are bringing their daughter—Aurea—you know—the one Arthur used to rave about. Do you know what her name is? Her married name, I mean? I never thought of it till Mrs. Howard had rung off, and then it seemed too odd to ring up again and say, "Pardon me, but has your daughter a name?" Don't say you can't tell me."

"Aurea Howard's name," mused Vanna's voice. "I must have heard it. I know, Palgrave."

Fanny scrawled the name in the spidery handwriting which is produced by writing with one hand on a pad which won't keep quiet, while the other hand is holding the telephone.

"Any more details?" she asked as he scrawled.

"Not that I know," said Vanna. "I used to know her as a young girl, and I have hardly seen her since."

"Did Arthur rave frightfully about her?" inquired the shameless Fanny.

"I don't know about frightfully," said Vanna. "I don't think he was old enough to know what he was talking about, and certainly she hadn't the faintest idea of being in love. I always thought her very nice, but a little bit dull and cold. Poor Arthur had some good imaginary suffering when she married very young, but that was all."

"Oh," said Fanny, rather downcast, "I thought it was much more amusing than that. I hoped that when I told him she was coming, he would turn pale and look silly, and perhaps moan her name in his sleep."

"Don't be dramatic, Fanny," said Vanna, and then they each laughed down their own receivers and the laughs very cleverly got past each other in the middle and reached the opposite end, and both Fanny and Vanna thought how amusing it was to be on such understanding terms with one's in-laws. After a little more conversation about the boys and their holiday plans, the telephoning came to an end. Then Fanny went out to lunch with one of her wealthier admirers, and very much disconcerted him by talking exclusively about her adoration of her husband, which was not in the least what he had ordered a very expensive meal for.

CHAPTER 2

It was the usual gray rainy April day when the Howards and Aurea Palgrave arrived at the station. Fanny was there to meet them, full of high spirits, in a very ramshackle old car which she drove about the country at breakneck speed, preferably with one hand. Luckily the local police were her bosom friends and, in the absence of better flirting material, she kept her hand in on them to some purpose. She had never actually been in an accident, but if she had, it would have been very difficult to get evidence against her. The drive to Waterside lay across flattish wind-swept country where lines of pollarded trees, cringing all in the same direction, showed what was the prevailing wind. Mrs. Howard got into the front with Fanny, and the other two sat behind. Presently Fanny, seeing a clear stretch of road in front, turned half around, flung her left arm over the back of the seat, and shouted to Aurea:

"You aren't a bit like what I thought you were."

"What did you think?" asked Aurea.

"Small, and dark, and very attractive," shouted Fanny.

All the others laughed.

"Oh, I don't mean that," added Fanny hastily. "Of course you are terribly attractive, but you are tall and not very dark—what I would call ordinary brown—and it was a blow."

"Fanny, dear," said Mrs. Howard, "I hate to interrupt, but will you, just for my sake, turn around again and look where you are going?"

"Sorry, Mrs. Howard," said Fanny, and turned around obediently.

But in a moment she slewed around the other way and shouted to Aurea:

"What did you say your name was?"

"What?" said Aurea, who had been talking to her father.

"Your name," explained Fanny loudly. "I did ask Vanna, and now I've forgotten it."

"Oh, Aurea, please," said Mrs. Palgrave.

"How sweet of you," yelled Fanny, and turning right around, blew a kiss in Aurea's direction. Mrs. Howard gave a ladylike scream, which had the effect of making Fanny face the wheel again with a jerk that would have upset a less easy-going driver.

"But what is Aurea's real name?" she asked Mrs. Howard.

"Palgrave."

"I love her," said Fanny. "She confirms me in my opinion that Arthur has good taste, even if he isn't clever. First Aurea, then me."

Mrs. Howard smiled but made no answer.

Meanwhile, under the roar and clanking of the engine, Aurea got closer to her father and said:

"Papa, I like Fanny, don't you?"

"Yes, Aurea."

"She is so nice and ready to be friends. Do you and mother see much of her and Arthur?"

"A certain amount. Of course we are rather quiet for them, but we dine there sometimes, and occasionally when Fanny is alone I have taken her out to dinner. She is usually intelligent."

"Oh, papa, is she your Fate?"

"No, dear, I wouldn't put it that way."

"I mean, do you have fun together?"

"Fun? Well, yes, I suppose we do. Fanny is very entertaining."

Fanny chose to be entertaining at that moment by swinging the car around abruptly and dashing up a narrow, muddy lane at the end of which Waterside stood.

"Make yourselves at home," shrieked Fanny, when they had got out, "while I see to the chickens," and putting the car into reverse she disappeared around the corner of the house, while her guests stood on the doorstep.

"I think I'll go around the garden," said Mr. Howard. "There's time before lunch." And off he went in the direction of the chicken run.

Aurea and her mother went indoors and found a blazing log fire in the sitting room. Making comfort was one of Fanny's gifts. Waterside was only an unpretentious farmer's house, with low square rooms, which Fanny had furnished in the days of their comparative poverty. As she couldn't afford luxuries she had concentrated on beds and chairs. Her rooms, therefore, combined comfort and emptiness.

"Isn't papa perfect with Fanny?" said Aurea affectionately.

"How do you mean, perfect?"

"Oh, you know, mother. Featuring old-fashioned courtesy, and being so devoted."

Mrs. Howard laughed. Aurea laughed. Obviously another case of relations understanding each other.

In a few moments Fanny and Mr. Howard came in, Fanny full of a new incubator which was shortly due for its first hatching. After lunch she insisted on dragging them all out to see it. At tea time Arthur arrived from town, and Fanny was able to enjoy with her own eyes the meeting of her husband and his early love. Much to her regret both Arthur and Aurea took it very calmly, and Aurea even went so far as to express regret that Arthur had grown fatter since they last met. This was more than Fanny could bear.

"Fatter, Aurea, is *not* a word for Arthur. Filled out, is what we say, and anyway it was twenty years ago, and I dare say Arthur was a thin misery of a wretch then. I remember when I first saw him I thought what a hideous starveling he looked, and indeed, Aurea, I took a dislike to him at first sight on account of his boniness, though, let it never be forgotten that he hated me because I was too fat, didn't you, Arthur?"

Mr. Howard saved Arthur the trouble of answering by assuring Fanny that she, more or less in the words of Queen Elizabeth, was neither too fat nor too thin, and Fanny, responsive to his rather

Victorian technique, immediately fell into a violent flirtation with him.

"Don't listen to Fanny, Aurea," said Arthur. "She is a good wife, but horribly untruthful."

Aurea smiled at him and then turned to her mother.

"Did I show you my cable from Ned?" she asked. "It only came just before we started."

Mrs. Howard looked anxious.

"He doesn't want you to go back to Canada sooner, does he, darling?"

"Oh, no, mother; the end of next month as we settled before—quite soon enough, though."

Mrs. Howard's face showed such anguish for a moment that Aurea quickly went on to talk about plans for the next few weeks, and possible combinations of people for dinner parties, and the letters from her boy and girl.

So that Arthur was, as so often happened, left out of it. In Fanny's gay, noisy parties he was as silent and remote as the schoolboy had been; but if he had not been there Fanny would have been far less gay and noisy. It was only on rare occasions that she was unable to prevent her adoration of him from being visible, and most of her friends had the habit of rather laughing at Arthur and calling him Fanny's background. He was quite aware of this, and was also aware that to be a background to her was to be a beloved necessity to a creature that needed life and much companionship. In abstract arguments with Fanny and Valentine, he would maintain that a wife should do as she liked, and no husband should keep a wife one day after she wanted to be free. But Fanny knew at the back of her wild but quite clever head, that with Arthur for a background she wouldn't be allowed to go too far, and that it was just possible he might even give her the beating she so richly deserved, if she tried him too severely—perhaps not an actual beating, though of that she wasn't quite sure, but at any rate a mortification and humiliation which she wouldn't at all like. So Arthur sat, and smoked his pipe, and watched his Fanny dancing a platonic minuet with Mr. Howard, and his first love discussing her children with Mrs. Howard.

It was curious to meet one's first love again. He had laughed at Fanny's hopes of drama, and certainly there had been none. Aurea, of course, was not a girl of eighteen now, but she looked very young still. It was always a curious feeling to meet an old friend again after many years. For a moment you saw a stranger with a look that reminded you of someone you had known. Then, like the troubling of still water, the old face trembled to life through the new one, and the years made no difference. I know she is twenty years older than when I last saw her, thought Arthur, but I suppose I shall always think of her as eighteen. It doesn't make any difference that she is married, and has children older than mine. I never knew that part of her life, so it means nothing to me. What made me lose the stranger in her and only see the long-lost friend? It wasn't when she smiled at me—I had found her again long before that. Was it perhaps her voice? Voices don't change so much as faces.

He looked across the room and saw Aurea unpinning some carnations from her dress, and putting them into a bowl of flowers on the table by her. One she kept in her hand and smelt it, and presently began to nibble at the petals without thinking. Suddenly Arthur saw in his mind the country garden where he and Aurea had talked so much for three days. It was hot June—difficult to believe now that there used to be hot Junes—and they had walked and chattered continuously all that weekend, ignoring the rest of the house party. There had been no lovemaking at all. Only those talks of profound depth and profound ignorance, and a joy in being together. Arthur had often wondered what would have happened if he and Aurea had been older, and she had not married Ned Palgrave next year. Had he really loved her, or was it only a delusion of youth? If he had really loved her, wouldn't he have said some word, made some sign, or asked for some sign? It was curious that, so far as he could formulate his feelings of so many years ago, he had never associated the word love with Aurea. She had been so delightfully fond of him, so obviously unaware of deeper emotions, that he had hesitated to betray himself in any way for fear of losing the fondness which she so openly showed. For which of them was it, he had often asked himself, that he was afraid? Was Aurea's presence such bliss to him that he was afraid to risk the exchange of what was so sweet for what might be either more or less sweet? A kind of cowardice? Or had he really thought of her with such drowning of self that he couldn't bear to cast even the thinnest silken web about her remote affection while she was so young and inexperienced?

While he thought again of these things, he felt the hot June sunlight on the grass where they sat. Larkspurs, incandescent blue, shining with their own radiance, were behind Aurea, and she had nibbled a carnation while he talked to her about heaven knows what—a very young man's ideas of life and books and people. He had been less silent with her than with most people. Then she had gone abroad. They had written to each other for six months very affectionately, and then Aurea had written to tell him she was engaged to a man called Palgrave, a journalist. He still didn't like to remember the agony of getting her letter and answering it and somehow going on living, though he was able to admit now that he had sometimes positively enjoyed that agony from a literary point of view, feeling his own pulse, and taking his own emotional temperature. The war had been not unwelcome, and his heart became stiller. Aurea was in Canada, where her husband was editing a newspaper, and he heard nothing of her. Then he had met Fanny who, several years younger than Aurea, had far more knowledge of the world and was not at all unapproachable. Arthur had been swept off his feet by the wild charm, and life had been very happy for them both. He had no regrets for what might have been, or what might with equal possibility never have been. The present was very satisfactory, and Fanny occupied his mind very exclusively. Only why did Aurea sit nibbling at a carnation, just as a girl had done on that hot June day? Not being able to answer the question, he suggested a walk before dinner.

Fanny, in pursuance of her unprincipled scheme, jumped at the idea, and sent Arthur and Aurea off together, while she stayed with the Howards, resolutely heading Mr. Howard off with his attempt to join the walking party.

"After all," she remarked, "they haven't met for nearly twenty years, and Arthur was so terribly fond of her, and I think it would be a good plan for them to get it all off their chests and have done."

"Really, Fanny," began the outraged father, but Mrs. Howard reassured him.

"You know Fanny well enough, Will, to know how untruthful she is. Probably you don't remember that Arthur and Aurea had a very boy and girl affair years ago. I don't suppose either of them ever thought of it again."

But she was quite wrong as far as Arthur was concerned, as we already know.

Aurea and Arthur had a long walk and talked very little. Arthur was normally rather speechless, and Aurea was thinking a good deal of her approaching return to Canada. As they neared home in the dusk, she pulled herself together enough to inquire about the ages and characters of his boys, and give a rapid sketch of her own family. Coming across the garden she stopped for a moment and said:

"Do you remember the garden at your mother's house, Arthur, and the larkspurs?"

Arthur said he did.

"Do you know we have never had a talk since then," said Aurea. "And heaven knows how much we talked in those few days."

Arthur agreed that they had.

"But neither of us was old enough to know what we were talking about," said she, "at least I know I wasn't." And she smiled at him.

"You haven't given up eating carnations," said Arthur abruptly.

"Carnations?" said Aurea, genuinely puzzled, and moving on towards the house.

"Don't you remember eating them?" asked Arthur.

"No," said she doubtfully. "No, I'm sure I don't. What a cannibal taste." And she ran indoors to dress.

Her bedroom was furnished in Fanny's peculiar style. There were two kitchen chairs. The dressing table was a packing case with as many yards of primrose organdie tacked around it as would make a ballerina's skirts. On it was sheet of glass, and an unflattering mirror in a tarnished gold frame. The bed, on the other hand, was large and voluptuous, with the latest thing in lightweight blankets, and one of the exquisite silk quilts which Fanny so surprisingly found time to make for all her bedrooms. The room was lighted by candles. Fanny came rushing in on her way to a bath.

"Darling," she cried, hugging Aurea, "you are perfect. Arthur looks a new man already. I'm dying to hear what you talked about."

"Nothing particular," said Aurea. "We were just walking."

"Oh, well, it will come later," said Fanny hopefully. "And I'm sorry there's no wardrobe, but you'll find two shelves in the dressing table under the flounces, and there's a huge cupboard in the passage where you can hang things and heaps of hangers, only don't take up all the room because Arthur will want some. And if you want a bath, darling, will you be ready in about ten minutes and I'll scream for you and you can have it before Arthur."

Aurea agreed, but Fanny's ten minutes had more than doubled themselves before the promised scream was heard.

It was a quiet evening inside and out. The garden was still, and the party in the house was pleasantly drugged with fresh air. Fanny had decided on the role of virtuous and innocent matron for the evening, and asked intelligent questions of Mr. Howard with such zeal that Mrs. Howard and Aurea nearly had the giggles. Mr. Howard enjoyed it immensely, and became what Aurea afterwards described to her mother as super-paternal. Arthur spoke little, watching his Fanny with loving and sardonic thoughts. Sometimes Aurea or Mrs. Howard tried to bring him into their conversation, but he quickly slipped out again, and sometimes drifted back into a June garden.

It was only ten o'clock when Fanny shepherded her ladies up to bed. After saying good night to Mrs. Howard, she accompanied Aurea to her room.

"I'm going to sit here and watch you brush your hair," she announced. "Long hair is still a curiosity. Didn't you ever want to cut yours?"

"No," said Aurea. "I know exactly what I'd look like."

Fanny cocked her impertinent head on one side and looked at Aurea.

"Perhaps you're right," she admitted. "Not the type at all. But I don't wonder Arthur was so in love with you. You are just the kind of person people fall in love with."

Aurea stopped brushing her hair and looked gravely at Fanny.

"But they don't," she remarked. "I never get a proposal at all. I don't think I'd like it if I did."

Fanny considered the statement.

"I suppose you are the kind that can't care for more than one man at a time," she said.

"Why should I?" said Aurea, plaiting her hair and throwing it back over her shoulder.

"So much more fun," said Fanny. "If you only care for one you'll always get hurt."

"Doesn't one get hurt anyway," said Aurea rather wearily.

Fanny came up behind her, and looked over her shoulder into the unflattering glass.

"Bad philosophy, my child," she said to Aurea's reflection. "Make up your mind that things won't hurt you, and they don't."

"But you have Arthur there, whatever happens. That makes you feel safe. I imagine, Fanny, that you could carry on with twenty gentlemen at once, just because Arthur is safely there. If he weren't such a safe kind of person, you wouldn't be so brave about being hurt."

Fanny gaped, as though assimilating a new idea.

"I believe you are perfectly right," she announced. "And that's why I enjoy life so much with Arthur. But you've got your Ned, so there's no reason for you not to feel safe."

"Yes," said Aurea. She paused for a moment and blew out the candles on the dressing table. "Yes," she repeated, "I have Ned; that's true."

"Are you happy?" asked Fanny shamelessly, but Aurea was winding up the traveling clock by her bed and didn't hear her—or did she? Fanny would not have allowed any situation to remain in a half light, and was on the point of pressing her inquiries, when her mind took one of its snipe-flights.

"Ah-h," she shrieked savagely, "did I or did I not tell Arthur to bring your father up to bed at once and not to sit still in the drawing room saying nothing, which is his idea of a host's behavior? Don't put the lights out—I'll be back again." And leaving the door ajar she flew downstairs. In an incredibly short time she reappeared.

"That's all right," she said. "They are coming straight up now. Darling, how lovely you look in bed with a pigtail. Arthur," she called through the open door, "come and look at Aurea in bed like Saint Ursula."

Arthur appeared at the bedroom door with a candlestick.

"Look at her!" cried Fanny. "Isn't she divine?"

"My wife has no manners," explained Arthur. "I apologize for her. Good night, Aurea."

"Good night, Arthur."

Arthur disappeared.

"No manners, have I?" said Fanny bitterly. "Let him wait."

With which remark she hugged Aurea and fled from the room, slamming the door.

Aurea read for a little and then blew out the light. Everything was silent with that loud quietness so disconcerting to a town dweller. Noises and rustlings in the garden, in the windless night, were like guns and the trump of doom. The splashing of a little stream on the far side of the meadow was the roaring of a cataract. Aurea felt very unsleepy. There were a good many unsorted impressions in her mind for sleep to tidy up, and if sleep didn't come her mind would go on thinking too much. Carnations. Why had Arthur asked her if she still ate carnations? Or why had she so completely forgotten it? Fanny. Fanny's evident affection for her at first sight. Fanny sending her off to walk with Arthur so obtrusively, calling Arthur to admire her in bed. Was this very modern, or just Fanny? Probably just Fanny. Fanny asking her if she was happy. What a breath-taking conversational opening. Though, if she had known Fanny better, she would have realized that she rather affected that question to people. With her friends it meant real interest. With acquaintances it was at least likely to cause a temporary embarrassment highly diverting to the questioner. "Are you happy?" Had Fanny meant it as a corollary to the mention of Ned? If so, she had made a good shot in the dark. To be happy with Ned, one would have to be rather different. Not that one didn't see his good points, his kindness, his good temper, his honesty, his affection for his children, even his adoration of herself. Yes; but how much of positive value was there in these qualities, thought Aurea bitterly. His kindness was so undiscriminating that it was almost self-indulgence, and was always letting Aurea in for meeting people and doing things which were distasteful. She would never be a good "mixer". Good temper; yes. Hardly ever had she seen his temper even ruffled, and heaven knows she must have put a strain upon it often enough. But could one really respect a man who was never angry with one? If one had been silly, or stupid, one needed pulling up, one needed a master. That was it; a master. And that was what Ned had never been. Honestly; yes, though it didn't seem much praise for a man to say he wasn't dishonest. As for the children, so long as he was not troubled about them, and Aurea spent her own allowance on their clothing and education, he was quite fond of them, and would keep them up much too late for his own amusement. Luckily they were both getting to an age when they could go their own way.

And he was very fond of her. He wrote by every mail, he who was such a bad correspondent, to say how he missed her, and how he adored her. Yes, thought Aurea, but I know exactly why he misses me, and why he wants me back. The adoring has only one meaning to him, and I would give it quite a different name. Aurea shut her eyes quickly and tightly, trying to escape remembrances of the many times when adoration had taken the one hated shape, of her own efforts to stave off the adoration, of the humiliating scene that always followed, of Ned whimpering, actually whimpering because she was not what he called "kind", of the utter contempt with which she finally gave in. A spasm of pain contracted her face alone in the dark. I suppose, she thought, I am a pretty bad wife. A person who, not to mince words, dislikes and despises her husband, can't be much of a success. And seeing his good side only makes it worse. It isn't much of an excuse now to say that I was very young when I married him. No one forced me to. I was just in love. I wonder if it is really a good plan to marry a person one is terribly in love with? Well, it's all over now, long ago, only one has to go on just the same. If I hadn't married Ned I might have married someone much worse, who beat me and took drugs.

Then she reflected sardonically that no one else had ever asked her to marry them, and laughed at herself, and felt better, and thought of Fanny again. Fanny showing her off to Arthur. Was Fanny right when she said that Arthur had cared for her so much? Probably not, for if Arthur had cared for her, surely he would have said something about it. She certainly had not cared for him except as a playfellow. She didn't even know then what being in love meant. She was young for her age and had had a very sheltered life as a girl. Ned was a good deal older than she was and carried her off her feet. She had been very happy at first, and that was always something to be thankful for. And then the children were such darlings, and so well and cheerful. No, it couldn't have been all wrong, whatever misery it might be now. If she and Arthur had been older, if she hadn't married so soon, would it have made any difference? No, none at all, she thought. She had been very fond of Arthur, and was still very fond of him, but there never had been any sentiment, and certainly there was none now. Certainly there was none; especially with Fanny being so kind, and taking one on trust as it were. One's husband's old friends were always a doubtful pleasure—she had vastly disliked one or two of Ned's old flames—but Fanny opened her arms to her.

And on this thought, warm with Fanny's quilt, and no longer conscious of the noisy stillness of the country, she slid into sleep.

Next morning she was woken by Fanny coming into her room with a tray.

"Tea, darling," said Fanny. "And then get up at once. I've got a job for you."

"What kind?" asked Aurea, sitting up.

"Orange juice," said Fanny.

"How orange juice?"

"Oh, we always start the day with it, and I want you to squeeze the oranges. My village woman is a bit half witted about breakfast, and I have to help her. Hurry up, darling, it's fiendishly cold." She tore out of the room.

Aurea got up obediently and looked out of the window. It was a gray boisterous day with a cold wind dashing spatters of rain against the panes. Dressing as quickly as possible she went downstairs and, guided by Fanny's voice, found her way to the kitchen.

"That's right, love," said Fanny, looking up from the stove. "I'm just taking breakfast in, and your blessed parents will be down in a minute. Strain all those oranges into a jug, and then pour it into the glasses and bring it into the dining room. Don't let any pips get in."

As she spoke she put coffee and milk on a tray and left the kitchen. In the dining room Mrs. Howard was standing near the large fire where the breakfast was keeping hot inside the fender.

"Good morning, Fanny," she said.

"Good morning, Mrs. Howard," said Fanny, putting her tray down. "Come and sit down. We never wait. Will you have kidneys, or eggs and bacon? The kidneys are very good because I did them myself and I don't waste any of the juice. It all goes onto delicious squashy, buttery toast."

"Kidneys, please then, dear."

"I let the woman do the eggs and bacon," continued Fanny, warming to her subject and putting a plate in front of Mrs. Howard. "I believe it's the only thing she can cook, but she does it well. She enjoys letting herself go over the bacon fat and fries scrunchy bits of bread in it. Coffee half and half?"

"Please," said Mrs. Howard.

"Would Mr. Howard like his breakfast in bed? I'll take it up if he would."

"No, he's just coming down. He doesn't want to miss anything of Aurea."

"When does she go back to Canada?" asked Fanny.

"At the end of next month."

"Yes, Fanny, we shall. But I hope she'll be over again the year after next."

"Oh, can't she come sooner? Or why shouldn't you and Mr. Howard go and see her? I'm sure he could give lectures in Canada and earn heaps of money and you could let the house."

"Thank you, Fanny, for arranging our lives, but he did lecture last year, you know, and he doesn't much want to go again."

"I didn't mean to interfere," said Fanny meekly. "But I was thinking of something nice for you and Aurea. Couldn't she come over next year instead of the year after?"

"I don't know," said Mrs. Howard in an uncertain way which wasn't at all like her. "It might be difficult. Ned naturally doesn't like being without her, and he finds it difficult to get away from his newspaper. And then there are her boy and girl."

"Is—Aurea—happy, Mrs. Howard?" said Fanny, pausing in her breakfast, and thumping on the table with knife and fork in her fists.

Mrs. Howard looked at her in desperation.

"We don't talk about it," she said. "And now, Fanny, I beg you to be quiet and control yourself, because Will is coming down and mustn't be bothered. Help us to pretend, child—that's all you can do."

Upon which Mr. Howard appeared at the door. Fanny got up to greet him, and was rewarded by a hand on each shoulder and a kiss on the forehead. Winking violently at Mrs. Howard, she went over to the hearth, while Mr. Howard sat down.

"Kidneys, or eggs and bacon, Mr. Howard?" said Fanny; "and did you sleep all right?"

"To your first question, kidneys, please," said Mr. Howard. "To your second, ah, yes, I may say that I slept excellently."

"Coffee half and half?" asked Fanny, sitting down.

"Yes, please. At least, to be perfectly truthful, I slept excellently when once I had got to sleep again. What was the uproar in the middle of the night?"

"Uproar?" said Fanny. "Oh, that wasn't an uproar. That was Val arriving in the village Ford. I told you he was coming, didn't I?"

"Val?" said Mr. Howard, with the cold voice of an unsatisfied examiner.

"Yes, dear," said Mrs. Howard. "You know Fanny told us that Arthur's friend, Mr. Ensor, was coming down for the weekend."

"Ah, Ensor," repeated Mr. Howard. "Yes, Ensor. At the bar, I think you said?"

"No—bank," corrected Fanny. "He often comes here. He and Arthur were at school together, so they sit and don't talk, and that brightens our evenings wonderfully."

At that moment something bumped against the door and Arthur came in with a scuttle of coal.

"Good morning," he said to the company generally. "Here's your coal, Fanny, and I've routed Val out and sent him to bring in some logs. It's frightfully cold outside."

"Your friend Val kept Mr. Howard awake all night," said Fanny accusingly.

"No, Fanny, not all night," corrected Mr. Howard. "I only said that I heard a noise. But after I had recovered from having my rest broken, I slept excellently."

"Here's Val; you can scold him yourself," remarked Arthur as Valentine Ensor came into the room.

"Good morning, Val," said Fanny. "Get some breakfast out of the fireplace. It appears that you kept everyone awake last night coming roistering up in the Ford as you did. Oh, I forgot. This is Mr. Ensor. This is Mrs. Howard and Mr. Howard. Mr. Howard never slept a wink last night because of your rowdy arrival."

Valentine looked down apologetically from his considerable height.

"I'm terribly sorry, sir," he said. "I didn't think I was disturbing anyone."

The Howards, feeling as uncomfortable as one always does when anyone is publicly scolded, hurried into the breach made by Fanny's bad manners.

"Please, Mr. Ensor, don't listen to Fanny," said Mrs. Howard. "It was only the noise of your car turning in the drive, and my husband went to sleep again almost at once."

"I am very sorry I ever mentioned the subject," said Mr. Howard. "It was nothing at all."

Valentine smiled. "Thank you very much," he said gratefully. "And for your ill-judged effort to make mischief, Fanny, no thanks at all. If I've told you once, I've told you a hundred times, that your drive wants widening. No Christian car can turn in it, let alone a Ford."

"Well, put the logs down for the Lord's sake," said Fanny, "and don't stand there grinning through a horse collar."

"Only a soft collar, Fanny," said Valentine. He put the logs in the hearth, filled a plate, and sat down with his back to the door.

"Kidneys *and* eggs and bacon, I observe," said Fanny kindly, pushing a cup of coffee towards him.

"I couldn't help it, Fanny. Your food is always so good, one has to take a bit of everything."

"Don't waste charm on me," said Fanny acidly. "Look at him, Mrs. Howard. Large and hideous as that man is, he can twist me around his little finger. And why? All because he has charm."

"Admit, Fanny," put in Arthur, "that you ask him to hold out his finger, so that you can twist around it."

"Thank you, Arthur," said Valentine. "The remark of a true friend."

"All right," said Fanny. "Wait and see. He will twist you, Mrs. Howard, and probably Aurea."

"Where is Aurea?" asked Mr. Howard, who had now finished his breakfast.

"Oh, Gosh," cried Fanny. "I left her squeezing oranges, and she is probably dead with devotion like Casabianca. Wouldn't it be a good idea, Mr. Howard, to write a book about the idiot boys of history who stay on burning ships and put their fingers into holes in dykes and don't tell Roundheads when they last saw their father."

"An excellent field for research, Fanny," said Mr. Howard. "But is Aurea coming?"

"Who is Aurea?" asked Valentine.

"Mr. Howard's daughter, of course," said Fanny, "and she is married to a man who runs a newspaper and lives in Canada and has some children older than mine, but not so nice, and is on a holiday with her papa and mamma, so now you know all."

"She is a long time," said Mr. Howard.

"Perhaps," said Arthur, "she has pricked her finger on an orange pip, and gone to sleep for a hundred years. Shall I go and see?"

Fanny was so obviously going to make a low-minded suggestion about the methods of waking princesses, that it was as well that Aurea's voice was heard at the moment calling:

"Please open the door for me, or I'll slop all the orange juice over."

Arthur began to move, but Valentine, who was nearer the door, got up first. The door opened inwards to that he was behind it as Aurea came into the room, with the tray in her hands.

"I am so sorry, Fanny," she said. "The pips were most intrusive, and then I had to wait while your charlady told me about her new teeth."

"Well, put the tray down here by me," said Fanny. "It's a bit late for the orange juice, but better late than never."

Aurea kissed her father and mother on the top of their heads, and got some food out of the hearth. As she stood up she saw Valentine for the first time, and looked questioningly at Fanny.

"Oh, of course you hadn't met," said Fanny. "This is Mr. Ensor. And how he expects to get on in society if he goes skulking about behind doors I don't know. Sit down and let the lady look at you."

"But I think I do know you," said Aurea. "Weren't you at that party that Arthur's people had, hundreds of years ago?"

"'Among those present,'" remarked Valentine "'was the fascinating and accomplished Mr. Ensor.' I thought I knew your face."

"And now you know Aurea's face, for God's sake put something into your own and get on with breakfast," said Fanny rudely. "Anyone who has finished can get up and last up clear the table. Oh, and everyone listen to me. Plans. Tomorrow Arthur has to go up by the early train, so he will have the village car to the station. I can drive anyone else up later. What about the Howard family?"

"I shall go up with Arthur," said Mr. Howard. "I have a meeting at eleven."

"And I think I'll go too, Fanny dear," said Mrs. Howard. "There are always things to be seen to on Monday."

"Then that's three for the station and three for the car," said Fanny.

"Sorry, Fanny," put in Valentine, "but I'll have to go by the early train too."

"Drat you, child," said Fanny. "I thought you would look after the women and children. Well, well, then that's only you and I, Aurea. Do you mind?"

"No, indeed," said Aurea, "I'd love to come with you, if mother and papa don't mind."

"Yes, you go with Fanny," said Mrs. Howard.

"Sure, darling?" asked Aurea.

"Yes, quite."

"Then, that's that," said Fanny. "And now, Mrs. Howard, would you like to help me with the incubator?"

"Not in the least," replied Mrs. Howard. "I'll look on if you like, but as for helping, no."

Fanny and Mrs. Howard went out. While Arthur and Mr. Howard stood before the fire talking in rather loud grown-up voices, Aurea and Valentine were able to go on with breakfast.

"Do you think we have to drink that orange juice?" asked Aurea anxiously.

Valentine looked at it with intense disgust and, picking up the tray, put it on the sideboard. Aurea thought she liked people to be tall as that and to have long hands. Certainly one wouldn't say he was good-looking, with that long upper lip, and such a high—or perhaps it would be less romantic to say slightly bald—forehead. But to look clean and tidy did count for something, and Mr. Ensor looked as if he washed a good deal, and went to a good tailor. If one of his shirt cuffs was a little frayed, that just came of living alone and having no one to look after one. And Aurea felt that foolish small gust of emotion which her sex feel at the sight of a dangling button, or a loose thread, in any fairly personable male for whom they have no direct responsibility. Not that she had shirked sewing on buttons in her own family, for a husband and two children can run through a gross or so of buttons in a year, not to speak of perpetual patching of school suits, refooting of everyone's socks, and a heap of darning which renewed its youth weekly. But any woman, old or young, can find emotion in a missing button when the owner is not her property.

Valentine, as he sat down again, was agreeably conscious that Aurea was attractive. Outside the bank, where he worked hard and intelligently and would be a partner by the time money wasn't much good to him, his chief interest was in attractive women. An unlucky beginning had not at all soured his feelings towards females. On the contrary, he felt a good deal of devotion for them, and was more than ready to meet them halfway. A detached man, even if not particularly eligible, is always welcome to hostesses. Valentine danced well and had, as Fanny put it, excellent technique. To watch the two of them playing at lovemaking was to see a display by highly skilled artists, though, to do Fanny justice, she never let her virtuosity carry her away. To endanger Arthur's feelings towards herself, or Valentine, would have made her wretchedly unhappy, so, partly selfishly, partly unselfishly, she kept Valentine well in his place. In return he told her about all his affairs, listened to her good advice, and sometimes took it. Several years of living in rooms, after having had a wife and house of one's own, however uneasy, had inspired Valentine with a wish for matrimony. Very ingenuously he would expound to Fanny his views about marrying again, and how delightful it would be to settle down and have a home.

Fanny always pricked his bubbles at sight. All this talk about settling down made her quite sick, she said. If he married again, heaven help the woman. He might talk of settling, but he was a confirmed, professional gadabout. He wouldn't in the least like to have one woman always with him. No one would ask him to dinners and dances any longer at his age, when once he was married. He would pine for these delights and lead his wife a wretched life. In fact, Fanny, who had had the advantage of hearing both sides of his matrimonial troubles in the past, was ready to declare that he had been quite as difficult to live with as Sylvia, his wife, only a trifle more restrained. He was, she asserted, of a roving disposition, and would be far more trouble in the house than he was worth. He didn't know his own luck in being free to live as he really wished, or would wish if he knew what was good for him. Besides, added Fanny, what had he to keep a wife on? No private means and a salary of which Sylvia had a good share. Therefore if he married, he would have to marry money, and to marry money was mercenary. He must marry for love, but a woman who had an income of her own. But if he would listen to her, Fanny's, advice, he wouldn't try marriage, as it would only make two people wretched. And having delivered her soul of this wisdom, she would select likely heiresses and ask them down for weekends when Valentine was coming.

Valentine, to do him justice, was not mercenary. His ideal picture of domestic bliss certainly included great comfort and a good deal of traveling, but this was all part of the dream. He didn't feel capable of making any particular effort to look for money. His rather easily-conquered heart was always at the feet of some charmer, but the charmers appeared to require a position more solid than any he could offer. And then the worst of it was that they were all so delightful, and as soon as he was quite sure he was in love with one, he found himself halfway in love with another. Philanderer, he told himself a little bitterly in his rare fits of introspection, was what he was. Luckily for himself, he seldom let his mind dwell on its own workings. He had once been hurt more than he would admit, and to protect himself he had covered the grave where first love lay; not with willow, but with a dancing floor where, without too much effort, he could walk smoothly and set to each new partner.

At the moment he was in the reaction of a violent affair with a clever woman, who had temporarily lost her head. No serious damage was done on either side, but Valentine, who had of late neglected his charmers, found himself in his turn a little neglected by them and was, as Fanny elegantly put it, spoiling for a new affair. To amuse him, and to amuse herself, she had invited Aurea; and she hoped Arthur would be amused too. This was not kind of Fanny. But she had little capacity for abstract kindness. Unhappiness, if it made a direct appeal to her, she could understand and help with capable devotion, and she would have been deeply outraged at the suggestion that she could be unkind. But, very secure herself in the affection which Arthur and she felt for each other, her imagination did not enable her to feel the sensitiveness of natures deprived of deep-rooted affections. It was all sport for her, and what was amusing was all right. Valentine would have agreed with her entirely, taking, as he did, his emotional life easily. No charmer disturbed his sound sleep, or his excellent appetite, however fast his heart might beat in the daytime, between meals. And no charmer had died, or shown the slightest symptom of dying of love for him, however furious the flirtation. So we may conclude that both Fanny and Valentine belong to the people who are described as being able to take care of themselves: and these people are apt to be selfish towards abstract needs. If Aurea, whose happiness Mrs. Howard would not discuss with Fanny, who would not hear Fanny's question about her happiness, fell into such company, there might be very little pity for her. Arthur, indeed, would feel pity, but he might also make demands. Altogether Fanny had prepared a very pretty kettle of fish for a wet weekend, but whoever may suffer, we may be sure it will not be Fanny.

Arthur and Mr. Howard had finished justifying their existence as grown-ups, and were talking in more natural voices about taking a walk before lunch.

"Have we all to go that walk?" said Valentine to Aurea.

"I don't know," said she. "One has to do what Fanny tells one, I imagine."

"Not if you are firm," said Valentine.

"But I'm not. I'm rather a coward, and if people make plans for me, I do as I am told."

"May I suggest a plan then," said Valentine. "That you should have a large chair opposite the fire, and spend the morning indoors."

"Alone?"

"Oh, no. It is quite understood that I should be there too."

"Aurea," said Mr. Howard, "Arthur and I are going for a walk. Are you coming?"

Valentine spoke first. "I hoped she was going to spend the morning indoors, sir," he said.

"Do you want to, dear, or will you come with us?" said Mr. Howard.

"Well, papa, I think I'll stay in just now," said Aurea, "and perhaps this afternoon you and Arthur will take me out."

"Just as you like," said Mr. Howard.

"She will be quite all right, sir. I will take care of her," added Valentine, quite unnecessarily.

"She—she—" said Aurea, looking at Valentine. "In the nursery we were told that "she" was the cat's grandmother. Arthur, I believe Mr. Ensor doesn't even know my name."

"I thought Fanny had done the introducing," said Arthur. "This is Mrs. Palgrave."

"I had hoped I might be allowed to call you Aurea, considering the length of our acquaintance," said Valentine, quite unabashed.

"Why, certainly, if you like," said Aurea. "But it isn't quite fair, because I don't know your christian name."

"It's rather a silly one," said Valentine, suddenly self-conscious.

"Never mind, out with it. We are all married people here."

There was a barely perceptible pause before Valentine said, "It's Valentine, if you don't mind."

"Valentine? Valentine?" said Aurea, slowly, as if she were tasting a wine. "No, I don't mind it."

"Well then, we'll see you again later," said Arthur. "Do you feel like starting now, sir? The weather has cleared a bit, and we might get out before it pours again."

The plans for a walk were nearly wrecked because Mr. Howard remembered that he had forgotten his stick, but on being offered a choice of Arthur's, he cheered up and began to get under way.

"Good-bye, papa," said Aurea. "If it's a nice walk you can take me the same way this afternoon. And now, Valentine, if you'll help me, we'll clear the breakfast things on to the sideboard and get the sofa around to the fire."

As she spoke she began piling up cups and plates on the table by the door. With Valentine's help the breakfast table was soon cleared, and they pulled the big sofa around at right angles to the fire. Aurea established herself in a corner with some knitting while Valentine put himself into a large chair with his feet on the fender, and lit a pipe.

"Are you enjoying yourself?" he asked.

"Like anything," said Aurea. "Fanny is such fun. Not a bit like what I thought."

"But didn't you know her?"

"Oh, no. I hadn't seen Arthur for years and years, and only knew he was married. But Fanny was so nice to me."

"Why not?"

"Oh, you know one's husband's old friends are apt to be a horrid bore. But Fanny didn't treat me a bit like a husband's old friend. She opened her arms to me at once."

"Is that such a rare experience?" said Valentine. "I should have thought you might find the whole world rather open-armed."

"Oh, no," said Aurea, and her voice sounded flat.

"No impertinence intended," said Valentine reassuringly. "Only an honest expression of opinion."

"I suppose "granted" is the right answer," she said. "But Fanny really is remarkable in the way she makes one feel absolutely at home at once."

"Yes," said Valentine thoughtfully, "she is a remarkable woman."

Aurea was counting stitches and made no further comment. Valentine was able to look at her. He thought he liked people to be that kind of tallness, and to have lovely hands and voices. It was rather a delicious face, he thought. Certainly not as pretty as the young charmers, but if people's eyes looked tired and had a little darkness under them; if the little hollow below the cheekbone lay in shadow; surely that was more interesting than the smooth untired faces that looked on him as a useful dancing man. If Fanny had been there, she would have taken one look at Valentine and said that he had found the affair for which he was spoiling. To Valentine it wasn't in the least as clear as that. He was conscious of the faint excitement which always preludes the chase, but he wasn't in the least sure of any response. Aurea didn't appear to be one of the coming-on females. Ready enough to meet him in talk certainly, and he looked forward to exploring the quality of her conversation. But would there be anything more? Arthur, he knew, had cared for her a good deal at one time, and Arthur cared so seldom, that Valentine respected his fastidiousness of taste. One would like a woman of her distinction to like one. It would be worth taking trouble about. Valentine's experience of charmers was that they did rather like him, without taking much trouble. They all knew about his black past and found it an attraction. Was one, he wondered, too ready to make capital out of a misfortune which, though it was safely buried, did not stop coloring one's life. It was so easy to get a woman to be sorry for one if she knew, or thought, that another woman had treated one badly.

Suddenly his mind went back to the moment when Aurea had asked his name. What she had said had taken him unawares. "All married people here." Yes, of course, they were all married people; Mr. Howard, Arthur, Aurea, and himself. At least they all were married now, and he had once been. But why had Aurea said it? She would hardly have called him married if she knew that he had been divorced. Some of his charmers might have said a thing like that, and either thought it funny, or not thought about it at all. But Aurea quite obviously wasn't a charmer of that sort. She would be kind. She would probably be so kind that it would not be fair to try to make her sorry for one. It was rather a cheap business getting sympathy from people. He wouldn't like to do anything cheap where Aurea was concerned. He would immediately like her to know him, and care for him as he really was. A hopeless business though, he admitted, because the more you try to explain to people what you really are, the denser grows the mist of words around you, and in any case they will always think of you as they have made up their minds to find you, so it is all waste of time. Women, he had found, were mostly ready to explain themselves at great length, partly in conversations, partly in very long letters. Their idea of love letters was a very detailed description of their own feelings. Perhaps that was inevitable when you came to think of it. They couldn't according to modern convention, express their temporary love by physical images of beauty. If they said "your eyes . . . ," "your hair . . . ," one would either laugh, or feel very uncomfortable. So it all went back into themselves, and they classified their feelings about themselves because they couldn't quite describe their feelings about you. As for men's letters—well, he had written some good ones himself, but on the whole it was too much bother. And after all, it was only saying the same thing to them all, from Amanda to Zacintha.

Now, as he looked at Aurea, she appeared to have got over the counting part and was knitting placidly again. Valentine felt he must get the position clear before Fanny—whose fault it really was for asking Aurea down and not explaining her fellow-guests to her—came in and destroyed all peace.

"When you said just now that we were all married people," he began, finding an unaccountable difficulty in speaking, "did you mean anything?"

Aurea looked up and wrinkled her forehead, mildly surprised.

"Mean anything?" she asked. "No, not specially. It's just a family expression—it means nothing particular."

"I thought perhaps you knew I was married," said Valentine.

It is a sad fact, and mortifying to the sterner sex, that while any bachelor has the possibility of romance about him till he takes the trouble to prove his dullness, a woman no sooner hears that a man is married than the charm of romance evaporates. She may subsequently find romantic charm in him—probably of her own inventing—but, for the moment, all his merits are hopelessly obscured by matrimony. Aurea had always felt quite a little romantic about Valentine, for no earthly reason except that he was an unattached man, but at his words romance crashed to earth and lay dead at her feet. In that fleeting moment his agreeable tallness, his long hands, his pleasant deep voice, his plain intriguing face, had all become the dull attributes of someone else's husband. So she very properly said:

"No, I didn't know, but I'm delighted. Fanny never mentioned your wife."

"I didn't say I am married," said Valentine. "I was married."

"I don't quite understand," said Aurea. "Am I being tactless?"

"No—not a bit. But I thought perhaps Fanny would have told you."

"She didn't tell me anything. Please couldn't you just explain, so that I won't go on apparently putting my foot in it."

Quite suddenly Valentine's heart hit him so hard that he was surprised. He got up and stood facing the fire, and spoke straight into the mantelpiece.

"You see I was married for some years. My wife and I didn't get on frightfully well. She was—rather promiscuous. We hadn't any children, so it didn't matter so much. Then things got worse and worse. So I let her divorce me. That's all."

There was silence. It was less embarrassing to go on looking at the mantelpiece than to look at Aurea. It was very unusual to feel embarrassed. Everyone talked and laughed about these things. Why should one suddenly feel as if one had dropped a frightful brick? Aurea was a grown-up woman. She had been living in America where people divorced each other like anything—or anyway Canada—the same thing. Why couldn't one realize it, instead of feeling that she was still a girl at home who oughtn't to hear about ugly things? Not that girls now minded ugly things; everything was alike to them. Perhaps it was because he had first met Aurea when she was so very young, and in those days most of the girls one met were ignorant of almost everything. Then meeting her again with her father and mother gave one rather a schoolroom feeling about her. Was it silly and ill-bred to have plunged into one's own history like that? He looked down at Aurea. She was still knitting, but to his horror and admiration, wave after wave of color was flooding her neck and face. Did women actually blush now? One thought that only happened in novels, and bad ones at that. But here was a grown-up woman, with a husband and children, flying the flag of a female in distress. What was one to do? One way, of course, would be to sit on the sofa by her, put one's arms around her, and squash the breath out of her body. But obviously that wasn't practical.

Aurea, hopelessly conscious of her mounting color, was enraged with herself. Would nothing ever cure her, she asked crossly, of being a ridiculous fool? It was uncomfortable for herself and annoying for Ned, who would have liked her to be more grown-up. It was not that she was shocked by theories; she read all the new books, she saw all the new plays, and was ready to discuss anything as an abstract idea. But the moment actual personalities intruded, she reverted to Victorian type and fatally blushed. Quick confused thoughts flew through her mind about what people did when they let their wives divorce them. Having to find someone who would respectably spend the night in a hotel with one. A man called Rochester whom she had known, who madly took his hireling help to Rochester for the night because he couldn't think of anywhere else to go. A vision—very distasteful—of Valentine somewhere in an hotel bedroom, pretending. And finally, an uncomfortable feeling that Valentine was waiting for her to say something, and the longer she waited the more difficult it would be. Forcing a very small voice out of herself, she said, "That must have been very horrid for you," and immediately felt a fool for having said it.

"Not so very horrid," said Valentine; "they arrange it all for you."

Aurea felt unequal to any further statement than "Oh", which doesn't commit one, but she was able to say it more naturally. Valentine, still looking down on her, said, "I'm sorry."

Aurea, knitting very hard, said: "If you would perhaps sit down again, we might be a lady and gentleman having a conversation."

"I'd like that of all things. I am rather good at conversation."

"And I am celebrated for my act of a lady entertaining a gentleman. Shall I begin?"

"I would adore it," said Valentine. Then they both laughed, and felt more comfortable, and asked each other questions. Aurea told Valentine how old her children were, and what they wanted to do when they grew up, and Valentine told Aurea about his lodgings, and how his landlady wasn't good at sewing on buttons. And as for shirts, he said, the number he had to give away just because the cuffs were frayed would appall her. Aurea became quite pale at this thought. It would be, she felt, almost unbearable not to see more of a man so romantically persecuted by fate.

"Do you think, Valentine," she asked, "that you would dine with us one evening if my mamma will have you?"

"When?"

"Would Tuesday be a good day?" she inquired.

Valentine said it would be a good day, shelving till later the problem of getting out of a previous invitation to dine with Arthur and Fanny.

"Mother and I are going to a party," said Aurea, "but not till half-past ten. So if you would dine with us at eight, that would give us heaps of time, and we would drop you somewhere when we go."

Valentine said that would be perfect, and could be dropped somewhere near South Kensington Station.

Just then Fanny burst in, followed by Mrs. Howard, who sat down near the fire demanding sympathy from Aurea. Fanny had kept her for nearly an hour in a shed among the incubators. It was cold, and there were only packing-cases to sit on, and finally Fanny had wanted her to help chickens out of their shells. But at such sticky pleasure she drew the line, and had insisted on coming in.

Meanwhile Fanny was complaining to Valentine.

"How foully stuffy it is in here," she said. "Val, you really are a most useless guest. I didn't ask you down here to sit and frowst by a fire all day. Come and help me to shift the incubator. I want it in the other shed, nearer the furnace."

"All right, you cowardly bully," replied her guest. "You know a gentleman can't refuse a lady when she is mean enough to ask him in front of other people."

"Come on, then," Fanny began, when Valentine interrupted her.

"Oh, by the way, Fanny, I'm so sorry, but I was a perfect idiot to say I'd dine with you on Tuesday without looking at my engagement book. I had an engagement already. Will it matter frightfully?"

Fanny looked at him with deep suspicion, but apparently reassured by the serene candor of his countenance she only answered, "Make it Wednesday, then," and dragged him from the room.

"And how did you and Mr. Ensor get on, darling?" asked Mrs. Howard.

"Very nicely, mother. Of course, it's a pity about his face, but that can't be helped."

"I see nothing wrong with his face," said Mrs. Howard.

"Did papa like him?"

"I expect so. He always likes young men who call him 'sir'."

"Well, in that case, mother, what about asking him to dinner?"

"Yes, darling, if you want to. Friday week would do nicely. Friday is always a good day for papa, but this week he is engaged."

"I thought perhaps something a little nearer than that."

"I hardly think you'd get him, Aurea. Fanny says he is out a great deal."

"Why was Fanny talking about him?" asked Aurea eagerly.

"She was on her eternal subject of matchmaking. She said she wanted to find a wife for him, but he was so much in debt that it must be someone with money. I do wish dear Fanny weren't quite so blatant. She worked herself up so much about it that she dropped an eggy chicken into my lap. The chicken was all right, but I couldn't bear any more, so I came indoors."

"Well, she isn't matchmaking this weekend. You and I aren't eligible. Mother, what about next Tuesday for asking Mr. Ensor to dinner?"

Mrs. Howard began to be a little surprised at her daughter's unusual persistency. "Well, darling," she said, with a slight note of patience in her voice, "your father will be out, and you and I, if you remember, are going to the Sinclairs' party."

"Oh, but it wouldn't really matter about papa, would it? And if we dined at eight we needn't leave till halfpast ten, and that would give us heaps of time to talk to Mr. Ensor."

If Mrs. Howard had possessed a lorgnon, she would have put it up. Failing this, she looked her daughter in the face. "I suppose what you mean, Aurea, is that I should go and finish dressing or write letters, and you should talk to Mr. Ensor."

"That was rather in my thoughts, mother," said Aurea meekly. "Do let us have him for Tuesday. It would be such fun, and I haven't much longer to enjoy myself in."

This appeal, of course, was bound to melt Mrs. Howard, and Aurea, one regrets to say, knew it.

"Very well, darling," said his mother. "You can ask him, but don't expect him to come."

"Oh, but I know he can come, mother, because I asked him."

"I might have guessed that," said Mrs. Howard with resignation. "You are very direct in your methods with your young men, Aurea, even if you do go roundabout with your mother."

"I love you more than the whole lot of them put together," said Aurea, throwing her arms around her mother with great vehemence. "If you'd rather not have Mr. Ensor, we won't."

"Silly child. Of course we'll have him." Aurea ought to have blushed now, but she didn't.

Then Arthur and Mr. Howard came back from their walk. Mr. Howard was enthusiastic about it, but on being pressed for details could give no comprehensible description of the path they had taken. His attention, he said, had been largely occupied by the delightful conversation he and Arthur had had about the recent excavations in Rome. Aurea turned to Arthur and said in a low voice, "Arthur, I admire you tremendously. How on earth did you keep your end up with papa about excavations."

"I didn't," said Arthur. "Your father held both ends up at once. I only listened, and saw that he took the right turning."

"Bless his heart, I might have known it," said Aurea, beaming affectionately on her father.

"Are you coming for a walk with me this afternoon?" asked Arthur.

"I'd love to."

Then the restless Fanny burst back into the room, announcing that there was time for some bridge before lunch. Mr. Howard exercised a damping effect on the party by stating that whist had been good enough for him, and settling himself obtrusively with a book, Mrs. Howard also preferred to read, so Fanny gave up her bridge plan for the time and turned her attention to Aurea, making various piercing inquiries as to how she had spent her morning. Aurea emerged from this catechism with credit, and Fanny announced that Aurea would be a good friend for Valentine.

"He needs a few female friends with economical tastes like you and me, Aurea. All the young women seem to expect dinners and theaters and dancing clubs and what not nowadays, and Val is hopelessly in debt."

"Fanny," said Arthur, "I shall take to beating you with a stick if you don't hold your tongue. My wife, Aurea, is a model of devotion and a perfect mother, but she seems to think every unattached young man she knows is created for the express purpose of taking her out for the evening. That is why most of her friends are in debt."

"Wasn't Mr. Ensor married once?" said Aurea with a little difficulty.

"Yes, Aurea," responded the ever ready Fanny, "and a great mistake it was. But now he is free again, and it is a shame that a really nice young man shouldn't be able to marry again simply because—"

As Arthur made an ill-advised attempt to stem this flow of confidences, she turned on him.

"Arthur, if you interrupt me before I have said what you may or may not think I am going to say, I'll BITE you. Simply, Aurea, because he is paying a whacking allowance to his wife as was, besides all the lawyers' bills. All right, Arthur, now you can stop me."

"But does he want to marry again?" asked Aurea.

This time Arthur got in first.

"Aurea, you mustn't listen to Fanny, she is incorrigible. Val doesn't want to marry anyone as far as I know, and it is no business of Fanny's, but she can't be happy unless she's meddling."

"Did you arrange his first meeting, Fanny?" said Aurea, with a shade of malice which was lost on Fanny.

"I did," said she modestly. "My first success."

Arthur gave up any further attempt to control his wife. "Success, she calls it—Oh, Lord!" he remarked in a private way.

"Well, Fanny," said Aurea with much spirit, "if that's all you can do for the poor man and then to get him down for a weekend with nothing but middle-aged married women about, I don't think much of your match making."

"He who lives longest sees most," said Fanny oracularly.

"Very true, my dear," said Arthur, "but singularly wanting in application to this particular case."

Fanny evaded the question by hailing Valentine, who came in at the moment, for a game of bridge. Valentine said she knew how he played, and if she didn't like it she could lump it. Arthur and Fanny began to wrangle about which cards to use, Fanny maintaining that any cards were good enough for friends, Arthur that practically no cards were good enough for guests. Under cover of their argument Aurea approached Valentine.

"I rather gather from my mamma that papa is pleased with you," she said, "because you are a respectful young man, and call him 'sir'."

"Anything else I can do to oblige?"

"Well, if you wanted papa to feel passionate devotion for you, could you say something about Roman excavations? I don't mean now—just any time. You needn't know much about them. Arthur can do it, so I should think you can."

"Are you asking me to fawn in a sycophantic way upon your father?" asked Valentine, nobly.

"Yes, please," said Aurea, quite deliberately doing what her mother would have called making eyes at Valentine.

"No Ensor ever refused a dare," said the representative of that name, and alarmed Aurea by going straight up to Mr. Howard.

"Are you playing bridge, sir?" he inquired.

Mr. Howard shut his book in a temporary way with one finger in his place, and looked up with a patient expression.

"No, Ensor. Whist was good enough for me. You young people amuse yourselves. I shall read."

This was not an inspiring beginning. Fanny and Arthur had finished their wrangle and were getting out a table. Valentine decided that a quick assault was his only chance.

"I expect, sir, you are interested in the new Roman excavations. I was in Rome for a few days last autumn and saw something of them."

Mr. Howard took his finger out of his book and removed his glasses. The folly of bridge was forgotten. "How very interesting, Ensor," he said, "most interesting. I've been wanting to run over myself, but I can't get away at present. I should like to hear what you thought of them."

Valentine had it on the tip of his tongue to say, "massive and concrete," but thought better of it. He had literally seen them, but had no scholar's knowledge of the subject, though he was good at picking information from other people. He looked appealingly at Aurea, but she was sharpening pencils into the hearth, so he faced the assault again.

"Well, sir, I only got a layman's impression of them—I know very little of the subject. But it would be a great pleasure to me to tell you anything I can. If you cared to ask me questions I could give you some sort of answer, and probably," he added, with his disarming smile, and incidentally with great truth, "you could make a good deal clear to me that I didn't understand."

Mr. Howard put the book down. All was going well, but Fanny called for Valentine and Aurea to begin the game. Valentine apologized for having to go and asked if they could have their talk later on.

"Never mind, Will," said Mrs. Howard looking up from her book. "You can pick Mr. Ensor's brains in the train tomorrow."

"Oh, I'm terribly sorry, Mrs. Howard," said Valentine, "but I'm not going up by the early train after all. Will that be all right, Fanny, if I come with you?"

Fanny, who attributed Valentine's change of plan to her own charms, said it would be quite all right.

"But if you'd let me come and call some time," said Valentine, "I'd be awfully pleased to tell Mr. Howard anything I can about the excavations."

"Of course we will be delighted," said Mrs. Howard. "Oh, but you are dining with us on Tuesday, aren't you?"

Unfortunately these words reached Fanny's ears. "But—but—" she began. Then all her better nature, or her love of mischief, came to the rescue, and gulping down the furious expostulation which was surging in her, she decided not to spoil Valentine's game. After all, she had asked Aurea down to amuse him, and if they had got off at once, she vulgarly said to herself, and Valentine wanted to dine with the Howards and throw her and Arthur over, why, it would be kindness to let him. So she contented herself with making a hideous face at Valentine, who looked deprecatingly at her and moved over to the card table.

Meanwhile, Mr. Howard was explaining that he would be out on Tuesday, and that though it was his house he got very little consideration in it. Mrs. Howard, knowing how much he enjoyed his attitude, expressed contrition.

"Oh, it's all right, Mary, quite all right. But I do wish you wouldn't change your mind so often." He put on his glasses and retired into his book.

The cards had been cut. Arthur and Fanny played together. "And please remember, Arthur," said his wife, "that I occasionally like to play a hand."

"Last time we were partners," said Arthur to the company generally, "I was dummy for every game but one."

"Indeed you weren't," answered Fanny, "unless you mean the evening you were asleep and I saved your life. Get on with the dealing, Arthur."

"That's very nice, Valentine, that you are coming up tomorrow with Fanny and me," said Aurea, "but I'm afraid you'll find you're rather squashed in the back seat with all the rugs and suitcases."

"I had a kind of idea," said Valentine, "that some of the suitcases were going in front with Fanny."

"Then, where do I go?"

"I had a feeling that you were coming in the back with me."

"If Fanny prefers the company of the suitcases, I suppose I might."

Fanny, who had been collecting ashtrays, heard the last words as she returned to the table.

"What's that, Aurea?" she said. "Do you want to go behind? Do. Arthur, for God's sake finish sorting your cards and let's get on."

Fanny was a born player of bridge, which she played with a poker face, a gambler's instincts, and invariable luck. None of the others played seriously, so there was bound to be trouble, which indeed began when Arthur, looking at his hand, said gloomily:

"A job lot if ever I saw one. No bid."

"What kind of convention is that?" asked Fanny tartly.

"No convention. A rotten hand," said Arthur defiantly.

Fanny was going to retort, when Aurea bid a heart. Fanny bid a spade, Valentine two hearts.

"No bid," said Arthur. Then, noticing his wife's expression, he added, "All right, Fanny, come and look at my hand if you don't believe me."

"No bid," said Aurea, but Fanny, invoking the shades of the Portland Club, gave a short and brilliant lecture on the laws of bridge to all who cared to listen. Arthur endured it with patience because he hated cards, and the longer Fanny talked the less time there would be for playing. Aurea and Valentine were both secretly and romantically struck by the fact that the game would probably be played, whenever Fanny chose to allow it to proceed, in hearts, their joint contribution. Each would have been ashamed to confess it to the other, but such trifles can pull strongly at unanchored minds. Valentine finally cut across Fanny's lecture by asking her if she had anything to say, which nearly deprived her of her reason with rage. So two hearts it was, and Fanny's lead.

Fanny played brilliantly. Arthur was perpetual dummy. Valentine and Aurea played in a dream. Aurea, in any case, was the kind of player who scores by copying from a next-door neighbor, taking great care to put the figures in the opposite column of course, so it is hardly surprising that the Turners won four and sixpence each from their guests.

While the party lay torpid after Fanny's excellent lunch, their hostess did some thinking. So far her plans had gone fairly well. The Howards were quietly enjoying themselves. Mrs. Howard would always fit in, and Mr. Howard had got a lot of pleasure out of disapproving of bridge. They wouldn't want to walk far on such a cold, wet afternoon. Aurea must walk, but with whom? Fanny's original plan had been to send Aurea out with Arthur to annoy Valentine, and though Valentine, in spite of his treacherous behavior about dinner on Tuesday, hardly looked as if he would be annoyed enough to make it worth while, she did not alter her plan. Accordingly, at three o'clock she ordered Arthur to take Aurea for a good tramp and be back for tea at five. Both her victims seemed content and set off in mackintoshes. Mr. Howard showed symptoms of wanting to go too, but Fanny, determined that her Arthur should have fair play, delayed him, and finally sent him for a shorter walk with Valentine.

"And that," she remarked to Valentine, when they were alone for a moment, "will learn you not to desert your old friends for the first young woman you meet."

"I knew I could rely on you, Fanny," was Valentine's answer, and Fanny was left wondering exactly what he meant. She went back to the drawing room to pump Mrs. Howard about Aurea, but was met by such bland imperturbability that she fell back discouraged, and took to needlework. Another of her lovely quilts was excuse enough for staying by the drawing room fire peacefully. So she and Mrs. Howard sat happily sewing and reading till the walking expeditions returned.

Mr. Howard, a good enough judge of men apart from their relations with women, had taken a liking to Valentine, who found that Mr. Howard by himself was very different from Mr. Howard rather fussed among his womenfolk. He was a scholar of wide learning and reading, with larger sympathies and a wider outlook than Valentine had realized. Ever since Valentine had, almost impertinently, spoken to him about excavations, he had treated him as a reasonable contemporary. This subtle flattery made Valentine show his best side; the side that was mostly trampled down under the dancing floor. He was not a scholar in Mr. Howard's sense of the word, but he had lived much among men of the world, and had traveled in most of Europe. His mind was well trained and supple, though apart from his work he gave it little to do, and it was like a machine racing in the void. He was quite intelligent enough to know this and dispassionately to deplore it; but too lazy, too easily led into easier paths by the charmers, he let year after year slip by without any full use of his powers. To Mr. Howard's tacit acceptance of him as an equal he responded at once, and talked clearly and cleverly about what he had seen in Rome.

"I wish I could have gone there myself this spring," said Mr. Howard, "but I will not leave England till my daughter has gone. We see so little of her."

"Has Mrs. Palgrave lived long in Canada?" asked Valentine.

"Her husband was offered a post there just after the War, and they have been there ever since. She used to visit us regularly, but it has somehow been more difficult of late years."

Valentine longed to ask why, but felt that Mr. Howard would resent such an intrusion.

"You must miss her, sir," seemed a safe thing to say.

"We do," said Mr. Howard. "You won't know what I am talking about, Ensor, but as we get older we feel through our children more and more. I suppose all parents except and claim from life a better and happier time for their children than they have had themselves; but it is a false hope. There is no continuity of progress in human lives. No experience that the parents can have will help the children. Every generation has to learn its own lesson, and the hardest lesson is the one that we have to learn towards the end of our lives: that we cannot help those whom we most love. Materially, yes. Spiritually, very little. It is all very well for the pelican to make a nest of its own feathers, but the young don't want it. They prefer to hurt themselves in their own way. The nest is left empty."

Mr. Howard looked so haggard as he spoke that Valentine was touched.

"At least, sir," he said, "Mrs. Palgrave is lucky to have you and Mrs. Howard to come back to sometimes."

"Perhaps, Ensor, perhaps. But children don't always want to talk to their parents, and then they keep away."

"Mrs. Palgrave was very young when she married, wasn't she, sir?" said Valentine. "I remember Arthur saying something about it years ago, just after I had left Oxford."

"Yes, she was very young and very dear," said her father. "Regrets,

Ensor, are of little use, or I should allow myself bitter regrets that I ever permitted it. She was too young to know what she wanted—what she needed."

"She is so young now," said Valentine.

"That's half the tragedy. She has seen too much and known too much in her youth. I don't know exactly what, but some kind of cruel impression has been made on her. I blame no one, but there is some kind of incompatibility in her life which makes me afraid for her. She is very reserved, very loyal, and in some ways very childish. She won't talk and she won't complain. She accepts things just as a child does, and doesn't try to protest. I know it is because she doesn't want to make us unhappy, but we know her looks and voice too well. I sometimes wonder if when her mother and I are dead she will be happier. Then there will be no one to hide her secrets from. Ah, well, it is useless to regret and useless to look ahead. You say you were at Oxford, Ensor—which college?"

Most agreeably Ensor had been at Mr. Howard's old college, so that fellowship was established, and the conversation didn't return to Aurea. Perhaps Mr. Howard felt he had said too much. But Valentine thought again, as they walked, of darkness under her eyes and a little hollow below each cheekbone, and wanted to be allowed to touch her face, once, very gently.

As they came in they met Arthur and Aurea. Aurea was windblown, untidy and wet. Arthur said she had sped along like a greyhound, landed him in a boggy meadow, and torn him to pieces by trying short cuts through barbed wire.

"I am enjoying myself frightfully, Fanny," said Aurea as they all came into the drawing room. "It was a heavenly walk, and tea to look forward to."

"What did you talk about?" said Fanny.

"Mostly nothing," said Aurea. "We just walked."

After tea Fanny's energy abated. She summoned Valentine to play duets with her on the piano, which were much like other duets, with loud countings, pushings and shovings, fights for the pedals, and moments of more acute agony when they scratched each other's fingers because their parts overlapped, or were written too close together. But all performances are more for the pleasure of the players than the audience.

The rest of the party were allowed to lie stretched on sofas, or wallowing in large chairs. Mr. and Mrs. Howard went gently to sleep in spite of the duets, and Fanny, seeing this, obligingly trampled on the soft pedal and kept it down in spite of Valentine's efforts to dislodge her. Apart from a belief that when once a note was more than two ledger lines above or below the stave it didn't matter what you played, she was a good sight reader. Valentine didn't read so well, but he had the unfair advantage of hands that could take ten notes easily with some black ones in between, and he kept accurate time. So that, on the whole, he and Fanny were pretty evenly matched.

"I am so happy, Arthur," said Aurea. "It's all perfect here. Food, fires and friends."

Arthur said nothing, but one was used to that. Secretly he rejoiced that his house was giving Aurea pleasure. What she had just said must be meant a little for him. She was lying quietly back in her chair watching the fire. Looking at her he was conscious of heavenly rest, a prevading stillness that turned all his thoughts to a deep, brooding affection. Her sensitive face was a mirror to her wandering thoughts of laughter, of anxiety, of fear. At last her eyes brimmed with tears, and she began to dab them furtively with her handkerchief. Arthur was appalled and looked around anxiously, but the Howards were safely asleep, Fanny and Valentine dealing with a slow movement that had far too many demi-semiquavers, and the room too dimly lighted for anyone to see Aurea's desolate face. She looked once at him and apparently reassured by his immobility, made no attempt to restrain the flow of her tears. He was afraid to move or say a word lest this strange unhappy confidence should be frightened away. He felt that Aurea had something to tell him, but what it was he could not guess. There must be some help for her silent grief, but one hardly dared to offer any. His long habit of silence could not be easily broken, and probably no words would be much good. He leaned forward with his pipe in his hands, screening Aurea from the piano. After what felt like eternity a thin voice said, "Thank you, Arthur. I am good now. It was about leaving mother and papa."

"I see," he said. He was shaken by this rediscovery of Aurea. All his thoughts of her as a brilliant unattainable creature were shattered. It was only a frightened and desperately homesick child trying to behave.

"You don't despise me, do you?" went on the tear-exhausted small voice.

Arthur would have given a good deal to break through his barriers of reserve. All he could say was, "No, I don't."

This seemed to reassure Aurea, who went on, "You see I simply can't bear to think of leaving them again. Would you mind if I go on talking a little."

Arthur said nothing, but pulled his sheltering chair a little nearer, and busied himself with relighting his pipe.

"You see, it's worse every time," said Aurea, who had stopped crying, "and I feel such a devil. Of course I know there are the children and I adore them, but one's children don't really need one, and one's parents do. It is so awful to think of them missing me. I could put up with it if it were only I missing them, but when I have got into that horrible ship going in the wrong direction I begin to think of them alone at home, so wanting me, and it's more than I can bear. I never ought to have left them, but what can one do? I married for love and what can a woman do more? It comes partly of being so respectably brought up. I always thought if you fell in love with a person you married them—just like that. It didn't occur to me to weigh anything, or think things over. And of course we didn't think Ned's newspaper would keep him always in Canada. Our plan was to make a fortune and come back, but the fortune didn't get made and Ned likes Canada. So there am I on one side of the sea, and mother and papa on the other. Arthur, every night of my life I dream that I am at home again, and when I wake up I'm not. It doesn't need much psychoanalysis to analyse that. And every night when I am over here I dream that I am back in Canada, and can't make out why, and I cry and cry, and then, thank goodness, I wake up and I am safely here. But soon I shall be back in Canada again with that other dream. Oh, dear!"

"You are still very beautiful," said Arthur.

Aurea managed a rather doleful smile. "Thank you, Arthur," she said. "Coming from a gentleman of your well-known unsusceptibility, of course one values it. But I feel terribly humble in front of you."

"Why?"

"Well, because of you being so happy with Fanny."

"But why should that make you feel humble?"

"Perhaps it sounds mad, but when one sees people being very happy and having successful marriages, one feels very out of it, and one respects something in them that one can't do oneself."

"Aren't you happy then?" said Arthur, looking at the fire.

"Oh, no."

"Could I do anything?"

"Nothing, thank you. There's nothing wrong that you could lay your finger on. Only if Ned were just comfortably dead it would not be very regrettable. Now I suppose you despise me."

"I don't change my opinion of you."

"Oh, thank you. I really am grateful for people being kind. Don't think I'm a heartless beast. It isn't Ned's fault altogether. I'm a poor kind of wife in some ways. We are just—different."

"How?"

Aurea looked as if she were going to speak, and then thought better of it.

"You can't shock me," said Arthur placidly.

"I wouldn't try. It's just nothing," she added, looking sombrely away. "Only things. Things I hate. Things I can't bear. At least, that's not true, because whatever you have to bear, you can bear. And if you can bear one thing, they, whoever they are, say, 'Ha-ha, she can stand that, can she? Very well, let's give her some more.'"

Enthralled by this philosophical flight, Aurea looked almost cheerful again.

"It is such a help to talk about myself," she explained, "and so very bad for me. I didn't mean to."

"I like it," said Arthur. "You see I know quite a lot about life—professionally—and you can say anything you like to me. It's safe."

"Do you mean not even tell Fanny?" said Aurea.

"Certainly not Fanny."

At this moment the duet came to a long-drawn end of interminable tonic and dominant chords. The Howards woke up. Fanny remarked in a loud voice that Beethoven never knew when to stop, adding kindly that it was doubtless because he was deaf. Then she took Mrs. Howard and Aurea to the kitchen to make amusing things for Sunday supper, and for the rest of the evening conversation was general. Aurea went quite happily to bed, but after an hour's sleep she woke suddenly and could not sleep again. There was a storm in her mind that she couldn't understand. The night felt like a century's delirium, where all thoughts, all remembrances fled faster than the wind, and returned in maddening recurrence. Reading was no good, for she couldn't understand what she read. It was useless to have drinks of water, or look out of the window. Nothing would stop the riot in her mind. It was not till long after that first rowdy and ill-timed chorus of birds, who have nothing better to do than to yell before dawn and then go happily to sleep themselves, leaving a wrecked and exasperated world hopelessly awake, that she closed her eyes. When Fanny called her next morning, she felt battered and spent. Fanny could have diagnosed it, but Fanny for once was blind.

CHAPTER 3

Mr. and Mrs. Howard and Arthur went off by the early train as arranged. Fanny, Aurea and Valentine idled away an hour or two pleasantly enough before driving up to town. Aurea and Valentine sat in the back seat, and Valentine regrettably took Aurea's hand.

"Do you know," she said gravely, "that this is a very common kind of behavior."

"What is?"

"Holding people's hands in cars."

"Then let's be common," said Valentine cheerfully.

So they were common till they got to London, where Fanny dropped Valentine at a tube station and drove Aurea home.

"Goodbye, and a thousand thanks for a heavenly time," said Aurea. "I expect we shall meet you at the Sinclairs' on Tuesday."

"No, I don't think we shall go. Val has chucked us to dine with you, and I don't like to go to a party with nothing but a husband." And having planted this barbed shaft, Fanny drove off, leaving Aurea rather uncomfortable. Had she perhaps been poaching on Fanny's preserves? Would Fanny really mind because Valentine had thrown her over? It would be horrid if she did, because one wanted Arthur's wife to like one, and one thought on the whole she did, in spite of her brusque ways. Would it perhaps be better to ring Valentine up and tell him to come another evening? But even as this foolish thought passed through her mind, she knew that whatever happened Valentine must dine with her on Tuesday. It was already one whole hour since she had seen him, and there were, roughly, thirty more hours to be got through before she could see him again. Anything might happen in that time. Valentine had broken one engagement to dine with her: mightn't he break his word to her for someone else? He has deceived his hostess and may thee, she remarked sardonically to herself. This made her laugh, but almost at once her laughter was swallowed up in anxiety. Even if Valentine did mean to keep his word, he might be unavoidably detained, or be ill. Or she might be ill herself, or her father and mother might be ill, or even worse the cook, in which case Mrs. Howard would certainly want to put Valentine off. Or it might be a mistake about the night. Ought she to ring him up and make perfectly sure that it was Tuesday? She ran downstairs and got as far as the telephone, when she had to stop for breath. Her heart was thumping so hard that she knew she couldn't speak naturally, and she had the horribly empty feeling which is experienced in a rapidly descending lift. She went slowly upstairs again to her room and knew at last, fatally, what had happened. This, she reflected, is being in love.

She sat on a chair, suspended in a whirling void, empty of all thoughts, all emotions; hurled skywards by great whirlwinds; dropping like a plummet to the depths of the earth; consumed in hidden fires; overwhelmed beneath roaring mountainous billows; deafened, blinded, deprived of all power to speak or feel. From her looking glass a strange woman stared at her. All values were lost and time had ceased to exist. Eternity passed in a few moments. After millions of years the winds and waves and flames subsided. Time was restored. Her own face looked at her from the glass.

The day passed in a trance. Night had no sleep; only waking dreams, where all her thoughts were of Waterside, reliving every moment again and again, listening to what Valentine said, reading fresh meanings into his words, tormenting herself with fears that they might never meet again, feeling sure that Valentine cared for her, but not knowing how much, longing to see him, fearing to see him, shaken and wasted as she had never been.

The next day passed as they always do. The world did not come to an end, nor had Valentine forgotten his engagement. He turned up at eight o'clock punctually, looking clean and distinguished. At the sight of him, Aurea thought perhaps it was all a dream from which she would awake heartwhole.

Mrs. Howard was inwardly almost as much perturbed as her daughter. Sitting at dinner between Aurea and Valentine, she observed them both anxiously. Aurea was quite obviously a little drunk with excitement, but then the child had a way of sparkling when gentlemen were about. Not, Mrs. Howard reflected fondly, that she had ever run after men, but she had a charming feminine reaction to their company. Mrs. Howard was all in favor of her daughter amusing herself, but this was something more alarming than Aurea's usual amusements. She would trust Aurea herself under any circumstances. The child had what used to be called good principles, and these would serve her well. But what about Mr. Ensor? She had taken a liking to him and had a vaguely protective feeling about him. If he were going to fall in love with Aurea it would do him no good. Aurea would always control her feelings, and Mr. Ensor was probably used to charmers who didn't. He would very likely be hurt, and it would make Aurea miserable. She didn't feel at all capable of handling either of them. It was particularly unlucky that he should have turned up near the end of Aurea's stay, when she was unhappy and needing distraction. She stole a glance at the unhappy daughter, who was looking extremely pretty and being very impertinently funny, but betraying nothing except what a mother's morbidly watchful eye might detect. Mr. Ensor, on the other hand, was in a quite alarming state. His excellent appetite was indeed in no way affected, but his eyes were nearly starting out of his head; he was talking quite incoherently, and had a general look of straining at a leash which might snap at any moment. Mrs. Howard sighed to herself at the difficulty of it all. It was hard work being a mother, she thought. One had a daughter, and she married and left one. Then she wasn't happy. It might be partly her own fault or not, but she was your own child whatever happened, and you could kill anyone who hurt her. Aurea had written less and less about her life with Ned of late years, and wouldn't talk about him. Mrs. Howard, as ignorant as only a happily married woman of her generation can be, had vague fears and suspicions from which she resolutely averted her mind. Aurea, she felt sure, did not care for any other man. She had loved Ned Palgrave as a girl, and was too honest to seek refuge from disillusionment in having affairs. Mrs. Howard knew her daughter had been dead for years as far as affection for her husband was concerned. Friends and children filled her life, and she had told herself they must be enough. There were worse fates, Mrs. Howard tried to persuade herself, than having a husband one didn't love. He might be a brute, or a drug-fiend, or an unlucky gambler, or unfaithful: though this last word was one which Mrs. Howard would hardly have said aloud. But Mrs. Howard was not going to sit by and see Aurea made more unhappy than necessary, and if Mr. Ensor was going to complicate her life she felt she would have to interfere, even at the risk of rousing Aurea's resentment. Perhaps Mr. Ensor, who was too nice to be hurt, would see reason on the subject. Vain faith of a mother and courage vain!

Mrs. Howard took her company into the drawing room, telling Valentine he might smoke there. Aurea went off to the other end of the room, and began making little noises on the piano. Valentine would obviously have liked to follow her, but politeness kept him by his hostess.

"Do you like your coffee black, Mr. Ensor?"

"Please, and two lumps, may I?"

"Will was so disappointed to miss you, but he hopes to have his talk with you another time."

Valentine's eyes were glued on Aurea and his attention was elsewhere. When his hostess stopped speaking, he brought it back with a jerk.

"I'm frightfully sorry," he said. "I didn't hear what you were saying. The piano distracted me."

"So I noticed," said Mrs. Howard drily. "I was only saying that Will was sorry he had to be out tonight."

"So am I," said Valentine effusively and untruthfully.

"But you must come again and have your talk with him."

"I'd love to."

"And I'd like to have a talk with you myself some time," said Mrs. Howard, "but just now you must excuse me, as I've got some letters that must be written. Aurea will look after you."

"That's splendid," said the distracted Valentine. "I mean I'm awfully sorry—I mean—"

Mrs. Howard gathered her scarf and bag, and rose in a slightly annihilating way. "Aurea," she said.

Aurea stopped playing.

"We must start about a quarter past ten."

"All right, mother darling, I'll be ready." She resumed her playing, while Ensor opened the door for Mrs. Howard. Then he lit a cigarette and came over to the piano and watched Aurea.

"Hello, Valentine," said she. "Has mother done her famous act of Mrs. Howard exhibiting tact?"

Valentine said nothing. His whole body and mind were in indescribable turmoil. This, he reflected, without considering how often he had previously made the same reflection, was quite unlike anything that had ever happened before. Here was this enchanting creature, older than the charmers, yet more attractive; far more experienced in some ways, yet of heartbreaking innocence; ill-mated, or so he had gathered from her father, but not asking for pity; confidingly friendly, but able to keep one at arm's length. How heavenly it would be to have her for a friend, to give her the cool affection which was so obviously all she needed, never to disturb her. A good resolution, but Valentine was a bad gardener, and could not resist the temptation to dig up his seeds and examine their progress. Quite suddenly, in a voice that wasn't his, he said, "Aurea, you have the loveliest hands in the world, and the loveliest voice."

Aurea stopped playing and looked up. Of course it was unavoidable that this should happen, but she must get time.

"You aren't by any chance falling temporarily in love with me, are you?" she asked lightly.

"No," said Valentine, so fiercely that it surprised them both. He turned his back on Aurea and walked to the far end of the room.

Aurea got up and went toward him. Valentine turned, and they met face to face.

"I can only say," said Valentine with a rapid thick utterance, "that I have thought of you consecutively for every single moment since yesterday."

Aurea was quite still. "I know, I know," she said.

"I thought I was old enough to be a man of the world, and have *savoir faire*," said Valentine, managing to laugh at himself a little, "and in general keep my senses. But I can think of nothing but you—you—you."

Aurea didn't move. "Yes, I know," she said.

"How do you know?"

"Because," said Aurea, speaking quickly, as if there were not a moment to lose, "there hasn't been a moment since Fanny and I left you yesterday that you haven't been in my thoughts."

"Then you have felt it too."

"I haven't slept all night. I have put it to myself in every possible way. I have thought how ugly it could all sound. Here are you, a man who has lately been divorced and, as far as outsiders know, for good reasons. Here am I, a respectable married woman with two growing-up children, away from my husband. One's friends could make it sound very unromantic, couldn't they?"

They stood an arm's length apart and looked at each other. Valentine, Aurea recognized rather wearily, was less under control than she was. She knew that she only had to move a step forward for Valentine to take her in his arms. But what then? It didn't perhaps matter so frightfully whether a man kissed one or not, but in Aurea there rose suddenly a passionate desire that Valentine should not be with her as he probably was with other charmers. They kissed and laughed and forgot. She would never forget, but she would not let herself have even a kiss to remember: as for laughing, that, thank heaven, one could always do. Valentine should never find her easy. He could think her cold if he liked, but she would die before she would betray her own answering ardor. I think, she said sardonically to herself, I care more for his honor than I do for my own. He will have to love me without touching me, or not at all.

"Sit down, Valentine, and talk to me," she managed to say. "Why did you tell me about yourself on Sunday morning?"

"I don't know. I had to."

"Do you usually find it a good opening with ladies?"

"You have no right to say that, Aurea," said Valentine furiously.

"How can I tell? Fanny says that charmers by the hundred are at your feet."

"Fanny," said Valentine, becoming a little more normal in manner, "is an untruthful, exaggerating minx. Aurea, I have a thousand million things to say to you and I can't think of one of them."

"Then try to answer my question. Why did you suddenly burst out at me with your life's story?"

"Aurea, I couldn't bear you to think me anything that I am not. I wanted you to know the best and worst of me. I adored you."

"Gentlemen don't usually adore one all in five minutes like that."

"No one could see you without adoring you. Give me your hand."

Not seeing any alternative, Aurea gave it.

"May I give you one very gentle kiss?" said Valentine, who was quite recovering his good spirits.

"Oh, no."

"Are you afraid that a flame will run through us both if I do?"

Aurea withdrew her hand and got up. "Oh, no!" she said, and then she walked up and down the room in great agitation, saying, "Oh, hell! Oh, hell!" in such a plaintive, helpless voice that Valentine couldn't help laughing.

"It's going to be much more hell before we have done with each other," he said cheerfully. "Sit down, Aurea, I won't touch you—truth and honor, I won't."

Aurea sat down. Valentine lit another cigarette. "Oh, heavens," he remarked, "why didn't I know you when we first met? I could have made you happy."

"I very much doubt it. Besides, you must remember that we are very near the same age, which means that when we were both about twenty, I was years older than you. You were only a fledgling then, while I was old enough to be married next year."

"By heavens," said Valentine, "I'd marry you tomorrow if you were free."

"But you see I'm not," said Aurea, finding the conversation distinctly easier. "In fact, I'm a perfectly respectable married woman, and likely to remain so."

"I adore you and adore you," said Valentine irrelevantly.

Aurea couldn't help laughing. "Dear Valentine," she said, "it is perfectly charming and terribly flattering of you to go on like that, and to goggle your eyes at me to that extent, but suppose you try to have about a pennyworth of sense."

"How can I with you about?"

He looked so ardent that Aurea hastily remarked in an abstracted way, "I often wonder what makes men breathe so loud when they think they are in love."

"I would like to shake you," said Valentine, with much feeling.

"Then want must be your master. Dear Valentine, do listen for a moment while I talk to you. You seem a little overwrought tonight, and you'll probably repent it all tomorrow morning. Let me make it easier for you. Couldn't you put your hand on your heart and say, "Darling Aurea, I have been an absolute half-wit and the victim of a divine frenzy. The frenzy having now abated, please forget about it, and be a very dear friend till you leave England." Couldn't you do that for me? I wouldn't think a pennyworth the worse of you for it—perhaps even a pennyworth the better."

"No."

"Oh, please do. It would truly be best, and later on you'll be quite grateful to me that things went no further."

"Don't," said Valentine, getting up and walking over to the fire. Aurea followed him and they stood looking at the flames.

"It's all so overwhelming and romantic and ridiculous," she said in a low voice, "and I never could resist romance."

"Is it only romance, Aurea?"

"No," she said, "it's something more."

She was trembling so, that Valentine could only control his burning desire to take her in his arms by remembering that to frighten her would be the worst thing he could do for himself, and certainly not the way to requite her mother's hospitality. So, without coming any nearer to her, he said: "Is it love?"

"I don't know," said she, never withdrawing her eyes from the flames, "whether it is you that I love, or only a thought that I have of you."

"My lovely darling," said Valentine in a voice of such peaceful tenderness that Aurea felt it like a sword in her heart. Summoning all her resolution, she looked at him steadily before answering, "I can't very well say that to you, can I?"

Valentine had to laugh. "Perhaps ape-face would be more to the point," he remarked.

"I do like to hear you being sensible," said Aurea, and sat down by the fire. Her danger point, she felt, had passed. She was mistress of herself, and could now give her mind to helping Valentine, who was still abundantly in need of help, as was proved by his next remark.

"Aurea," he said in an exalted voice, "this marvelous thing has come to us both, and we must go through with it to the end, whatever it means." And a sillier remark, even by a man in love, has seldom been made.

"My poor Valentine," said his adored one, "your brain must be made of cotton wool. Let me explain to you again, firmly but kindly, that I am nothing if not respectable, and that everything comes to an end for me when I sail for Canada. Need I say it again?"

"I suppose not," said Valentine, and then foolishly added: "But you don't mind being friends till then?"

"It's such an elastic word, Valentine. Friends, yes, with all my heart, but only as far as a line which I draw. I don't want you to have anything to regret when I am gone, and you sometimes perhaps think of me."

"My dear, I know, I know, that there can never be anything between us such as every lover must long for, but I can't help adoring. Will you let me?"

"I don't seem to have very much control over what you do, or don't do," said Aurea piteously. "Oh, dear, how very upsetting it all is. If only I could cry."

"I couldn't bear to see you cry," said Valentine earnestly.

"Selfish beast."

"I'm so sorry. Do cry. Would you like to cry on my shoulder?"

"Of course I should," said Aurea promptly, "but I'm not going to. Do you think I have no principles?"

"I wish I did."

"I can't think," said Aurea, striking out a new train of thought, "why I don't feel wicked or remorseful, but I really don't in the least. But perhaps," she added hopefully, "it will come in time."

She looked so delighted at the comforting thought, that Valentine's heart smote him for the grief he was so abundantly bringing to this beloved creature. But it was only a temporary smiting. The telephone bell rang, and Aurea went to the receiver.

"Hello," she said, "yes, darling, yes, we are going. You are? I thought you were staying at home tonight. Wait a minute and I'll ask mother." She put her hand over the mouthpiece and turned an agonized face to Valentine.

"Valentine, it's Fanny. She says if you can change your mind so can she, and they are going to the Sinclairs after all and want to pick us up. I don't know what to say. I wish she wouldn't, but she knows you are here, and I don't want to seem rude."

"Pretend you are cut off."

"Have you yet met the telephone that could get cut off if Fanny wanted to talk? I'll have to say yes." After a little more talk she put the receiver up.

"She and Arthur are coming around directly," she said with gloomy resignation.

"They would," said Valentine.

Conversation languished. What more was there to say? Both were so shaken with passion that speech was nothing but a barrier. But as the barrier had to be kept up, speech was necessary.

"I must tell mother that Fanny is coming," said Aurea.

"Wait a moment, Aurea. I've got to see you again. When can it be?"

"Whenever you like."

They both spoke in low hurried voices as if enemies were watching and listening.

"May I take you out to dinner tomorrow?"

"I thought you were dining with Fanny. You can't very well throw her over twice."

"Thursday, then?"

"I'd love to."

"And may I call on you tomorrow rather late?"

"You may."

"And may I ring you up tomorrow morning?"

"Do."

"I'll be here then with a taxi at half-past seven on Thursday."

"And may I remind you," said Aurea, "that taxis are apt to have rather an intoxicating effect on gentlemen of your sex?"

"You needn't have said that," said Valentine gravely. "Give me your hand." He raised it to his lips, and let it go. "That," he said firmly, "is what I think of you."

"You are rather an angel," said Aurea. They moved apart as Mrs. Howard came in, anxious because Aurea wasn't ready. Aurea told her that Fanny was coming, and was sent upstairs to tidy herself.

"Come and sit down, Mr. Ensor," said Mrs. Howard. "Did you and Aurea find things to talk about?"

"Quite a lot," said he. "We got on very well. I hope you'll let me take her out to dinner on Thursday."

"I'm sure she would like it."

"And then may I take her to a show, and perhaps to supper?"

"Yes, I suppose so," said Mrs. Howard, rather surprised. "Don't you young people usually make your own plans without consulting us?"

Valentine looked a little confused. "You see, Mrs. Howard," he said, "Aurea is rather different."

"She is; though I shouldn't have thought you were old enough to notice it."

"One couldn't help noticing it. She isn't a bit like anyone else. Not like Fanny."

"I should think not," said Mrs. Howard, bridling, if any one bridles now.

"You see," said Valentine, frowning with the effort of unwonted thought, "Fanny is grown up and Aurea isn't."

Mrs. Howard was taken aback. Aurea's quality of un-grown-upness was obvious enough to her father and mother. They loved it because it was herself, and deplored it because it left her so fatally unprotected against life. But they didn't think it was so noticeable to the first comer. To her liking for Valentine, Mrs. Howard began to add a certain respect for his insight into her child.

"Yes," she sighed, "it is difficult to remember that Aurea is a grown-up person with responsibilities."

"And meeting her in your house makes her seem even younger," said Valentine. "It is ridiculous to think of her with growing-up children."

"And a husband," said Mrs. Howard.

Valentine nearly jumped at these words. Had Mrs. Howard said them pointedly, or was it just a statement? When you have been making love violently to a married woman, your conscience may be a little uneasy in front of her mother with whom you are dining. More had been said or implied between him and Aurea than could ever be undone, and if Mrs. Howard was meaning to warn him, it was too late.

"Yes, I know," he said, rather lamely.

Mrs. Howard looked at him searchingly. The excitement which had made him behave so oddly at dinner was certainly not so acute, but he still looked as if he were walking on air and seeing something over people's heads. Thoroughly exalted and romantic, she thought. And perhaps very upsetting to Aurea. She longed to ask exactly what had been said or looked, but how difficult it was to ask a young man pointblank if he had been making love to your daughter. So obviously it was his affair and Aurea's, not hers. But if Aurea was going to suffer, she would commit any rudeness to save her. Perhaps this hadn't gone very far, and Mr. Ensor seemed understanding enough not to take amiss what she wanted to say.

"Mr. Ensor," she began, "I don't believe in interfering, but I am going to for once, and you must forgive me. You and Aurea seem to have fallen into friendship rather suddenly. Have you looked ahead at all?"

There was a pause. Valentine was half annoyed, half remorseful. He fully realized the justice of Mrs. Howard's question. Naturally he hadn't looked ahead at all. One never did with these affairs, for if you did you would never begin them. But Aurea couldn't be called an affair, that would be insulting. One might call her a revelation of beauty, an answer to every question in life, heart's delight, beloved child; but never an affair, Valentine went hot as he remembered how foolishly he had said to her that they must go through with it whatever happened. That was not looking ahead with a vengeance. It would be the basest kind of treachery to try to lead so inexperienced a creature farther than she wanted to go. The kindest thing would have been never to have spoken. Now it was too late. One couldn't draw back; that would only bewilder and grieve her, and perhaps make her feel that she had been too forward. What then could one do? Would it be possible to cherish this miracle of dearness for the short time that she remained in England, and yet leave her with no worse heartache than a few weeks would heal? One's own heartache, of course, would never heal—although it had healed often before—but that would be of small account if she could escape unhurt. After all, if one had to suffer slow torture on her account, wasn't she worth it?

"No, I hadn't," he said at last, adding rather boyishly, "but I will now."

Mrs. Howard would have liked first to snort and then to groan. To snort on account of the extreme folly of his remark, and to groan because his last words showed her so plainly that it was too late. Exactly what had been said she would never know, but there had been some kind of explanation between them. She prayed that Valentine would be the one to suffer, if suffering there must be. After all, it was possible that Aurea was temporarily carried away, but wouldn't take it all too seriously. If Valentine broke his heart, there would be, according to Fanny, plenty of charmers to mend it. But if Aurea loved too blindly, what hope was there for her?

"Mr. Ensor," she said desperately, "I am going to undertake the very ungrateful task of giving you good advice. When you said that Aurea wasn't grown-up, you said something very true. In spite of a husband and children, she is only a child herself in many ways. I don't know if I ought to say what I am going to say, but I trust you. Aurea's married life has not been a success. She adores her children, but that isn't enough. Her holiday here has been bliss for us all, but she has rooted again in England very strongly, and the wrench of parting with us—even with her children to look forward to—is going to be almost unbearable. If anything else happens to make her more unhappy, it would almost kill her father and myself."

"I would rather kill myself than make her unhappy," said Valentine.

"That wouldn't do much good; and it may be too late."

"What do you mean?" said he quickly.

"My dear Mr. Ensor, I am not blind. You must forgive me for talking to you like this, but she is my only child, and mothers are notoriously fierce when roused. It is so difficult to talk about a subject like this without being either priggish or melodramatic. It isn't that I want to inquire whether your intentions are honorable, because in the first place I think you haven't got as far as having any intentions at all, and in the second place I believe you could love a person unselfishly. I want to ask you, even if you can't stop caring for that child, to do your very best to keep things on such a footing that she won't be made far more unhappy than she need be. If a woman has an empty place in her heart, and a man can fill it who has no right to, it can only mean intense misery for everyone concerned."

Valentine looked so wretched that she hastened to add: "Now I've finished, and if you can forgive me, you must."

Valentine was genuinely touched by her courage. "It's rather fine of you," he said slowly. "I'll do my best, but you don't know how difficult it will be."

Mrs. Howard looked relieved. "Perhaps I don't," she said. "Mothers have to be a nuisance sometimes, but I don't want you to feel that I am meddling. I shan't talk about it again."

"Then do you think, Mrs. Howard, it would be possible for me to take Aurea to this party tonight? If you and she go with Fanny and Arthur, I shan't have a chance of talking to her again."

"I suppose," said Mrs. Howard in a resigned voice, not without a hint of laughter, "that you are twisting me around your little finger, as Fanny said you would do."

"Well," said he apologetically, "I don't want to be a bore, but Fanny really doesn't leave much room for anyone else when she is about."

"I'll see what I can do," said Mrs. Howard, torn between inclination and duty.

"Thank you ever so much. It's great fun to have anyone think me worth scolding."

"My dear young man," said his hostess rather sharply, "I assure you that I certainly wouldn't think you worth scolding, nor should I presume to do it, if it weren't for Aurea. I like you, but I love her."

"I'm glad you like me," said Valentine, quite genuinely. "It's a lonely life sometimes."

"But I thought you had heaps of friends."

"So I have, and I go out a lot. But after weekends or parties there is always an empty bed-sitting-room waiting for one. It's rather a bore."

Mrs. Howard felt the same pity which Aurea had felt about a frayed shirt cuff. The thought of a nice young man alone in lodgings does so melt female hearts, though it is probable that the young men are quite happy, and have deliberately chosen this independent form of life, rather than live at home and have their parents fussing. Besides, what a delightful form of independence, with none of the drawbacks. If you want to go away, you simply shout down the kitchen stairs, "Oh, Mrs. Wilcox, I don't know when I'll be back—Monday perhaps," and you slam the front door. Whereas in your parents' comfortable home they want to know what meal you will be back to because of cook, and may even ask where you are going and what the telephone number is in case anyone wants you, which they certainly won't and you wouldn't want them if they did. Intolerable petty tyranny! Not that Valentine had a family to live with, consisting as it did of a very disapproving sister who inspected factories and had heaps of women friends. He was guiltily conscious that he was again asking for sympathy on false pretenses.

A loud noise was now heard outside the door. It sounded like Fanny. Valentine got up. "I'm sorry," he said, "I didn't mean to be sentimental. And I'll really do my best."

Fanny and Arthur came in; Fanny worked up and heated about something, Arthur evidently under a cloud.

"How do you do, Mrs. Howard," said Fanny. "Do look at Arthur in a black tie, and I've told him it's a white-tie party till I'm black in the face, and all to what purpose? Hello, Val."

Arthur shook hands with his hostess, and then turned on his wife, pointing out that Valentine was in a black tie too.

"Black ties are as worn this week, Fanny," said Valentine. "Haven't you read your fashion page?"

"That's only sour grapes, Val, because you aren't invited to the party."

"But Arthur is," said Valentine pleasantly. "My dear Arthur, you are going in unsuitable attire to an evening party at which, I am given to understand, a string quartet will perform. You will have to stand at the back of the room—your wife having, if I know her, immediately deserted you for some more congenial and sartorially correct companion—and you will be excessively bored by the music, and but little comforted by observing the mirth which your attire will excite among your wife's friends. Don't you wish you were coming with me to my club instead?"

"I do," said Arthur, with heartfelt emotion. "And what's more I will. We can drop Mrs. Howard and the others at the Sinclairs', and then go on to your club. I can come back and fetch you, Fanny."

"I dare say you can, Arthur," said his wife truculently, "and arrive half an hour after the party is over and find me miserably outstaying my welcome. Or else I shall have to take a taxi home and sit on the doorstep as I haven't a latchkey."

"Then take mine."

"And then have to get up and let you in at heaven knows what hour of the night. No thank you."

"Arthur," said Valentine, endeavoring to keep the peace, "you really don't seem to know what is good for you. Fanny, will you relent and take him to the party in his black tie?"

"Isn't that exactly what I am doing?" said the exasperated Fanny, whom Valentine could always rouse to frenzy. "Little credit as he does me, let it never be said that I left him out of any fun that was going."

"Fun! String quartets! Oh, God!" said Arthur bitterly.

Fanny inquired for Aurea and was told she would be down soon. Mrs. Howard inquired about Fanny's chickens. The news was not good. It appeared that someone, as yet unidentified, had bumped an incubator and broken a lamp, and a lot of eggs had died a chilly death before it was discovered and mended. Valentine's conscience suddenly smote him. "I'm awfully sorry, Fanny," he said penitently, "I did give it one bump when I was moving it for you, but I never thought it was broken."

"So it was you who broke it," said Fanny. "It will be many a day, Valentine Ensor, before you are again invited to our well-appointed country residence."

"Can't you do something with the eggs?" said Valentine hopefully. "Scramble them?"

"For those who like dead chickens in their breakfast, the advice is excellent," said Fanny coldly, and turned to Mrs. Howard. "I wish Aurea would hurry up," she said. "Where can we drop you, Val?"

Valentine cast an appealing glance at Mrs. Howard. "Oh, anywhere," he said. "Don't bother if the car is too full."

"I think we shall be rather a squash, Fanny," said Mrs. Howard with great presence of mind, "and you know I don't like being crowded. Suppose you and I go in a taxi, dear, and Arthur can take the others."

Arthur appeared to approve of the plan, which would have meant driving with Aurea. His approval immediately roused Fanny's suspicions. She saw in it a treacherous intention of dropping Aurea at the party and going with Valentine to the club after all, and she announced the fact.

"Very well, dear," said Mrs. Howard, who at last saw a way of gaining her point, "then Mr. Ensor can take Aurea in a taxi and take it on wherever he wants to go, and I'll come with you and Arthur."

Aurea had slipped in during the conversation, and smiled gratitude at her mother.

Just as they were moving to go, Mr. Howard came in unexpectedly from his meeting, so they all delayed their departure. Mr. Howard was evidently in the initial stages of a heavy cold and only too ready to make much of it. He expressed gratification that Mr. Ensor was there, and promised himself much pleasure in continuing their talk when the others had gone. Valentine and Aurea exchanged agonized glances. Mrs. Howard, under the pretext of putting Aurea straight, whispered to her, "Are you very determined to go with Mr. Ensor, darling?" Aurea said she was.

"You aren't going to be hurt by this, are you?" said her mother anxiously. "I couldn't bear it."

"Darling, don't worry so much," said her daughter, hugging her. "I am old enough to take care of myself."

"I wish I thought so," said Mrs. Howard with a sigh. "But never mind." And wondering to herself whether she had Sir Pandarus of Troy become, she set her wits to get her party disentangled. Ignoring Arthur's suggestion that if Val wasn't coming they could all go in his car, she addressed her dear but trying husband, and elicited from him the fact that he had been brought home by friends in an open motor. That meant, of course, that he was in for one of his Important Colds, which made more noise than anyone else's and required special treatment, firm handling, and much sympathy. Mr. Howard confessed that it was foolish of him to have allowed it, and sneezed portentously in confirmation. Hot whisky toddy was recommended, refused, and finally accepted, in which Mr. Howard asked Valentine to join him. Words cannot express the despair of Valentine and Aurea as they saw him doomed to spend the evening with her father, whom he respected, but did not passionately love. Fanny put on her cloak, and was just taking Aurea off, when Mr. Howard sneezed again six times running in an unrestrained way that confounded the senses. Mrs. Howard, seizing her opportunity, ordered him to go straight to bed. Ordinarily he would have resisted, but so appalled was he by the magnitude of his own sneezes, that he was inclined to follow his wife's advice. Mrs. Howard sent Aurea to order the materials for boiling toddy to be put in her father's room, shepherded Fanny toward the door, and told Valentine to ring up a taxi when Aurea came down. He looked expressively thankful. Arthur nearly held everything up by offering to go and sit with Mr. Howard, but Fanny forcibly dissuaded him, remarking that there were people who were less than no good in a sick room, and that among them he held no mean place.

"Good night, Val," she shouted. "Tell your taxi to drive around by Streatham Common."

"Witty woman," said Valentine politely, wondering how much she really meant it. Her voice died away on the stairs, and Valentine was left alone. He sat down and lit a cigarette. There was something silky and furry on the back of his chair; Aurea's cloak which she had left there when she went to see about her father's hot drink. A faint perfume in it brought her vividly to his mind. What was going to come of it all he asked himself. And there was absolutely no answer at all. If one isn't a professional seducer what does come of things? Muddle, heartbreak, a life disoriented, memories deliberately kept alive, or deliberately forgotten. A sterile business. A sweet torment, a bitter delight, a fruitless blossom, a flame that sears and never warms. More than anything he longed to hold Aurea in his arms and see her eyes closing with excess of love. But that was not to be. She knew so little and he knew too much. Could he possibly use his knowledge to help her? Could he, so skilled in easier charmers, put aside his arts before her simplicity, and not let her know what she meant to him? She knew he loved her, but he thought she understood more with mind and sympathy than with bodily passion. It might still be possible not to let her hurt herself past cure. He buried his face in her silks and furs, loving and adoring the faint scent, so like the perfume of her hair.

Aurea, having seen her father properly established, came back to the drawing room, and saw Valentine with her cloak to his lips. Unbearable pain and bliss. Not till he turned around did she make her presence known, when with as careless a voice as she could manage, she said that he had better ring up a taxi now. The number, she added, was written on the outside of the book.

Valentine jumped to his feet. "I thought perhaps the taxi would like to wait a little before it was rung up," he said.

"Oh, no, I think not. You see, mother has been very noble tonight, and I don't think it would be fair to be late at the party. She'll want me."

"But I want you," said Valentine with the fine selfishness of his sex.

Aurea looked afraid. "Oh, please," she said.

"All right, then," said Valentine and he rang up the taxi stand.

"Now I know what your voice is like when you're telephoning," said Aurea in a slightly imbecile way.

"Do you approve?"

"Is that the voice you have for the charmers?"

"No, I have a much better one for them."

"And for me?" said Aurea, which wasn't at all playing the game.

"I haven't anything good enough for you," said he, following her lead. But he wasn't at all prepared for the voice in which Aurea said, "It will do," nor for her look. Doing one's best was not going to be at all an easy job.

"Why do you make me feel like a driveling idiot?" he complained. "And now the taxi will be here in two minutes, and I have said nothing."

"Of course," said Aurea, "if you liked to be extravagant and afford twopence more, it could wait a little."

"I adore you. Where would you like to dine on Thursday?"

"Oh, anywhere, only not dressing, please. I shall feel more private like that."

"And shall we go to a play—or if you aren't dressing, would you prefer a cinema?"

"I'd love a cinema," said Aurea. "Only let me remind you, Valentine, that cinemas have rather the same effect on gentlemen as taxis."

"Rather intoxicating?"

"Yes."

"If I said I wouldn't be intoxicated—truth and honor?"

Aurea looked gravely at him and answered, "I would believe you. Oh, Valentine, isn't it funny that we could have met before and not known each other? When I got home yesterday I looked up some old diaries, and I found a lot about that weekend with Arthur's people, but nothing about you. I'm beginning to wonder if we ever really met at all. The moment I saw you at Waterside, I knew I had seen you before, but now I can't remember anything that happened before Sunday morning."

"I remembered you the moment you spoke, though I hadn't thought of you for all those years. I just remember someone who seemed very cool and far away."

"Oh, go on thinking that."

The taxi hooted outside. Valentine promptly opened the drawing room window and putting his head out, shouted to it to wait.

"You are extravagant," said Aurea, "throwing away twopences like this."

"That's the dashing kind of character I am."

Aurea picked her cloak up. Valentine made a movement to help her, but she was rather nervous, and got behind a chair and put it on herself. The disadvantage of having gone behind a chair was that one was so hemmed in. Valentine was between Aurea and the door, and she wondered if she could get out without an exhausting wrangle.

"Aurea," exclaimed the enamored swain, "I must have something of yours to remind me of you."

"How very material you are," said the adored one.

"A glove, a handkerchief, anything," and Valentine began to look distracted again. Aurea looked in her bag. "Here is a handkerchief," she said meditatively, "but it doesn't seem to be a very clean one. Oh, here you are—a perfectly new handkerchief." She handed it, neatly folded, to Valentine, who took it with an expression of passionate imbecility and put it into his waistcoat pocket. At the same time

Aurea slipped out toward the door, remarking, "It has no name on it, so when the other charmers see it, they won't know whose it is."

"How dare you?" cried Valentine in a fit of indignant virtue. "I was perfectly right. You *were* cool and far off—the coolest and farthest off person I ever met."

Aurea, safely near the door, made one last attempt to return to sanity. "Oh, Valentine," she said piteously, "you must think me a perfect half-wit, but I don't know what to do. You see, I've never been in love with a gentleman before, except getting married, and I don't know the rules. I know I'm a fool, but I do see that this is what is called playing with fire, and it is very foolish and wrong, and should be discouraged. Couldn't you possibly help me?"

What should a gentleman do in such a situation? Valentine was for once completely at a loss. If it had been one of the other charmers—but with them the situation would never have arisen. They liked you to put your arm around their waist, and if you did kiss them they didn't much notice it, except in so far as it deranged hair or make-up. Never before had he been asked to lay down the lines on which a love affair should proceed, and he was completely baffled. What he wanted to say was, "To hell with everything," and take Aurea straight off to Havana, or Sicily, or some equally practical and convenient place. But there seemed to be so many obstacles. It was late; the banks would be shut; one couldn't get a berth or a passport at midnight; and, anyway, one hadn't any money. One couldn't pick her up and take her to one's bed-sitting-room; equally, one couldn't spend the night here. Mrs. Howard was expecting her daughter; the taxi was ticking up twopences; Fanny—blast Fanny—knew where one was and would be full of indiscreet questions. And all the time, there was the idol of one's heart, looking distracted, and asking for guidance which one was incompetent and quite unworthy to offer.

If those two foolish lovers had known it, there was such a simple way out. If Valentine, knocking down a chair and tripping up on the electric light wire, had taken Aurea in his arms, squashed the breath out of her body, and kissed her unmercifully, it is probable that much misery would have been prevented for everyone concerned. Aurea's emotions worked largely in her head, the other kind being stiff with disuse. Her mind was terrified of a kiss or an embrace. Her heart—or whatever one chooses to call that part of one that isn't mind—had told her quite unmistakably what it wanted. One doesn't feel as if one were sitting under a millrace for nothing. But the poor half-wit, as she very properly called herself, didn't understand what her heart was saying. And if she had, she would have told it to be quiet and hold its tongue, and remember she was a lady. If Valentine had taken no notice of her appeal and taken her in his arms, it would have done her all the good in the world. She would have been terrified, then furious, then forgotten to be a lady and smacked his face, then burst into floods of refreshing tears, then had hysterics, and then quite genuinely laughed at herself. Then she would have stopped being frightened, and made great friends with Valentine with much less sentiment involved. They would have danced together, and dined together, and come home in taxis late at night, and no harm done. And when Aurea went back to Canada, she would think of it all as a pleasant spring night's dream.

As for Valentine he would have got what he wanted and, as far as the hysterics were concerned, what he deserved. If a gentleman who has great experience in affairs chooses to set his wits against a lady who has no experience at all, and is handicapped by good principles, the odds are all in his favor. But if to his experience she opposes quite infuriating and dense stupidity and innocence, all his arts are discounted, and serve him right. There was plenty of good in Valentine to respond to any lead in the right direction. His worst fault was that he frittered all his time and energies and emotions away when he wasn't at work. A frightened and hysterical Aurea would have made him pull himself together faster than anything else. And he would have felt a little ashamed and quite unrepentant, and they would have had such fun together. But poor, silly Aurea didn't know this any more than he did, and without meaning to she was leading him on far more than the most expert charmer could have done. Courage was needed, and unfortunately though she had plenty of it, it was of a negative kind. She would refuse to let Valentine touch her or take her hand, though she died a thousand deaths in refusing. But she could not tell him to go. Valentine had too much good feeling to attempt what she so obviously feared, but it was asking too much to expect him to renounce Aurea on the spot.

"My dear," he said, very kindly, "there are only two ways out. One is impossible, and doesn't come into this story at all. The other is that I should put you into your taxi and say goodbye to you now—and forever."

Aurea again disconcerted her admirer by blushing apparently from head to foot. "Oh, I suppose I know what you mean," she said doubtfully, as though her recognition of his meaning might be taken as a proof of innate viciousness. Then the horrible thought of never seeing him again wiped out everything else.

"Oh, but I couldn't say goodbye to you now," she cried. "I haven't the strength of mind. It will be quite bad enough when we *have* to say goodbye."

"It will be far, far worse then, my dear," said Valentine.

"It couldn't be worse than it is now," said Aurea, so drowned in grief that she had forgotten her fears, and laid both her hands on Valentine's arm. He very gently took them off and didn't hold them.

"Ten thousand times worse," he repeated. "But you shall do whatever you like. And now I have spent my twopence, and we must go."

"A lady and gentleman going to a party," said she without moving.

"Is that what you want?"

"I suppose so. Yes, please."

So the lady and gentleman went downstairs and got into the taxi, and Valentine behaved like a perfect gentleman and Aurea like a perfect lady. An outsider would have noticed that they both talked in highly unnatural voices and were quite incoherent, neither knowing what they said themselves, nor what the other said. But no outsider was there to applaud their behavior. Valentine left Aurea at the Sinclairs', and went to his club, and wrote letters to Aurea and tore them up till he was turned out.

Aurea went through the party in a dream. Fanny was, as usual, to the fore, with a group of cavaliers to whom she talked with great ignorance and effrontery about music. Aurea discovered Arthur morosely smoking on the landing. The string quartet had far exceeded his worst fears. Not only were there four foreigners playing stringed instruments, but there was another fellow with an oboe, and worst of all, a woman singing. People might call it Bach, said Arthur bitterly, but he didn't think it was the kind of thing to ask people to hear. Aurea was incapable of hearing anything intelligently, so she agreed with Arthur and suggested that they should go down to supper before the rest of the party got loose. So they went downstairs and found a little table in a corner, and Aurea drank quantities of champagne, which to her great astonishment, had no effect upon her at all.

"I usually get drunk on practically nothing," she explained quite unnecessarily to Arthur, "but tonight I seem to have a three-bottle head."

"Drunk," said Arthur scornfully. "You don't know what the word means. If ever you had drunk so hard that you had to pull up at once or go under, you could talk. I drank far too much once for a few months, and I had to stop myself short because it wasn't doing me any good; and that was no fun at all."

"You weren't really a confirmed drunkard, were you?" said Aurea, looking so alarmed that Arthur began to laugh.

"No, goose," he said. "But when the girl you love goes and marries someone else, you must work, or walk, or drink. I had just enough work then to keep me in London, so I couldn't get away and walk. But there wasn't enough to keep me occupied all the time. So I drank."

"But you don't now," said she anxiously.

"Oh, no—it's too expensive for a married man with a family."

"I hope it wasn't at all my fault," said Aurea hesitatingly. "I couldn't bear to think that I had ever made you unhappy."

"That's all right," said Arthur, "you didn't." Aurea felt secretly rather disappointed. "But," he added, relapsing into his usual somber mood, "I think you would make anyone very unhappy that you didn't care for."

After this he became speechless, and Aurea was not sorry when a round of decent applause proclaimed the end of the music, and the audience began pouring into the supper-room. She was glad to see her mother safely escorted by their host. Then Fanny with three gentlemen in tow appeared at the next table.

"Hello, Aurea," she shouted across the tumult, "Why didn't you bring Val?"

"He wasn't invited," shouted Aurea, "and I'm not a gate-crasher."

"You took long enough getting here, anyway," said the unabashed Fanny. "What were you doing?"

"Making love, of course," said Aurea desperately. The remark was a complete success, and from that moment Fanny's suspicious mind was entirely at rest. She insisted on having her table pushed up close to Arthur's so that they made one party. Her companions, belying Valentine's prophecy, did not despise Arthur for being in a black tie, and Arthur took occasion to point out to his wife that their host was also in a dinner jacket. When the quartet came in, they all turned out to be friends of Fanny's, and kissed her hand and added themselves to the party. Fanny was enjoying herself frightfully with seven admirers around her, and managed to flirt outrageously with every one of them. Aurea was delighted and amused by Fanny's brilliance, and entirely unenvious of what she couldn't hope to emulate. Arthur, she thought, looked suddenly tired. It must sometimes be difficult to work hard all day and keep up with Fanny at night. Arthur had absented himself, as he so often did, from the noisy surroundings, and was leaning back, wrapped in his own thoughts. Now and again his eye fell tolerantly and admiringly on his wayward wife. He knew that she would not notice that he was tired, but if he could force himself to be so far articulate as to hint to her that he was, she was capable of getting up in such a whirlwind of repentant haste as to upset the table, and taking him straight home. Therefore, he said nothing. Aurea, he thought, looked very lovely, and he rejoiced to see her looking so happy. The memory of her silent tears had been with him, uncomfortably, ever since Sunday.

Then people began to go, and Aurea said goodbye and went off to find her mother. As they drove back, mother and daughter were silent. Mrs. Howard was wondering whether she had better tell Aurea about her conversation with Mr. Ensor. On the whole, better not, she thought. One could trust Mr. Ensor to say nothing about it and it might, not unnaturally, annoy Aurea. When they were home Mrs. Howard did summon up courage to say, "Is it quite all right about Mr. Ensor, darling?" and Aurea answered, "Absolutely all right, darling. We are terribly in love and it is going to be a tremendous affair." Then she kissed her mother and ran upstairs and, overcome with excitement, emotion and champagne, went to sleep at once. As it is the last good night she will have for many weeks to come, it is just as well that she should sleep soundly now.

Mrs. Howard looked softly in at her husband's door, and found him peacefully asleep. She went to her own room, wondering about Aurea's last words which had partly alarmed and partly reassured her. If by any conceivable chance Aurea were speaking the exact truth, how appalling and hopeless. But that was impossible. She knew Aurea too well. From a child she had had an ostrich way of hiding her emotions which made them but all too visible. She had never been able to pretend that she didn't care for people well enough to deceive anyone. If she really cared for Mr. Ensor, she wouldn't be able to talk of it so lightly. In fact, her whole attitude to him from the beginning had been so open that there couldn't be much in it. What had probably happened was that Mr. Ensor had made some kind of declaration and Aurea, who was really good at keeping people off, had laughed him out of it. And what Aurea had said was just her customary exaggeration, to make it sound important. Probably she would be a little beside herself for the next few weeks, and rather in a whirl of lunches and dinners and taxis, but that would keep her from thinking of her departure, and Mrs. Howard could not bear the moments when her child forgot to forget and her face suddenly became haggard and lined. Mrs. Howard was a kind woman, but she sometimes wished to herself, as her daughter had wished, that Ned Palgrave were just comfortably dead. But he wasn't, nor was he likely to be, so one must make the best of things, and be glad that Mr. Ensor had taken one's perhaps quite unnecessary interference so nicely. She sighed, took up a book, and read herself to sleep.

CHAPTER 4

The next few weeks were to be the happiest and the unhappiest that Aurea had ever known, or was ever to know again. As she explained to Valentine, "The trouble is, Valentine, that I loved you before I had time to know if I liked you. I quite thought I was going to like you very much at Waterside, and then suddenly this love business had to get in the way and I loved you so much that I simply couldn't see straight, and I haven't the faintest idea whether we could be friends or not. I think possibly not, but now I shall never know." It didn't matter in the least, Valentine assured her; but Aurea didn't take much notice of what he said, because she knew he was wrong. She had made him into an idea, and ideas are quite fatal to women. If they get abstract ideas they become magistrates, or run the local branch of the League of Nations Union, or found a new Women's Institute if they live in the country, and they take their object very seriously, and do their work far too conscientiously, and without any of that necessary sense of the ultimate worthlessness of everything one does. Still, it keeps them happy and out of mischief, and at least does no very serious harm. Mrs. Howard had for years had an amiable idea about the poor, and had tired herself very much by committees and visiting, putting so much personal interest into it that she would usually finish the day on the sofa. Then she had overheard a chance remark by one of her poor women about a lady who was visiting the poor, and entrapping mothers to bring their babies to a clinic to be weighed weekly. Waste of time, and worrying to the mothers, thought Mrs.

Howard privately. In my time if a baby slept all night and didn't cry, all was well. Now, if it doesn't put on the Board of Health standard number of ounces in the week, the mother is wildly anxious for the next seven days, and that doesn't do the baby any good. "Poor thing," the woman had said of the visitor, with the large and tolerant philosophy of the poor, "she likes it and I let her." That was about the ultimate value of ideas.

But there was a far more dangerous idea for women and that was a personal one. Body and mind appeared to be far more mixed up in women than in men, so that one didn't quite know the difference between a mental attraction and a physical one. But if once your mind was possessed by an idea it might drag your body into anything. Aurea knew, fatally and dispassionately, that Valentine was not suitable for her, not quite worthy of her. It might sound conceited to think that, but it was true nevertheless. She knew that if Heaven had suddenly seen fit to remove Ned and make her a widow, incidentally providing either her or Valentine with a large income, things would have been little better than they were. She and Valentine could never live in peace together. Even making allowances for the fierce jangling of nerves which their present inharmonious relations involved, they were too different ever to mix. Putting aside all talk of intellectual interests, or tastes in common, physical passion was, if one looked straight at things, the only way they could at all understand each other. And in that Aurea had little faith, having already experienced its transitory qualities. Already she was aware, though she didn't like to think of it, that she cared for Valentine, fatally, more than he could care for her, and that this would always be the case. Not that she questioned the real sincerity of his love, but she knew, as well as if she had seen it in a magic mirror, that Valentine was, luckily for himself, incapable of living on the passions of the mind. When they parted, he would be wretched beyond speech, and suffer deeply. But the end of it would be a scar that had healed, and quite possibly oblivion when another woman had crossed his path, who had a right to give all that Aurea could not and dared not offer. Her own case would be different. Love, she concluded, was like red hair, or a deformity of some sort.

You had it; and that was that. Nothing but death could part you; as for after death, useless to discuss that. Eternal rest would be enough, if one could only be sure of getting it. Her love would not be a scar that had healed. It would be something that was always with her. There would be days, later, perhaps, weeks and months, when it would lie quiet in her breast. Then for no reason, called up by one of the thousand chances that stir the chords of the heart, it would blaze again and be the torture one so well knew it to be. Then for weeks, days, perhaps months, one would be so consumed, so shaken by the mere thought of a man whom one had never even kissed, that the world would become distant and veiled. No one ever to talk to about it. And in a few years one would be too old for him to care for one, even if he had remembered. A man of forty would have his life before him. A woman of forty would have done her work, which was, after all, having children, Aurea supposed, and trying to bring them up. After that your children took you in hand and brought you up, and you were lucky if they were even interested enough to do that. But as for love, it would only be silly—the kind of thing one laughed at in other people. No, there was nothing for it but to grin and bear it, and to be extraordinarily glad that one hadn't gone through life without this experience, even if it brought no kind of happiness with it. And what in the name of heaven was happiness? Certainly being in love wasn't happiness; it meant every kind of torture, only inexplicably, one wouldn't have it otherwise. Perhaps it was only another idea. One made an idea of a person in one's head, and then decided that everything to do with this idea must be happiness. Then one accepted gratefully all the pains that it involved. So that the only way to get through life comfortably would be to have no ideas at all, in fact, to be an idiot. And that's what I am, thought Aurea, only the wrong sort, without any of the advantages.

One of the great drawbacks to living in London, Aurea and Valentine discovered, was that there were so few places where one could court in comfort. The streets were abominably well-lighted. Taxis were repellent to her taste. Gone were the days of happy silent movies, where one sat in warm emotion drenched silence, whispering, under cover of a gentle orchestra, the more idiotic phrases of love. No restaurant, however cheap, appeared to cater for people who wanted to hold hands unseen—for she had found herself forced to abandon her intransigent attitude about holding hands (though further she conceded nothing), and appeared to Valentine to find great comfort in clinging to one of his fingers. It felt safer like that, she said, than if he held her whole hand. That would be one of the small things to remember her by, later, and would send a pang to Valentine's heart—till he forgot it.

Their first outing together was only a sample of the trials that beset middle class London lovers who are being very honorable. Valentine fetched Aurea in a taxi as he had promised, and took her to dinner at a pot-house in Soho. This is always rather a test of a cavalier, because to be taken out by a man who boggles over the dinner and doesn't command the affection and awe of the waiter, is a horrid disillusion. Aurea was pleased to find that Valentine took the whole matter in hand without hesitation, ordered food and wine without consulting her, and immediately became the lifelong patron and esteemed friend of the waiter. Aurea was deeply impressed with Valentine's fluent Italian, though he hastily explained that it was really only of the hotel railway variety.

"I wish I could take you to Italy, Aurea," he said, not wasting any time on preliminaries. "There people really understand love. Here they marry and have children and live and die, and never know what love means."

"Oh," said Aurea, feeling inferior to people in Italy.

"You, of all women," said her adorer, warming to his subject, "ought to know what love can be. Probably you have been hurt and mauled—I don't know and I don't ask—but I could make you forget all that if you were my wife."

Seeing that Aurea looked a little frightened, he obligingly stopped. She wasn't quite sure what Valentine meant, and was wrestling with a vision of him and a bevy of Italian mistresses, all in bright colored aprons and striped scarves, like Masetto's wedding festivities in *Don Giovanni*. And however little one may wish to be a gentleman's mistress oneself, it is mortifying to imagine him with forty or fifty of them, both sopranos and contraltos. And she wasn't quite sure if she approved of Valentine's calm assumption that she would be his wife. Even if Ned were comfortably dead, she mightn't want to marry again. Besides, being in love with another man's wife was one thing, and actually asking her to marry you if she were a widow, was another. And then two stepchildren. No, it was all too complicated.

The waiter had taken the fish away, and there was a gap in the dinner. Aurea looked up carefully at her host. His whole countenance was suffused with that dusky hue of passion which besets gentlemen who are violently in love and have to control themselves in public places, and his eyes were fixed on her. She looked steadily at him with equal passion, and practically nothing but the arrival of the waiter with the bird saved them from some kind of explosion. "Oh, hell! Oh, hell!" she said in her plaintive voice. "Yes, hell," responded Valentine earnestly, adding as an afterthought, "my own lovely darling."

"But I'm not," said Aurea, making valiant efforts to get her food down her singularly dry and constricted throat.

"Well; missing out the first two words," said Valentine, in a businesslike voice, and eating very fast.

"Darling," said Aurea for the first time, and the waiter was so entranced by the signore and signora—for he always looked at a lady's left hand to avoid tactless mistakes—that he hovered solicitously over them hoping to hear more, which forced Aurea to talk about a party she had been at the night before, and Valentine to give her a lot of really valuable information about banking. It was, she was to remember afterwards, as something foolish and lovable, his habit to bridge over moments of intense emotion by dissertations on the ramifications of international banking, with special reference to the law of averages. On this last subject he maundered about so long that even his loving Aurea at last said, "For God's sake do stop talking."

The waiter, disappointed, entirely through his own fault, in the love scene, hopefully anticipated a row, but again the strange English let him down. The signore only smiled amiably and asked the signora where they should go and she said anywhere where there were comfortable seats. So these two fools walked up and down London Town till they found a good cinema, and got into the last row of the stalls and sat there in blessed semi-darkness, though alas! not in silence, for a gentleman with a brazen voice was conducting them through Burma, taking advantage of the journey to let off an incredibly large number of very hoary wisecracks.

"The best place in a cinema," said Aurea in a whisper, "is to get behind an enamored couple, because they lay their heads close together, and you can look around either side, with a good wide gap."

"It is a pity we are in the last row, then, with no one behind us who wants to see," said Valentine, and took Aurea's hand. One cannot make a row or struggle in the three-and-sixpenny seats, so this was the moment at which Aurea had to reconsider her decision about handholding. Valentine, rapid as ever in his methods, was amusing himself by unbuttoning her long glove and pulling it off.

At this moment the wisecracker ceased and the lights went up. Aurea nervously pulled her hand away and sat bolt upright, as did nine-tenths of the female members of the audience, so leveling is the tender passion.

Professor Prokoff and his Twenty Musical Hussars were then announced on the screen. They all came up from the basement on a moving platform with pink limelight on them, and tripped lightly on to the stage where, in a bower of cardboard trellis and paper wisteria, a large white grand piano was awaiting them, together with a quantity of musical instruments of all kinds. The Hussars turned out to be of the female persuasion. They wore rather dirty white tunics, most of which were misfits, obviously passed on from one member of the troupe to the next, lancers' helmets and leatherette top-boots. They all looked good, respectable, tired, conscientious, and—as far as their union would allow it—underpaid. The professor himself wore a velvet smoking coat and a loose, flowing tie. His long hair was shining with grease and fell repellently upon his shoulders, but was not sufficiently brushed over the large bald spot on the top of his head. Aurea was indignant. "I think with all those wives," she said to Valentine under cover of A Pot Pourri of Old Favorites with the professor conducting on his violin and the Head Musical Hussar at the piano, "one of them might see that his hair is properly brushed."

"But they aren't all his wives," said Valentine, rather shocked.

"Oh, yes, they are. Look at them. They couldn't possibly be anything else. Respectable wives, I mean; and they all live together in the boardinghouse and look after each other's babies and do a little washing and a little practicing, and the professor works frightfully hard at getting engagements for them and leaves the rest to luck."

It was at this moment that Valentine, filled with admiration for his idol's insight into human nature, tried to take her hand again. Aurea, thinking attack wiser than defense, took tight hold of one of his fingers and held it through the rest of the performance. Valentine was so amused and touched by this piece of childishness that he submitted cheerfully to it, and indeed came later to expect it.

The Hussars having played the Old Favorites, now obliged with New Favorites in which the solo part was played by each of the Twenty in turn. After giving an entirely unwanted encore, they all got back onto the platform again, and were carried away to their dressing rooms and the tube and the boardinghouse and, let us hope, a good supper. For they had worked hard, and if they had given little or no pleasure, why, it is difficult to give what you have not got.

The lights died down again and an enchanting film began. It was about Benvenuto Cellini, sometimes pronounced with a hard "C" and sometimes with a soft, the Great Italian Medieval Lover and Craftsman of All Time. First came a silent prologue in which the Tower of Babel, the Pyramids and the Parthenon figured prominently. "But," said the caption, "the Master Craftsman had not yet come." There followed short and unconvincing scenes from the loves of Solomon, Helen and Cleopatra. "But," said the caption, "the Master Lover had not yet come." This led by easy degrees to a cabaret scene in the Coliseum under The Popes (unspecified), where Cellino made his first appearance as a gay prentice lad with a maiden on his arm. "And here," said Doge with a strong American accent, who had come over to Rome for the party, "is Kelleeney, master of those who ply the silversmith's noble craft."

"Nay, sire," said Kelleeney, who spoke refined English, "not master yet, but soon to be."

"How so, Selleeney?" asked a real hunchback, who had been put into the crowd for local color.

Selleeney made no answer, but seizing a mug from the hunchback and drawing a small hammer from his pouch, transformed the vessel in a few moments to a goblet of exquisite art design. Upon this the crowd all shouted "The master, the master," and the picture faded out.

Valentine looked down at Aurea to see how she was enjoying it.

"Valentine," she said, "I oughtn't to be holding your hand."

Valentine, instead of telling her affectionately to attend to the film and not be a morbid little silly, entirely lost his own sense of humor, never perhaps very marked.

"Aurea," he said tensely, "you are wronging no one, you are depriving no one of anything by letting me have your hand."

Aurea felt very grateful at having her mind made up for her. The film waxed and waned to its appointed close. Selleeney fell in love with, or was fallen in love by, several historical though hardly contemporary ladies. He defied the Popes and the Kings and from time to time threw off some little triumph of the silversmith's art to show who he was. His final exploit—a midnight ride on a white car thorse from Rome to Paris, through hordes of condottieri, lazzaroni, sbirri, alguazils and freemasons, all thirsting for his blood—ended in his marriage with a lady called La Belle Duchesse, and the picture faded out on him with one arm around the duchess, and the other lovingly fingering his latest work, a gigantic candelabrum, cunningly fitted for electric light.

Aurea and Valentine went out blinkingly into the street. What were they to do now? Apparently one must eat all the time if one wants to make love, and supper seemed to be the only possible way of seeing more of each other. So Valentine took her to another pothouse. It was incredible, she thought fondly, that anyone who was in love as much as he was could enjoy his meals to that extent. As for herself, between excitement and exhaustion, it was all she could do to drink black coffee, and even then, her hand shook so that she could hardly hold the cup steady. There seemed to be nothing to talk about either.

When you care for a person as much as that, you naturally want to talk to them about nothing else, but partly you are rather shy, and partly there are other people so near at other tables, and waiters show far too much attention.

But she couldn't help saying what simply has to be said, "How much do you love me, Valentine?"

Valentine looked around in case anyone was listening.

Aurea laughed. "Coward," she said, "did you think I hadn't looked around myself before I spoke? Tell me, how much?"

"As much as the new Argentine loan," said Valentine in a very besotted way. How much was the loan, Aurea asked. It turned out to be such an extremely large sum of money, even allowing for a country which counts in pesos, that Aurea felt he really must love her very much indeed.

Then the wireless began, that curse of modern society, part of the great democratic movement for helping people not to think. It broadcast a jazz band. People began to get up and dance.

"Would you like to dance?" said Valentine. Seeing Aurea look undecided, he added, "You needn't be afraid that our steps won't suit or anything."

"No, thank you, I'm rather tired," said she. How could you explain to a gentleman in a public place, with the wireless blaring away so that it hurt the back of your throat to talk, that the reason you wouldn't dance was that you couldn't trust yourself to keep your senses so near your heart's love; that you would probably disgrace him by fainting, or near enough to make no odds?

"I'm a brute," said Valentine with melancholy satisfaction, "keeping you up like this. Come home at once."

Once more they found themselves in a taxi. "Put your dear head on my shoulder," said Valentine, "and rest."

"No, thank you. Not that I wouldn't like to, but one must draw the line somewhere." Also, as she well remembered from old days with Ned, the position was far from restful. The taxi jolted about, and instead of one's dear head resting, it banged about on what was after all a very bony part of a gentleman's body. And if there were an unusually bad jolt it might hit the gentleman's chin, causing him an agony so acute that even affection could barely control his blasphemy. Besides which one was always sliding away from him on the shiny seat and having to be hitched up again. No; decidedly an overrated form of entertainment.

Like conspirators they stopped the taxi at the corner of the street where the Howards lived. "I can't very well ask you in," said Aurea. "Mother always keeps awake for me, and she would wonder why we were so long downstairs."

"Angel!" said Valentine. "Am I to go then?"

"Couldn't we go for a little walk," said Aurea, though she was dropping with fatigue.

Luckily the Howards lived just around the corner from a large leafy square with a church in it. So Aurea and Valentine walked around and around the square which, like the rest of London, was abominably well lighted, even in the part that hadn't any houses overlooking it, but only a high wall. Valentine put his arm around Aurea's shoulders, but as she had on a tweed coat with a fur collar, it didn't seem so wrong to her. Of course it made walking rather uncomfortable for them both, because they were so very close together and impeded each other's progress; but it appeared to give satisfaction.

"I suppose I couldn't kiss you," said Valentine hopefully.

"No, no. And the policeman would see you if you did."

The policeman, in fact, was taking very little notice of them. Nocturnal couples were a natural accompaniment of his night's work, and this couple were evidently good class, not the kind who stood inexpressively glued together under a lamppost for half an hour at a time.

Aurea would probably have gone on walking all night if not discouraged. She was so tired that she walked mechanically and had quite stopped thinking. Valentine, on the other hand, began to feel that something must be done. He couldn't walk around a square all night with this heavenly lunatic, and the recurring meetings with the policeman began to embarrass him. It had been a perfect evening, of course, but very unsatisfactory. Dinner with a hovering waiter; a cinema where the lights were always coming on; supper with more waiters and people; the drive home with Aurea always keeping him at arm's length; then this walk where he could put an arm around a coat, but no more. Always restless, unsatisfying, exhausting. Were things always to be like this? Something ought to be done about it. Longer and darker cinema performances, where only silent films should be shown, with a real orchestra playing, not too loud. Much more comfortable seats. Perhaps seats for couples without that annoying arm in between them, and rather larger arms to separate them from the next couple. Or even little partitions like old-fashioned pews. One would willingly pay extra. Then probably the censor would object. Oh, damn, why couldn't the poor court in comfort? He felt a vague surge of kindness towards the democracy, and Serpentine bathing, and hiking, and chaste Polytechnic weekend outings.

Aurea's pace was gradually slackening till as they reached the high wall she stopped. "I think I'm too tired," said a small voice. Valentine stopped, looked down at a small tired face, took it in both his hands and kissed it. But because he was in a hurry, and Aurea was an unpracticed kisser, it really hardly counted. Indeed Aurea's chief impression was of her hat being pushed backwards.

"Let me kiss you again," said Valentine, thoroughly annoyed by the bungling job he had made of it.

"Oh, no," said Aurea and put her hat straight. Then she started determinedly homewards. Neither of them spoke till they got to the front door, which was unfortunately in the full glare of a street lamp. Here these two idiots lingered for nearly half-an-hour, saying first one thing and then another, and every time Aurea tried to shut the front door Valentine remembered something else to say, and every time Valentine said he really must go Aurea found another valuable remark to make. But at last the front door somehow got shut, and she heard Valentine run down the front steps and walk away down the street.

Mrs. Howard called out from her bedroom, as was her custom. Her erring daughter went in and found her reading in bed. "Have you had a nice time, darling," said Mrs. Howard.

"Yes, very. We had dinner and went to a cinema, and then went to a place for supper, which made us rather late." Then she made her mother laugh by a brilliant description of the film. But of the walk around the square she said nothing. So Mrs. Howard went to sleep happy, and Aurea went to bed, but not to sleep, because when you are too tired you don't sleep, and if you have been kissed there is a good deal to think about. She resented it, not because she minded Valentine having done it, but because it had been all on his side. If a kiss there had to be, it seemed very unfair that he should have all the fun of it. There was no fun in being kissed when you weren't expecting it, and nothing to show for it but your hat and hair all untidy. Men had the unfair advantage that their hats and hair did not matter. Yet perhaps it was all just as well, for if one had been forewarned either one would have evaded it, or else one would have put one's whole soul into it, and what then? Oh, if only one dared to put one's whole soul into it. But one couldn't. One would feel wicked afterwards, and it would upset mother and papa very much if they came to hear of it. As for Ned, the respectably married woman never thought of him once. All night long she lay awake, and no nearer deciding anything than she had been when she went to bed. Her last thought, before she fell into an uneasy sleep at dawn, was that if one were being judged by the kisses one had given or received, this one certainly wouldn't count.

CHAPTER 5

After this shattering experience the unhappy pair tacitly agreed that evening meetings were too difficult. When everyone sits restraining him or her self, breathing hard, or looking swooningly imbecile, for four or five hours, the strain is too great. So they took to lunching together. Valentine would have liked to take her to expensive grills, but Aurea refused because she said he couldn't afford it. Also she secretly rather hated Valentine to spend money on her. She would have liked always to be the giver, and then she had visions of him starving on bread and cheese in the evening if he had given her oysters and white wine for lunch, and this was unbearable. Common sense occasionally poked her head up, and told Aurea that if he could afford to take charmers out for the evening who expected much, surely he could take her out to lunch who expected little. But common sense was quickly pushed back into her hole. Besides, lunch saved one from the obvious dangers of taxis.

About a week after the fatal evening Aurea arrived at five minutes to one at the pothouse chosen for that day's lunch. She was always too early and Valentine, rather curiously, for it didn't seem to be in keeping with the rest of his ways, was of meticulous punctuality. Aurea chose a table in a corner, and sitting down, she took out of her bag a piece of paper which she studied industriously, her lips moving from time to time as if she were rehearsing a speech. Precisely at one Valentine's tall figure appeared at the door, and Aurea put her paper away. It was one of the drawbacks of love that it made one so blind.

How true the poets are in all they say about that disturbing emotion; though Aurea's blindness was a purely physical kind. To her idol's many moral defects her eyes were perfectly open, but to his personal appearance they were sealed. She could never visualize him when they were apart, and when they met he always looked rather different from the Valentine she had tried to remember. It had always been the same with anything she really loved. Each year in spring she had vowed to look at the young green of the trees, the enameled hawthorn boughs, the dripping laburnum, the mist of bluebells, with such intensity that they would be stamped on her mind through all the year. Yet the more and the harder she looked, the more it seemed to her that she looked right through the earth's beauty to something beyond. If the something had been a vision of an even lovelier spring, some green May morning in Paradise, it would have been worth while, but it definitely wasn't. Nothing lovelier than an earthly spring could ever be, and it was most annoying that one's eyes couldn't look with enough concentration to make it one's own forever. And so with Valentine, she always saw beyond him to some idea of her own, and try as she might, his visible form and face were never clear to her. When they had been separated, she thought it was even possible that, meeting again by chance, she would not know him, unless it were by his height, or a note in his voice. It is improbable that Valentine thought much about it one way or the other, not being given to introspection, and having a very sane conviction that what people had faces for was to recognize them by.

Valentine began by telling Aurea about the bank rate for the day. Aurea felt herself growing more stupid and dumb every moment. It was really too awful to be a tongue-tied fool when one had so many million things to say.

"I have something for you, Valentine," she managed to say at last.

"Angel, what?"

"Oh, just a little snapshot of me that I found."

"You darling. I will put it very safely away with the others. Do you know where I keep them?"

"No."

"Under my shirts," said Valentine, in a proud voice, like a hen who has laid an egg in a secret place, "so that no one will see them."

This seemed to Aurea such a proof of chivalry and incarnation of romantic feeling that she nearly fainted. But, controlling herself, she looked long and devotedly at Valentine, trying to make out what his face was really like.

"When you look at me like that you melt me," said Valentine, and ate a very large mouthful of chop and drank a very large gulp of beer.

Aurea fished in her bag and pulled out a small snapshot which she handed to Valentine. As she did so, the piece of paper which she had been studying fell on the floor. Valentine stooped and picked it up. "It is in your writing," said he rapturously. "May I read it?"

"Oh, yes, if you like."

Valentine looked at the paper. On it was written:

Lecture.
Fanny after?
Horsham.
Ch. letters.
Bankers–pension?

"What is it about, darling?" said he.

"Things to talk about," said Aurea, going bright red all over.

"Darling, how lovely of you to look like that," said the besotted gentleman, "but what sort of things?"

Aurea looked as if she were going to cry, and then said in a choked voice, "I can't ever talk to you, Valentine, because I love you so much, so I thought I'd write down some things to help me."

"Tell me some more about it," said Valentine, very kindly, giving her back the paper.

"Well," said she, trying to pluck up courage and laugh a little, "you can't think how difficult it is to talk when you are in love. So I wrote down some things that I thought might interest you, and then I could look at them from time to time when conversation flagged. First there is about a lecture that papa and I are going to this afternoon, and then we are going to tea with Fanny afterwards, and I thought you might perhaps drop in—it won't be till late. And then I am going next weekend to some people near Horsham, and I thought we could talk about that a bit—I could ask you if you knew that part of Sussex, and you could say No, but you knew another bit. It all helps. And then I had some letters from the children, and I thought I could read extracts to you, and you could pretend to be amused. That was all, Valentine. Do you think it foolish?"

"Dear darling," said Valentine, adding, "What about bankers' pensions? You had that on your list too."

Aurea looked as if the Inquisition were clutching at her. "Oh, it was only something that I thought might interest you. I was going to ask you if bankers got pensions, because I thought it would be nice for me to think when you were too old to work you had something to live on."

Valentine was so overpowered by this instance of loving thoughtfulness that he drank all his beer at one draught, and had to order some more.

"I shall be quite all right when I retire," he assured her. "I shall probably be a director, or a partner, or something, and live in luxury on ill-gotten gains."

"Oh, Valentine," said Aurea, taken with a new idea, "when you retire couldn't we go a tour of Europe together? It would be quite respectable then, and it would be such fun. You could do all the business part about hotels and things, and I would share the bills with you."

"Of course we will, only you shan't pay a penny. It will be my present to you."

"Oh, thank you, thank you, Valentine. Is that a promise?"

"Truth and honor," said Valentine. But Aurea said to herself that it would never happen, though she loved Valentine for thinking of it while he still loved her.

"And what about looking in at Fanny's this afternoon, after your work?"

"Of course I will. Not for long, because I'm going on to dine with some people. Darling, do you really find it so difficult to talk?"

"If you ask me that with your conquering male voice," said Aurea with sudden spirit, "I shall have no difficulty at all. Damn you,

Valentine Ensor, don't come your airs over me, and anyway it's time you went back to your office. Shall I come with you on a bus?"

So she did. And when they got out Valentine had to take her across the road to get her bus back to the other side, by which means they were enabled to stand arm in arm, blissfully close together, on an island, what time the policeman closed and opened the sluice gates of traffic four times. Which was quite an unnecessary waste of time.

Aurea was to meet her father at a learned society which gave lectures on Wednesday afternoons at half-past three. She got there a little before the time, and was directed to go upstairs. The society was not rich enough to have rooms of its own, so it borrowed the rooms of the Independent Union of Clerical Teachers. The lecture room was paneled in pitch pine below and distempered sage green above. On the walls hung enlarged photographs of members of the Union, all full of zeal, with the corners of their mouths inhumanly drawn down and their Adam's apples sticking out over their collars. The chairs for the audience had fat leather seats which looked as if hundreds of cats spent their leisure in sharpening their claws on them. Aurea took a seat at one side, and surveyed the early arrivals who were mostly of the female sex. Two or three incredibly hideous elderly ladies, with enormous features surmounted by plumed hats, sat together, sharing a railway rug. A number of earnest middle-aged women had note-books. Here and there were a few elderly men whose dusty shoulders and crumb-sprinkled waistcoats proclaimed them to be scholars. One of these pounced on Aurea and inquired if it was her father that was lecturing. She said no, but he was taking the chair.

"And is your father engaged on any work at present?" asked the scholarly man, whom Aurea suspected of being the very boring Professor Osgood, but didn't dare to address by that name in case she were wrong.

"Well, he is always doing something," said Aurea vaguely, "but he isn't doing anything very special at the moment."

"Nothing more on Polybius, ah-ha?" said the possible Professor Osgood. As Mr. Howard had recently published an edition of Polybius, embodying the work of a lifetime, it was hardly probable that he would immediately produce another book on the same subject, but Aurea just said she thought not.

"I saw your father not so long ago at the dinner of the Milton Society, where our old friend Bennington was speaking. You wouldn't know Bennington. He very rarely leaves Cambridge, unless it is to come up to town and see his widowed sister-in-law," said the putative Osgood.

"Oh, yes," said Aurea, "I believe he did go," and felt that she wasn't shining. Luckily at this moment a snag in a bottle-green coat-frock trimmed with lace braces came up, and disentangling her eyeglasses from some embroidery, begged Professor Bolton's pardon, but Dr. Alice Jupp would so much like to meet him. The professor followed obediently, and a just judgment fell upon him for being so dull, for he was thrown alive into the jaws of Dr. Jupp, an American lady in a tartan mackintosh, who had just written a book on Gray, which consisted entirely in rewriting his letters in *oratio obliqua*, occasionally adding, "Gray may well have thought . . ." or, "we may imagine Gray's sensitive mind. . . ." For this piece of research or, as it was called in the university which gave her a degree, *re*-search, she had been made a doctor, and enjoyed it very much. Aurea was thankful that she hadn't addressed the professor as Osgood.

Then her father came in with the lecturer, whom he introduced with great charm. The lecturer, poor young man, had been working in the British School at Rome, and imagined that he was going to create the classical and literary event of the year by lecturing to the learned society. If he had been older and more experienced, he would have known that lectures, especially afternoon ones, are attended almost exclusively by women. If he had been younger, he would have remembered what women students at Oxford were like, and not expected any intelligence or humor from his audience. Aurea felt heartily sorry for him as he ploughed his way through his lecture to rows of earnest female faces. She did her best to help him by laughing at his jokes, but it was a hollow sham when no one supported her. Women students don't think that a serious lecturer would do anything so silly as to make a joke, so they aren't prepared with their bright sense of humor.

While he spoke they sat grim and motionless, unless he happened to mention a date, when they all hurriedly took it down. Professor Bolton, I regret to say, sniffed all the time, and the hideous elderly women stared unblinkingly while the lecturer fumbled his way along for an hour and a quarter. Mr. Howard moved a vote of thanks in as few words as possible, and was seconded at infinite length by Professor Bolton, who took occasion to try out some very dull anecdotes of Oxford in the seventies, the chief point of which seemed to be that everyone was very rude to each other, and someone made a witty little poem about it, which he could not quite remember. After this, Dr. Jupp descended upon the lecturer, and petrified him to that extent that he consented, quite against his better judgment, to go back to her hotel for tea and meet two very rare and cultivated women whose acquaintance she had made on the boat coming over.

"There, papa, that's done," said Aurea, taking her father downstairs. "Shall we walk to Fanny's and get some fresh air?" Mr. Howard was quite agreeable.

"I was sorry for the poor little lecturer," said Aurea, when they got out of the noisy street into the comparative quiet of the park.

"I can't think why I consented to take the chair," said Mr. Howard. "I ought to have known better. First that young man who, although I must say he knows his subject very well, spoke for seventy-five minutes, which is unpardonable, and then that old ass Bolton with his stories. A silly scholar is a most humiliating sight, and very mortifying to those who have to listen to him."

"At least, papa, you were spared Dr. Jupp."

"Dr. Who? Oh, the American woman. Doctor, indeed! They all buy their degrees for ten dollars," said Mr. Howard, unjustly.

"Oh, papa, she might be honest. I expect she is just Ph.D. That's the easiest sort, isn't it?"

"Ff-dee?"

Aurea explained. "But you might be kinder to the young man, papa. He was doing his best, and I expect he was all flustered with you being there."

This not very subtle flattery produced its effect, and Mr. Howard smiled grimly, saying, "I will say for him that he had the root of matter in him, though he still has much to learn. I certainly must get out to Rome myself and see what is being done. Perhaps in the autumn."

"Are those the excavations Valentine was telling you about?" said Aurea, finding great difficulty in saying the beloved name.

"Valentine?" said Mr. Howard, who had an annoying habit of repeating one's statements as a query, thus putting one hopelessly into the wrong.

"Yes, Valentine Ensor, you know, papa. He was in Rome last autumn and saw them, and he was going to tell you all about them that night we went to the Sinclair's party, only you had that frightful cold and mother sent you to bed. Don't register denseness, papa."

"Ha, yes, Ensor. I like that young man."

"Which young man, papa? The lecturer?"

"I think it is you who are registering denseness now," said Mr. Howard disconcertingly. "I mean your friend Mr. Ensor. You see a good deal of him, don't you?"

This was more disconcerting than ever. Could it be possible that papa, who never noticed what was going on, and indeed drove everybody mad with irritation by his habit of plunging uninvited into the middle of conversations to which he had no clue, and wanting to know what it was all about; could it be that papa was noticing that she and Valentine were in love? That would be dreadful. He was quite capable of suddenly becoming a Victorian father and forbidding Valentine the house. That would be the right expression. Not that it would make any difference, as one just took no notice of the blessed darling when he came the heavy father. It was very funny, thought Aurea, how one's parents never thought of one as grown-up. Mother still threw fits, as Aurea inelegantly expressed it to herself, if her daughter was home late from a dinner party, or even a tea party. And as for papa he had absolutely no sense of fitness where young men were concerned, and could be confidently counted upon to descend benignly upon Aurea's tea parties and paralyze conversation. And, even more annoying, would stay on, showing every outward sign of boredom, till the young men were driven away, and then wonder why they went so soon. But he was such a darling that one couldn't be angry. Now he seemed to be upon his hind legs—again his daughter's way of putting it—about Valentine. It was largely her own fault, she admitted, for mentioning his name at all, but heaven knows what the temptation was to say that dearest of names aloud, even if one got oneself into trouble by it. Mother had been successfully sidetracked, so that she did not worry if Aurea was out with Valentine. Papa must be headed off now.

"Yes, papa, quite a lot. You see, he is at Fanny's a great deal."

"Is he one of Fanny's young men?"

"Yes, one of her collection, papa."

Again a shock. Why on earth should papa, ordinarily the blindest of men, suddenly develop acute eyesight about Valentine of all people. Oh, if only she had never mentioned his name. If papa touched on any piece of gossip it must be on its last legs with age. As a rule, he lived on mountain heights with the classics, but occasionally he made these terrifying eagle swoops into the realms of ordinary life and women's talk, and appeared to relish them exceedingly. If he spoke of Valentine as one of Fanny's young men, it must have been said a thousand times already before it reached him. Of course Fanny had swains by the score, so it didn't mean anything particular—only it hurt. One was in such a helpless position if people spoke of Valentine as anyone else's property. One couldn't say "He is not: he is mine," and throw down a gauntlet or wave a flag. To begin with one would be far too self-conscious to do such a thing. Then, what right had one to say it? What real claim had one on Valentine? Only the claim of loving him hopelessly forever; only the claim of being loved with exhausting intensity for a few weeks. Probably not a claim that a man would recognize; certainly not a claim that he would recognize. Aurea had already noticed in him a certain shy aloofness, a fear of some quite imaginary attack upon his freedom of mind and habit. He hated to be asked to make engagements, though he would be eager in making them himself. He had never, she reflected, broken any engagement for her since that first evening when he had thrown Fanny over. If she had suggested any time of meeting that clashed with his plans, he always explained, carefully and kindly, that he could not break his word to go to such a lady's dance, or such a charmer's dinner, or such a nymph's cocktail party. Aurea, on the other hand, had never told him what her other plans were, but ruthlessly hacked and hewed at them, so that he might find her ready whenever he wanted her. He would ring up from his office for long talks, and Aurea would hang about the house till he had telephoned; but he didn't much like her to ring him up, saying that it was sometimes rather awkward. What a poor position one is in, she thought, if one is the person that loves most. It simply cramps one's style and hampers one in every way. What fun it must be to be a heartless charmer, and throw gentlemen over right and left without a thought, and have them always clamoring for more ill-treatment, while I give my whole heart and must be content with what crumbs I can get. All the same, I would rather be like that. It is something to know that I love Valentine more than he does me, and I think I would prefer it so. The giving is all.

Mr. Howard had not pursued the subject of Valentine, and they walked on, sometimes silent, sometimes talking idly, till they reached Fanny's house. Fanny was lazily at home working on one of the quilts. There was a fire though the day was not cold, and a lamp though the afternoon was barely darkening, and every sign that Fanny meant to be comfortable. Her mobile marmoset face lighted up at the sight of the Howards, and she threw herself upon Aurea with tender embraces. To Mr. Howard she turned what the French call a candid front, and upon this front he imprinted a paternal kiss, holding her at the same time with a hand on each shoulder. Fanny managed to wink at Aurea.

"Arthur will be back soon, and he specially said you weren't to go, Aurea, till he came. And Val rang up to say he would look in later for a cocktail. So there we all shall be. Dear Mr. Howard, come and sit here on the sofa with me, and Aurea, I'm going to put you in that large chair near the fire to have the pleasure of looking at you, and then Arthur can talk to you when he comes in."

They had hardly finished tea when Arthur arrived and, according to plan, was told to sit by Aurea. Neither of them had much to say, but talk was quite unnecessary while Fanny held the field. Aurea asked Arthur how the children were. He said quite well.

"And what's far worse," said Fanny, "the holidays begin soon and I am getting quite thin at the very thought of them."

"You don't look thin, my dear," said Mr. Howard, with courtly foreign grace, "you look delightful."

"You could see every bone in my body if you looked," declared the fond mother. "And look at my hands. All my rings are falling off. I lost my wedding ring last week."

Mr. Howard was slightly shocked. "Lost it?" he repeated. "But you don't mean to say you have been going about without a wedding ring all this time?"

"Well, you see, I hadn't got it, so I couldn't wear it, could I?"

"But—isn't it a little unsuitable? I mean—mightn't people think . . ."

"Oh, no, I don't think they would."

"But what are you doing to do?" asked Mr. Howard, quite puzzled. "You must ask Arthur to get you another."

"He would be so cross," said Fanny, instantly becoming the oppressed wife. "It's the second time I've lost mine, not counting the one I took off and threw at him and it went in the fire."

"This is indeed a bad habit to form," said Mr. Howard.

"Yes, isn't it? And I don't quite know what I'll do this time, because Arthur will be so annoyed and it would look so peculiar to go into a shop and buy a wedding ring for oneself. Of course there's always Woolworth's. You can get an awfully good ring there for sixpence, or three for a shilling."

Mr. Howard was upset by Fanny's attitude to the symbol of matrimony. "Really," he said, "it is a more serious matter than that."

Fanny looked across the teatable to the other side of the fire. Arthur was showing Aurea some old photographs of their young days, with Aurea in incredible frocks and her hair puffed out all around her face. They were giggling over them and discovering old friends and enemies among the house party. So, feeling safe from interruption, she became contrite, and even managed to put a suspicion of tears into her voice as she said, "Yes, I know it's serious. But you can see how awkward it is. And as you said, people might say all sorts of things if I went to buy a wedding ring alone."

"Would it be a help if I came with you?"

"Oh, Mr. Howard," said the innocent Fanny, opening her large dark eyes very wide. "How good of you. But I couldn't dream of bothering you."

"No bother at all, my dear. Suppose we go one day next week, unless you have found the old one by then."

"Oh, I never find them. I dare say this one slipped off at Waterside while I was cleaning the car. If it did, I shan't find it again till the machinery sticks."

Mr. Howard registered surprise, but mastering himself, suggested Tuesday next week. Fanny offered to pick him up in the car.

"Thank you, Fanny. Say about eleven then?"

This wasn't at all what Fanny meant. "Wouldn't that be a little early?" she said meekly. "I mean, if you were lunching in town or anything, you would have such a long gap to fill in and none of the cinemas are open except the educational ones about insects coming out of cocoons, all very indelicate and uninteresting."

So Mr. Howard quite agreed, and they decided on half-past twelve, with lunch to follow, and Fanny, out of pure devilry, said that she would ask Mrs. Howard too. That lady's husband said it would be delightful, but that was the day she would be at Dorking, and would Fanny ask her another time.

Aurea and Arthur had enjoyed themselves with the photographs. Arthur had been thinking of Aurea a great deal since their last meeting at the Sinclairs', and weighing it all with a scientific mind, had come to the conclusion that he loved her deeply. With a man's happy capacity for caring for more than one woman at a time, he combined a steadfast devotion to his Fanny with a rekindling of old fires. How he reconciled the two devotions was his affair. He was, luckily for himself, almost devoid of conscience as far as the paralyzing and inhibiting effects of that ill-arranged organ are in question. He did not greatly concern himself with the right or wrong of his feelings. What he felt was a fact; it had happened and therefore one accepted it. A great simplification of life's subtler troubles. Fanny was there, beloved, his wife, unassailable. Aurea was there, a warm and enchanting ghost from his youth, once loved, always loved, unhappy, inarticulate, asking nothing, unconsciously demanding everything. If these two loyalties clashed, there was no doubt to which of his loves his stronger allegiance would be. But that did not keep him from worshipping this once adored girl, this presently adored woman, whose delicate face showed humor and unhappiness, who was so childishly and totally unfitted to deal with life. Aurea's presence recalled his early passion so strongly that he felt like a young man, half adoring, half afraid to speak. And all the time there was his Fanny flirting outrageously with Aurea's father, and nothing could shake his loyalty to Fanny.

He got up, drew the curtains and turned on more lights.

"Ring the bell, darling," said Fanny, "and say cocktails, because Val is coming and he'll want a drink."

Tea was cleared away, cocktails brought, and almost immediately Valentine arrived.

"Come and have a drink, Val," exclaimed his hostess, "you know everyone."

Valentine smiled at everyone. Aurea smiled back, her heart banging about so furiously that everyone must see it, she felt.

"We've had a lovely tea party, Val," continued the irrepressible Fanny, "and Aurea is looking so lovely. Look at her there, Val. Isn't it a face anyone might fall in love with?"

A more ill-judged remark in mixed company even Fanny had never made. Valentine managed to say, with the requisite absence of conviction, that it was. Poor Aurea blushed again and hated herself. Arthur saw the blush and misinterpreted it. Mr. Howard felt a lamentable want of taste in his dear Fanny's remark. There was a moment's uncomfortable silence.

Aurea spoke first. "I think papa and I ought to be going now. He has to go to town, and I am going home."

"I'm dining with Vanna," said Fanny. "She wants to see you some day, Aurea. That's in your direction; we could start in a taxi together. What about Val?"

"I am dining in Chelsea," said Valentine.

"Then you can give us both a lift. I'll split the taxi with you and Aurea, but mind, I'm only the extra sixpence."

She fled upstairs to get her hat and coat, and was down again in a moment. "Come on, children," she cried, "we'll pick up a taxi."

"Goodbye, Arthur," said Aurea. "I loved seeing the photographs."

"Oh," said Arthur.

A taxi was soon found, and all three got into it. "Drop me first," commanded Fanny, "Vanna is only a few streets off." When Vanna's front door had shut on her, Aurea turned happily to Valentine. "This is fun," she said. "Now you can drive me home first. I thought we would never have a chance of seeing each other."

"Aurea, dear, I am so sorry, but I am almost late already where I am dining. Do you mind if we go there first, and you take the taxi on?"

"Oh, but, Valentine, it won't take you long to drive me home first."

"Darling, it will. You know how difficult it is to say goodbye to you. I shall spend at least ten minutes on your doorstep, and be frightfully late."

"Oh, Valentine, they wouldn't mind if you were a little late. Oh, do come home with me first."

"Dear child, I would adore to, but I am so late already. I know you will understand."

One of the world's silliest remarks. No one ever understands—at least, not in the way one means. And probably they will misunderstand more than ever. Aurea stiffened. She did not understand—not at all. If Valentine didn't care enough for her to be a few minutes late for dinner—and not a formal dinner either, as he wasn't dressing—what was the world coming to? Why should it always be she who gave in?

"Oh, all right, have it your own way," said she, rather rudely shrugging her shoulders.

This rude attitude of hers put Valentine more or less in the right, but he very foolishly gave his position away by saying, "You don't mind, darling, do you?" which is another of the world's silly remarks, and immediately makes one mind very much indeed, besides unnecessarily reopening the argument.

"Of course I do," said Aurea sharply. "What difference would it make if you took me home first? And we shan't be seeing each other again for two days, Valentine."

"You know I'd love to, darling," said Valentine, a little too patiently, "but one must keep engagements, mustn't one?"

"Yes, to everyone but me," said Aurea, turning like a tigress upon her lover, as far as is possible in the limited space of a taxi. "Just because you know I am always waiting for you, you think I am not to be considered at all. It serves me right for being such a fool. It's not fair."

"Darling, darling, do be reasonable," said Valentine in his most affectionate voice. "You do see that one can't play fast and loose with one's friends, don't you?"

"No, only with people that love you," said Aurea furiously. The taxi had just reached the bottom of Sloane Street, and was whisking around the maelstrom of Sloane Square, so that she was thrown heavily against Valentine, but in her miserable fury she didn't even notice it. "Stop this taxi, Valentine. I can quite well go home by myself, thank you, if you don't care to take me."

"But, Aurea, do be sensible. . . ."

Sensible! She banged on the glass and stopped the taxi. Before Valentine could recover from his astonishment, she had got out and told the driver to go on. The traffic was held up, and she took advantage of this delay to put her head into the taxi and say coldly, "At least you might have got out yourself and taken another taxi to your beastly party, instead of leaving me alone in the middle of London like this." The taxi moved on. Aurea had to wait a long time as the buses were very full. Luckily it was dark by now, and if one had a quivering lip and brimming eyes it didn't matter. Nobody knew one. She got home in time for dinner and made a valiant effort to behave in front of her mother. Friends came in after dinner, but she could hardly see or hear for misery. Oh, why couldn't Valentine be kind when there was so very little time; when she would have given up every engagement in the world for him. How could he be so cruel? How could she have been so impatient and horrible? And now perhaps he was annoyed, and wouldn't want to have lunch with her the day after tomorrow, which would be unbearable. She didn't know the name of the people he was with—he was very reticent about his friends, and she was not curious—and couldn't ring up. And if she did, he probably wouldn't like it. What to do, oh, what to do? Before she went to bed, the foolish, distracted creature did what her silly sex will always do—wrote to beg her lover's pardon for being in the right.

> "Forgive me" she wrote, "for a word spoken in haste. One's nerves are raw. I couldn't help it. Please, please ring me up tomorrow. Always A."

As for Valentine, he was much taken aback by his gentle Aurea's revolt. He was genuinely horrified that she should think him capable of deserting her in the middle of the road and going off in a taxi; but after all, he had not turned her out of the cab, it was she who had got out of her own accord. He ought certainly to have stopped the taxi and gone back, but he might not have found her again in the dark, and anyway, it would have meant beginning the argument afresh. He would have had to give in, if only as an *amende* for his involuntary impoliteness, and then he would have been later than ever. Besides, the unreasonableness of the woman. He did love her more than anything in the world, and would do anything for her in the way of (rather vaguely) protecting her from nothing in particular, or dying under slow torture (a contingency so remote as not to come under serious consideration) for her sake. But if one lived in the world, one must keep one's commitments to it, and being punctual at dinner was one of them. So he put Aurea safely at the back of his mind, and next morning when he got her pitiful, ill-advised note, he called himself a brute, and rang her up, and said it was all forgotten. Aurea nearly burst with indignation at this calmly superior attitude, but was afraid to annoy him by insisting that he had really been in the wrong by being so discourteous. So when he said, "Dear darling, I had to go on to those people, really, hadn't I?" the poor fool melted to his voice and said, "Of course you had, darling." And the rest of their conversation was nauseatingly dull to anyone else, and does not concern us. But alas for the proper pride of womankind!

CHAPTER 6

Not long after this Arthur's mother rang Aurea up, asking her to dine that evening. Aurea wasn't sure if it would be amusing or not, till she remembered that Valentine was apt to drop in between work and dinner. So she accepted Vanna's invitation. Then she thought she would like to make sure of seeing Valentine, so she rang him up.

"E. and S. Bank speaking," said the competent female voice.

"Oh, could I speak to Mr. Ensor?" said Aurea, while all heaven's lightnings crashed in her head, and she felt empty all over. This was only the effect of being about to speak to Valentine.

"I'm sorry, he's in conference," said the voice.

Fanny would have walked over the voice and got through at once, but Aurea was afraid of the competent voice, and also a little afraid of bothering Valentine.

"Could you take a message for him to ring up Mrs. Palgrave?"

The voice wrote down the name and telephone number and rang off. Aurea walked restlessly about, played a little on the piano, ate a biscuit that she didn't want, and did a little knitting. Presently the telephone bell rang. It was Valentine, introduced by the competent voice.

"Oh, Valentine," she said, in a polite voice, in case anyone was listening in the bank, "I am dining with Mrs. Turner this evening. If I went a little earlier, do you think you would drop in after work and stay a little later?"

"Darling, I'd love to, but I have promised to go to some people who are having a cocktail party, and then I'm dining out."

"Oh, Valentine, couldn't you just manage to look in, only for a few moments?"

"Darling, you know I'd love to, but I have to get home and dress, and I shan't have a moment."

"Couldn't you perhaps dress five minutes earlier and look in on Vanna on your way to your party?"

"I'm afraid I simply can't, darling. I'll see you tomorrow at lunch, anyway. I must go now—there are six highly important people waiting for me, any one of whom might sack me if he wasn't pleased. Bless you, bless you, darling, goodbye."

Aurea was left with the receiver in her hand, feeling emptier than ever. She hung it slowly up, and went upstairs, and sat down in front of her glass and looked at herself. Gradually the glass became misty, and her image was dissolved in tears. "Oh, Valentine, Valentine" was all she said.

But life has to be lived, so she had her hair washed, which is very restoring, and thought of having a face massage but didn't feel in spirits, for you must be feeling rather nice before you can take trouble about making yourself look nice, and went out to dinner. Vanna lived by herself in a delightfully small house with about a pennyworth of garden, which she kept well stocked by buying plants from Mr. Woolworth. Aurea hadn't seen her since the memorable weekend party, and found her looking much the same.

"You don't look a bit grandmotherish, Mrs. Turner," she said.

Vanna looked gratified. "How long is it since I saw you?" said she.

"About—oh, about nearly twenty years. It sounds frightfully grown-up, doesn't it? Arthur was just leaving Oxford then, wasn't he?"

"It must have been that year, or the year before. I think we had house parties both years. But Arthur will be able to tell us when he comes."

"Oh, is he coming tonight? I didn't know." One might have had he face massage after all.

"I didn't know either till a few minutes ago. Fanny is off for the evening with one of her admirers, and Arthur rang up to ask if I could have him."

"How nice," said Aurea while she thought, "Which admirer? Is it Valentine?"

"Arthur said you looked no older than when he last saw you," said Vanna, "and I am inclined to agree."

"That," said Aurea, "is by artificial light. By daylight my second name is Gorgon."

Arthur came in and kissed his mother.

"How nice that you are here," said Aurea politely. "I didn't know you were coming."

"I wasn't," said Arthur.

"Who is Fanny out with?" asked Vanna.

"I didn't ask her. She rang me up at my rooms, and said she was going to a cocktail party and then to dinner with some friends, so I thought you would take pity on me."

"Of course, dear," said his mother.

"How very nice for us," said Aurea. But, oh, to what cocktail party had Fanny gone? with whom was she dining?

The evening passed pleasantly enough. Vanna was an easy talker, and Arthur expanded with his mother, and they made Aurea laugh. Vanna's summer in a caravan had become a legend in the family, brought out and elaborated from time to time for the entertainment of discerning guests.

"You can't think, Aurea, how ashamed of me my son was when he came down to visit me."

"Hardly surprising, mother, considering how disgraceful you looked," said her dutiful son. "Aurea, can you imagine Vanna with bare legs and clogs, an old black satin dress covered with a hessian apron, and one of her very respectable dear-old-lady mushroom hats, stirring a devil's cauldron of game—bought, I believe, from a poacher—with a toasting fork?"

"At, least, Arthur," said his mother with some dignity, "I was not wearing canvas shoes slashed across the tops with my toes sticking through, nor a hat without a crown. And as for poachers, who shot at least two pheasants out of season?"

"One must live," said Arthur sententiously, "and to live one must eat, and pheasants are food. Also, mother dear, if you had come fifteen miles out of your way on a walking tour, on a sweltering hot day, to see your adored mamma, your feet would have been even more swollen than mine and you would have cut your shoes to ribbons. As for my hat, that," he concluded lamely, "was my own affair."

"I'd love to have seen you both," said Aurea. "My family do a lot of camping, Mrs. Turner, but I don't like it. I am all for beds with four legs, and a table to eat at, and hot baths."

"Sensible woman," said Arthur approvingly. "I hate uncivilized females like Vanna."

"Then why do you let me bring up your children?"

"That's Fanny's doing, mamma. She believes in an uncivilized childhood. So do I, if it comes to that. I was brought up far too civilized. Vanna is terribly selfish and inconsistent, Aurea. She brought me up with hideous Victorian straitlacedness, and when she had ruined my character and launched me in life, she went savage herself, and does all the things I'd like to have done. But unfortunately I am full of inhibitions, implanted by her, and therefore the moral wreck you see me."

"But it seems to have been quite a success in your case, Arthur," said Aurea.

"Thank you, Aurea," said Vanna. "You see, it was really altruism. I knew Arthur was the kind of character that has to react against something, so I thought I had better give him something to react against. It was really very noble of me, because in repressing him, I had to repress myself, too. As you say," she looked fondly at Arthur, "he is rather a success now, and I can enjoy myself being what he calls savage with my grandchildren."

"I can't help being a little sorry for Arthur, though," said Aurea, "I was brought up very repressed and Victorian myself, only I never got loose, so I have to face a post-war world with a pre-war mind."

"You do it very nicely."

"Thank you, Arthur, it may look nice, but it doesn't feel nice. It is so mortifying," she added plaintively, "to see other people of one's own age doing cocktails and free love and self-expression, and to be quite incapable of it oneself, however much one might wish it."

Vanna and Arthur both burst out laughing. "Don't try any of them," said Vanna kindly, "they wouldn't suit you."

"On the contrary, mamma, I think they would suit Aurea very well, and she ought to have a go at them. I am quite ready to encourage her!"

"Oh, Arthur," said Aurea, "would you really?"

"I'd do more than that for you, but we'll make a beginning."

"When?"

"Tonight, if you like. I'll take you to a night club."

"That's very kind of you. Would I like it?"

"We can only try. Of course, Aurea, you are far too critical. You look at everything with a suspicious eye before you leap, and then you don't leap at all, or if you do you are dissatisfied. You spoil life entirely for yourself by asking questions all the time, and trying to fit facts to some extraordinary standards of your own. It is no good being behind the times, Aurea. If life isn't what you like, take it in both hands and make it what you want. You seem to think that everything you want must be wrong, but it is just as likely to be right. Have a little courage."

"Oh, but I haven't. I think," she went on, frowning, because it is so extremely difficult to say what one means when one does not usually take the trouble to formulate one's thoughts, "I think some people get hold of life first, like you, Arthur," she said admiringly, "and some people are got hold of. I was got hold of by life a long time ago, and I feel I've been pulled and pushed along all my life, always a little faster than I could run. All I really want is to be allowed to stop for a moment at a nice place and look at the view; but it isn't allowed."

"I know one or two quite good views, if I could persuade you to stop and look at them."

"Oh, do you? Well, I don't quite know what you mean, Arthur, but thank you very much; only as I've never managed to stop yet, I don't suppose I shall now. I suppose," she added, looking confidingly at Arthur and Vanna, "you both think I'm a bit of a half-wit?"

"No, dear, I don't," said Vanna. "You only have an inward eye, and that's a misfortune in life."

"What do you mean by inward eye, mamma?" asked Arthur.

"Aurea can't see very far in front of her, and what she sees doesn't really exist," said Vanna comprehensively. "She couldn't as a girl, and she can't now. She lets ideas fill up the foreground, and spends her time pretending that facts are like ideas, which they aren't. She can only see what is inside her own imagination. When you met her again the other day, Arthur, you told me that she hadn't grown up very much, and that's why. When she meets facts she runs away from them mentally, or winds them up in a cocoon of imaginings. She lives, I should say, largely in an idealized past, or an imaginary future. You can't change her, Arthur, so don't try."

"I don't want to, Vanna, not the essential Aurea, but she does need shaking sometimes," said Arthur chivalrously.

"So do you, Arthur, and it wouldn't do you the least good, nor her. Leave her alone, and take her as she is."

"Please," said Aurea, "I am in the room, if you wouldn't mind remembering it."

"You must excuse my mother, Aurea. She is quite uncivilized, as I mentioned before. She has a passion for dissecting her friends, and doesn't care in the least if the corpse is present or not."

"Oh, I don't mind at all—I just thought I'd mention that I was here. As a matter of fact, it all sounded rather true. How on earth can you know so much about me, Mrs. Turner?"

Well, Aurea, I saw a good deal of you for a few days years ago, and I happened to notice you rather specially."

"But why?"

Vanna hesitated for a moment. "I had a reason. Perhaps you interested me more than young men. At any rate, I had some definite impressions about you, and I remembered them very well. You have changed very little since then, that's all."

"Don't pay any attention to Vanna," said Arthur, rather quickly. "Living alone, she takes to thinking aloud, don't you, Mrs. T.?"

"Graceless cub," said Mrs. T. majestically, and she and her son began to laugh, both feeling that a danger point had been passed. No one but Vanna knew about Arthur's early love, and even that was more than half guesswork with her. She had seen them together through a long weekend, idling in a punt, sitting in a garden, talking endlessly, and she had formed her own conclusions and her own hopes. Though she made a practice of announcing her readiness to accept any wife whom Arthur chose to marry, there were undoubtedly types that she preferred. Aurea would have been a daughter-in-law after her own heart. Arthur would have been very kind to her and quite sufficiently firm, and Aurea would have gained strength and confidence, and made him very happy. Vanna had thought, looking at Aurea with the eye of a prospective mother-in-law, that life would go hard with the child unless she married a man who could worship her and govern her at the same time. Arthur was wrong when he accused her of want of courage. She would have boundless courage to endure, and it was quite plain that she had had to call deeply upon these reserves of strength; but equally plain that, living among her imaginings as she did, she would rarely make any determined effort to change the course of her life. It was all a question of wanting hard enough. Aurea would long for things or people with a fruitless longing, but she lacked the vitality to want them in a way that would force life to serve her. Poor child. How curious it was that Arthur could love two such absolutely different types as Aurea and Fanny. They had so little in common that they might belong to different worlds. Luckily, Arthur was very happy with his brilliant Fanny, who knew so exactly what she wanted and invariably got it. Vanna would have liked sometimes to feel that he was more needed by Fanny, but even her affection did not grasp the very deep bond of interdependence which united her son and his wife. Their lives would often run in separate channels for days and weeks, but each had complete confidence, and drew strength from the other at need. Perhaps, thought Vanna, things are as well as they are; but she felt sorry for Aurea, and sighed.

Aurea said she must really go now, because it was nearly half-past ten. She thanked Vanna very much for a delightful evening.

"Arthur will see you home," said Vanna and kissed her very kindly. "I am very glad to have seen you. Good luck, child, and don't break Arthur's heart again."

Aurea, occupied in collecting her bag and cloak, wasn't quite sure if she heard the words rightly. In any case she didn't attach much importance to them, unless they were a sort of joke. So she smiled vaguely, and kissed her hostess good night.

"Shall I get a taxi?" said Arthur as they went downstairs.

"No, let's walk and find one." So they walked along and found one.

"Where are we going?" asked Arthur.

"To mother's house, of course."

"Shan't we go somewhere more amusing?"

Aurea thought for a moment. It had really been such a pleasant evening that she had been able to forget about Valentine several times. Perhaps to go on somewhere would help the forgetting, and it might encourage one to free love and self-expression. So she said "Yes, where?"

Arthur told the man to go to the Vampire in Gerrard Street.

"Why do we go to a Vampire, and what is it?" asked Aurea.

"It is a kind of cheap and respectable night club we belong to," said Arthur, "where I can feed you for much less than at more gilded haunts of vice."

"How amusing. I expect papa will ramp when he hears about it."

"Never mind," said Arthur, "you are with me tonight, not with your revered father," and he tucked Aurea's arm under his.

She looked at him with wild fear in her eyes. An instant afterwards she had collected herself, and her face became blank. "Don't be an ass, Arthur," she said, disengaging her arm, "or I'll stop the taxi and go home. I can't stand being touched."

"Oh?" said Arthur.

"In fact, I'm not sure if I won't get out at once," said Aurea, beginning to let the window down.

"You don't like being touched?" said Arthur in an interested voice.

"No," said she, wrestling with the strap.

"It was only a friendly action," said Arthur calmly.

"If that's your idea of friendship, I call it a pretty sloppy one."

"I don't like the word, but of course, if you don't like it, I won't do it again."

Aurea felt she was being silly and making a fuss about nothing, so she sat back. "All right," she said, wrapping herself up tight in her cloak, and sitting bolt upright in a corner. They both began to laugh.

"You're not very romantic," said Arthur.

"Oh, not at all," said she. Where, oh, where was Valentine? With whom was he dancing or talking now? For whom was the high star of romance shining?

The taxi drew up before a narrow passage. They went into a small entrance hall with a lift in it. Arthur rang, the lift came down, they got in, and the lift went slowly upwards. Aurea counted five stories before they stopped. Arthur couldn't get the door open. "Damn this thing, it's always sticking," said he, rattling the handle. Someone below pressed a button and they went down again. Arthur put his finger on the button called STOP, and pressed it. The lift stopped. Aurea began to giggle.

"When a lift stops in mid-air," she announced, "you should prepare for the worst. If the machinery breaks, you should get ready to jump the moment it reaches the bottom, otherwise your legs will be driven right up into your chest."

Arthur's determined concentration upon the button marked six finally overcame the people downstairs, and the lift shot up again. The door at the top was violently opened by a young man who said, "Why the devil are you playing tricks with this blasted lift?"

"Ask this lady," said Arthur courteously. "The mistake was hers." The young man went bright red, gobbled hopelessly, plunged into the lift and disappeared. Aurea found herself in a hall so small that she nearly fell head foremost into a hole, which was where the gentlemen's coats and hats were kept.

"That won't take you anywhere," said Arthur, taking her by the upper part of the arm and propelling her to the right.

"That's the way the lower middle class always take their womenkind across the road," said Aurea condescendingly. "Our class don't do it."

"Don't they?" said Arthur. He let her go, and opened a swing door. They entered a large room with a bar, and tables, and a sound of music. Arthur led the way to a seat near a door at the further end, explaining that they could feed in one room while they looked at the dancers in the other.

"I wonder why one has to eat all the time if one wants—" said Aurea and stopped short.

"Wants what?"

"Oh, I mean, one does seem to eat a lot, doesn't one, in the course of an evening?"

"Does one?" said Arthur and beckoned a waiter.

While he ordered supper Aurea looked through into the next room. The theaters were not yet out, so there were not many people dancing. A few couples were sitting at tables around the wall, and a band was wailing in a perfunctory way.

"How do you like our Vampire?"

"It's very nice, Arthur," said Aurea, who privately thought it dull and noisy, and wasn't at all inclined for another meal. "It's has—lots of looking-glasses, hasn't it?"

"As I said before, you are much too critical."

"I'm not critical. I only said it has lots of looking-glasses, which it has. I think it's charming—all the people look very nice."

"Do they?"

Aurea turned around and faced Arthur. "Well, if you will press me, Arthur, I think they look as if they all lived at Ealing, and came up to Kensington for the day to look at the shops and have a permanent wave, and then came on here to see life."

"Quite right," said Arthur. "I always felt that myself, but Fanny thinks it is real vice, bless her."

"And look at their clothes," said Aurea, encouraged by this sympathy. "Some in coats and skirts, and the ones in evening dress all wearing bridge coats so that you shan't see their naked arms."

Arthur advised her to suspend judgment about clothes till the theater people came on.

"Would I see real vice then?" she asked hopefully.

"I'll give you the chance, anyway."

"What fun!"

Food came.

"When do you go back?" said Arthur.

"Thank you for your tactless reminder, Arthur, I go today week, damn and blast it."

"I like to hear you curse," said Arthur placidly.

"All right then. Damn and blast leaving England, and curse it and damn its bloody eyes to hell. That's the best I can do," she said, not without a modest pride.

Arthur laughed quite loudly for him.

"All right. Laugh. But I mean what I say."

"Poor girl. Cheer up, it will be better on the ship."

"Oh, will it? Well, Arthur, that's just exactly about all you know about it. It will be wet and windy on the wharf, and then the steamer will be icy cold with damp decks on top, and centrally-heated till it blows your head off below. The bar won't be open, and the head-waiter will despise me because I am traveling alone and can't afford to tip heavily. The head steward will put me at a table with the ship's Sister to keep me good and quiet. Also I'll be lucky if I get unpacked before we start rolling, and when we do, I don't care what happens to me. Let me tell you, Arthur, that on an Atlantic crossing you discover depths in your stomach that you have never dreamed of."

"Then you must be a bad sailor."

"Marvellous, my dear Holmes."

"Well, never mind, Aurea. It won't really be so bad. You'll soon be coming back, I expect."

Aurea's exuberance subsided. "I mout and then I moutn't."

Arthur looked questioningly at her.

"Brer Rabbit," she said explanatorily.

"Oh, I see. Aurea, all your friends will be wanting you to come back."

Aurea was looking straight in front of her, and didn't answer for a moment. Where was Valentine? At what theater, at what dance? Where was Fanny? With him? Would either of them be among the friends that wanted her to come back? No, that would not be.

"Will they, Arthur?"

"One will, at any rate."

"You, do you mean?" said she uninterestedly. "Thank you, Arthur. But that doesn't make leaving mother and papa any easier."

"There will be your children," said Arthur in a comforting voice.

"Oh, yes, bless them. And they need me, which is something."

Arthur was pleased with this small success. Unfortunately in his desire to comfort Aurea, he continued, "And your husband."

Still without turning her head Aurea said gently, "Always tactless, Arthur dear."

The memory of their talk at Waterside came over Arthur in full flood. Of all the inconsiderate, cruel things he could have said, this was perhaps the worst. He cursed himself for his stupidity. All evening he had been behaving like a perfect beast. First worrying Aurea by taking her arm in the taxi, then reminding her of Palgrave whom she obviously wanted to forget as long as possible. Why she so much objected to being touched, he couldn't think. It had meant nothing; only a friendly gesture, but apparently to her profoundly repugnant. It must be that an unsuccessful marriage had made her man-shy. Unhappiness drove women to extremes—some drowned care in rather indiscriminate love-affairs as Valentine's wife had done. Sylvia and Aurea; there couldn't be two more different women. Sylvia screaming loudly for sympathy and getting it with an arm around her waist and a tearstained collapse into any gentleman's embraces; Aurea freezing and shutting herself up alone. He saw again the momentary terror in her face when he had taken her arm. She had mastered it quickly enough, for her manners were very good, but it was there. If she could be frightened by such an ordinary action on the part of a very old friend, she must have been more frightened than anybody knew. He couldn't make himself believe that it was he in particular who was repellent to her. She had shown in so many ways her pleasure at seeing him again, getting to know him again. It must be that the poor child was suspicious of all men. What waste it seemed of that beloved creature. He had only wanted to have her arm through his, and show a friendly spirit—or, to be quite candid, was it a living spirit? He didn't feel equal to deciding. Why need she have taken it so seriously, and even tried to stop the taxi as if he were a white slaver? There was only one reason that would make a woman shun one so fiercely; that she found one physically disgusting. But no, there was another possible reason. What a fool he had been not to think of it before. Or no, it would have been fatuous to consider it, it was fatuous to consider it now, except that it fitted so well with everything that had happened. He knew Aurea well enough to recognize that she would have a high, ridiculously and impossibly high, standard for herself. Wasn't it just possible that if she cared a good deal for a man who wasn't her husband, she would deliberately set herself to suppress her own feelings; to be far more distant and unkind to him because she loved him, than she would be if she didn't care? He had seen that she was strained and unlike herself since Waterside. Was this cool, far-off creature trying to hide an ardour that matched his? Did she refuse to be touched because her conscience made her refrain from what she desired? Lovely, silly, muddle-headed, unfortunate woman. Arthur caught his breath at the thought.

"It's like that, is it?" he said gently.

Still without moving she said, "It's like that."

It was a confession. But of what? Of her inward separation from Palgrave and no more—of an empty heart? Or of a heart already given, though fearing to let it be known? A quarter of an hour ago he could have asked her why she avoided him, and got some kind of answer out of her, but now the rooms were filling up, tables near them were occupied, already they had both recognized friends, and intimate talk was too difficult. He hazarded a question.

"I suppose inquiries aren't wanted—or sympathy?"

Aurea turned her head at last and said lightly, "The first wouldn't be answered, and the second would make me cry."

"I see," said Arthur, unsatisfied.

"Marriage is what you might call a tossup," said Aurea, with the air of one making a general reflection, "but it is better to be married than not—for a woman, I mean. It gives one some kind of background, and that's what women need unless they are abominably clever and strong-minded, or quite unprincipled."

Arthur tried again.

"Did you ever think what it would have been like, Aurea, if you had married me?" he said.

"But you never asked me," replied Aurea, interested and very much surprised.

"I couldn't very well. I hadn't a penny, and your people wouldn't have heard of it. But I would have, later."

"Oh, Arthur, I'm terribly sorry, and touched, and upset," cried Aurea. "How enchanting of you!"

"You don't mind?"

"Mind what? Your having had a young love for me? But of course not. It is always flattering when people say they were in love with one, though mostly they only imagine it in a fit of sentiment, and would never really have asked one. Thank you so much, Arthur dear. I think it quite adorable of you." She beamed on Arthur, and patted his coat-sleeve affectionately. "And now I can tell you," she went on, "that I have always felt terribly romantic about you. Not being in love, of course, or any rubbish like that, but just because it was such a nice weekend, and the garden was so heavenly, and we were so young."

"So you did feel romantic about me?"

"Why, of course. And that's why I was so pleased to see you again."

"You couldn't feel at all romantic about me now?"

"Now? Oh, Arthur, of course not. I'm terribly fond of you, but romantic—no. Do you know what I'd do if I felt romantic?"

"What?"

"I'd never see you again, of course."

"But why?"

"Because of Fanny. She has been such a dear to me. She might so easily have snubbed one of your old flames. Do you think I'd poach? Oh, no, I like my own sex far too much to want to annoy them, and

Fanny I'd certainly never annoy. But, anyway, that's all ridiculous nonsense. It's very nice to know that you thought you liked me, and that's that."

That was that with a vengeance, Arthur thought. With many women this appalling frankness might only be a subtle form of flirtation, but with Aurea he sadly felt it was probably the truth. He rather wished he could think that she was leading him on. If only she knew how little Fanny would mind, and indeed how she would approve her gentle poaching, it might encourage her. But one couldn't say, "My wife will be enchanted if you flirt with me." Aurea's taste would be shocked, and she would withdraw fastidiously. He looked at Aurea and saw beyond her, in the dancing room, his Fanny enjoying herself in the arms of a tall cavalier. He pointed her out to Aurea.

"Where, where?" said Aurea looking eagerly about. Her annoying insubordinate heart was battering at its walls again in the expectation of seeing Valentine, and her eyes were clouded.

"Over there, with that tall man who has his back to you.'

Still she couldn't see well, and one tall back in a tailcoat looks vastly like another. Not till Fanny and her partner had circled the room twice, did Aurea catch a glimpse of a very good-looking face bent over Fanny; therefore, thank God, not Valentine. At least, not altogether, thank God, for one wanted still so desperately to know where he was. Her steadfast gaze must have attracted Fanny, who suddenly caught sight of her, and with a shriek disentangled herself and her partner from the dance and came into the supper room.

"My dear, what fun to find you and Arthur here," she cried. "I have had a ravishing evening with Mr. Graham—this is Mr. Graham—and we came on here to dance. Why aren't you two dancing?"

"Men always want to eat," said Aurea.

"Too true," said Fanny. "Here, Arthur, get food for Mr. Graham and me, and we'll sit with you."

"It's the first time I've been here," said Aurea politely, "and I think it's charming."

"Mixed lot," said Fanny, "but amusing. Mr. Graham wants to join and I'm going to put him up. Who's seconding you, Ronnie?"

Ronnie Graham, who does not come into the story except as a make-weight, said he had spoken to Ensor about it.

"Oh, that'll be all right," said Fanny. "Val is a very good person to second you. He practically lives here and knows everyone."

"Fanny is off again," said Arthur parenthetically to Aurea.

"Off what?" inquired his spouse. "Well, you know as well as I do, Arthur, what Val said to me about the Vampire," and she began to laugh.

"When he snubbed you, as you well deserved," said Arthur.

"Oh, I say, he didn't snub you, Fanny?" said Mr. Graham.

"Oh, yes he did, though."

"What happened?" asked Mr. Graham, who was obviously in a fizzling state of devotion.

Fanny began to laugh again. "Twice I was having lunch here and saw him treating a female—a different one each time, of course—so of course I went and spoke to him."

"You would," said her husband.

"Yes, Arthur, I would, and why not? Am I not a matron? Well, Ronnie, next time he came to see me, he asked me not to talk to him when I saw him at the Vampire with a lady, as I would be apt to compromise him."

"Oh, I say, Fanny, you wouldn't compromise anybody," exclaimed Mr. Graham enthusiastically.

At this ill-judged remark Fanny cast a withering glance at him. "It's just as well, Ronnie," she said, "that you failed in the diplomatic exam. Business is about all you're fit for. My charms have not yet waned to that extent that I couldn't compromise anyone I wanted to. What Val meant, my poor fool, was that I would probably, in my frank and open-hearted way—or in my cups, if you prefer it—ask after one lady in the presence of the next: and take it from me, Ronnie, they don't like it."

Mr. Graham made profuse apologies. Arthur had relapsed into his more customary silence. Aurea wanted to run out of the room screaming, or have hysterics on the spot. Why, why must people say things that hurt one so? Was she just another of the many ladies that

Valentine liked? It was silly, she knew it was silly, to mind. After all, why shouldn't Valentine take as many ladies out to lunch and dine as he chose? If he didn't take her, it was only because neither of them could bear it. But it was cruel, cruel, that the ladies who didn't really care for him should have all the fun, while she, who would give her heart's blood for him (if it weren't, of course, for the children) had nothing but anguish and sickening anxiety. Just then Mr. Graham, who had recovered from his lapse, said to Fanny, "There's that Mounsey girl."

"What Mounsey girl?"

"The goodlooking one that goes about a lot with Ensor."

"Val never told me about her," exclaimed Fanny indignantly. "Where is she, what's she like?"

"Over there, in blue," said Mr. Graham, but as this description fitted half the ladies in the room, Fanny nearly danced with rage.

"Of course she is in blue, you idiot. Everyone's in blue this season. Who is she dancing with?"

"Ensor, of course," said Mr. Graham, delighted to have some gossip that Fanny didn't know.

Aurea turned her face from the door towards Arthur. She wouldn't look; she wouldn't look. Valentine could dance with all the girls in blue in the world, and go about with them till Kingdom Come; she didn't care, not she. But she must hear more. Luckily Fanny's curiosity demanded full details.

"You started this, Ronnie, and you've got to tell me more. Why didn't Val tell me? Ungrateful hound, dropping in five evenings out of seven and then biting the hand that shakes his drinks. Who is the Mounsey? Are they going to be married?"

Mr. Graham looked embarrassed. "I really don't know as much as that, Fanny," he said. "They just are a lot together at present. She has pots of money."

"That's one good thing," said Fanny. "I'll get the rest out of Val, the sneaking, low-down dog. Aurea, why didn't you keep Val out of this mischief? I thought I had provided a nice quiet, safe friend for him, but you are no good at all."

Nobody must know what she felt. Nobody must see that she was walking with bare feet on red-hot ploughshares, pierced with a thousand swords, struggling in tempestuous waters, beaten to the ground by black storm winds. "You ought to have found someone younger and more amusing that I am, Fanny," she said. "I'm not quite up to Valentine's standard, I think."

"His loss," said Fanny briefly. "Well, Ronnie, are we to sit guzzling here all night?"

The obedient Mr. Graham got up. Fanny blew a kiss to Aurea and Arthur, and whirled off with her swain.

"Had enough?" said Arthur.

"Yes, please," said Aurea. Then suddenly it was more than she could bear. She moved closer to Arthur and said, "Arthur, I can't tell you about it, but I am so unhappy—unhappier than you can ever know or guess."

Arthur felt a pang of hope and joy. What had seemed too exquisite to be possible, might be true after all. "Can I help?" he said very kindly. "Couldn't you tell me about it?"

"Oh, no; not you; never you."

Be still, fast-crowding, heavenly thoughts. She is unhappy; she longs to tell you; but you are the one person to whom she cannot speak.

"My dear, may I guess?"

"Oh, yes, if you like—it doesn't matter one way or the other. Nothing can help me."

"Do I come into it at all?"

"It was quite a good deal your fault."

Fast-crowding, heavenly thoughts, come thicker, come faster. Her unhappiness is your fault. She loves where she may not, dare not, love.

"Is it anything I said or did?"

"No—and not animal, vegetable, or mineral. Oh, Arthur, I can't explain, I can't."

"Was it the weekend when you and Val were with us?"

"Yes—partly—oh, it's no good. Don't ask any more," she said, so piteously that he had to be silent. But his thoughts soared and raced above him. She cared and would not tell. His touch had roused her blood. But because of Fanny she would be silent. And he would be silent, too. If that darling creature could silence her love for loyalty's sake, why so could he. For him a double reason for silence. Never to let Fanny know, and never to make it harder for Aurea. They were both worth it, and if his unhappiness would do either of them any good, by heaven, they both deserved it.

"Come along now, Aurea ," he said, getting up. "I'll put you into a taxi, and walk home. I need some fresh air."

Her eyes averted from the dance, Aurea left the club with Arthur. He told the commissionaire to get a taxi, and put Aurea into it.

"Thank you so much, Arthur, it was a lovely evening," she said, and held out her hand through the window. Arthur kissed it. It was very cold. He walked home with a vision of a tired, unhappy child going away alone into the darkness.

CHAPTER 7

Vanna is quite right about the inward eye. There are many ways of dividing one's friends besides Mr. Max Beerbohm's piercing definition of hosts and guests, and one of them is the inward or outward eye. Most of the people who were involved in the ill-starred folly of these few spring weeks possessed the inward eye, though in very varying degrees, and not always consciously. For hardly anyone can escape that mingled curse and blessing, unless it is Mr. Graham, who simply found his eyes useful to see things with, or recognize his friends by, or to express a passionate devotion with a fish-like stare. To him things are exactly what they seem, so perhaps he is the truest philosopher.

First comes Mr. Howard because he is the oldest, and the most to be respected. In him there lived both scholar and poet, and the inward eye saw its own visions. All that was wanting to make him complete was a larger acquaintance with the marketplace. His acutely critical mind shrank from contacts that would disturb his fastidious taste, and for the most part he had made his own circle, and lived entirely inside it. Hence, it came that, while his wisdom could be profound, noble, and without any affectation, he could not always apply it successfully to common life, or if he did, he would apply it so absolutely that it frightened lesser minds. His perception of right and wrong was so finely stern that it could be exercised practically in nothing short of a vacuum. In him there was also an ardor for truth and justice, which in any less easygoing country than England might have led him into difficulties. From time to time he felt called upon to testify, in a way which was excessively alarming to his family and friends, but he was so much loved that his outbursts were received with tolerant affection. In fact, his younger admirers among the scholars and writers of the day rather looked forward to what Aurea undutifully called "papa featuring John Knox," and took it with beautiful seriousness. Papa would never be really happy, Aurea continued, until he had got his whole family imprisoned or exiled; or better still, encouraged the Government, with a Roman gesture, to cut her (Aurea's) head off, offering at the same time to wield the axe himself. One could see darling papa terribly hampered by a toga, sacrificing his daughter with one hand, and decently veiling his face with the other, so that no one should see how much he was enjoying his own nobility. Which was all very irreverent of Aurea, but not entirely untrue. Unfortunately—or at least from a purely philosophic point of view, one supposes it must be accounted a misfortune—cheerfulness was always breaking in, and the stern Calvinist or Roman was at the same time the tenderest and most loving of fathers.

Life had been very good to him, except in the matter of his only daughter's marriage. In spite of his theoretical acceptance of things as they were, he sometimes blamed himself bitterly for having allowed Aurea's marriage—though what a father can do to prevent his daughter marrying nowadays, one hardly knows. Aurea was good and obedient enough, but when she became possessed by an idea she showed astounding powers of blindness and obstinacy, and was as if driven by some inward force which would stop at no obstacle. It was a subject which his pride would never let him discuss, so that Ned Palgrave's name was only mentioned on necessary occasions. In Aurea he saw his own image again (though it is improbable that he recognized her obsession by ideas and her obstinacy as an inheritance from himself), but without the support of the philosophy and the deep though undogmatic religious sense that had been his mainstay through life. Aurea was, he saw, what, coining a phrase, one might call *anima naturaliter pagana*. She was immune to any help or comfort of faith, and would always have to rely on her own strength entirely. And strength has hard work unsupported.

But though he lived on mountain-heights, he could, as Aurea well knew, make disconcerting swoops into lower air. He knew far more about his daughter than she imagined. He had seen, as Vanna and all other people who cared for the girl had seen, that marriage was Aurea's only vocation. Home, husband and children would fill her life. Only in love and safety could she discover herself, and grow in beauty and strength. But if marriage went wrong, it would go hard with Aurea and those nearest to her. Though he had not cared much for Ned Palgrave, he had felt that Aurea must make her own life. There was nothing against Ned except that he was too easily pleased, and with all his charm, hadn't quite the fineness of fiber and perception that his Aurea would need. However, the child had been very happy at first, and he had stifled his misgivings. Now, one of a woman's worst misfortunes had happened to her; she had grown out of her husband, as Mr. Howard had feared. Her face this time was a little harder, her mouth a little more set, her ways more restless than a father would wish to see. It cut him to the quick to see his daughter's delight in being a child at home again, and her shrinking from returning to her husband, much as she missed her children. Long habit of silence about emotional things made it impossible for him to ask questions or give counsel. He could only watch Aurea in silent anxiety, with loving watchful eyes. Things were not well, but one mustn't ask too much, and they were well enough till she had met Ensor in an unlucky hour. Mr. Howard had judged Ensor and approved him, but no good could come of what he called to himself Aurea's infatuation. He trusted her sense of duty absolutely and had no fear that she would deviate, but he felt a certain lack of dignity in her complete submission to an idea. By a kind of inverted pride, he ignored the very large part which Ensor had played in precipitating the affair, and blamed Aurea for everything. He did not attempt to explain this attitude to himself, but if he had put it into words, he would probably have said, "My daughter, because she is mine, is so strong and fine a thing that she can bear every burden of the world. No harm can touch her save by her own weakness. If any man who is not her husband, loves her, it is only through her own will. Her spell is upon him, but she should walk untouched in mind. She has descended from her starry height to let a mortal love her. Hers is the blame." Which was all very glorious, but put poor Aurea a little too high. She, too, needed the marketplace, and was sadly unexpert in the ways of men in love. A certain virginal quality about her had let her pass through life with only one love affair—the man she married. When, therefore, to an empty heart treasures of love were offered, she had no arts to turn aside the gifts, and not to be outdone in generosity, gave all she could in return. It did not diminish her troubles when she began to realize, by what her father had said as they walked across the park, that he might look on her as the temptress, and Valentine as the innocent bleating victim.

In those few weeks she longed for a confidante. People in novels always had a female friend to whom they could safely confide everything: look at Diana of the Crossways and her dismal Emma, or even Tilburina. Or sometimes it was a man, older than themselves, to whom they told all their difficulties over an expensive lunch, receiving stores of ripe wisdom to guide their conduct. But in real life these confidantes appear to be rare. Aurea could think of several people who would be very sympathetic, but none who could be relied upon not to spread the news. Also it was so very difficult to talk about Valentine at all, because the moment one began one's voice became strange and affected, one's tongue was suddenly much too large, or so dry that it wouldn't work; one felt one's face looking tight and strained. She had tried to say something to Arthur, who was such a safe old friend, but nothing had come of it. If only he had said to her, "You and Val are in love, aren't you?" it would have been such a help. Of course, one would have felt terribly embarrassed, but at least the ice would have been broken, and one could have begun to talk. Even with Valentine himself it was no easier. One could write pages and pages of explanations and outpourings, but she was very doubtful whether Valentine was interested in them, or indeed in anything she said. Some essential part of her meant everything to him, that was clear; but like the rest of his sex he had marvelous powers of ignoring what he didn't want to know, and entrenched himself behind a double barrier of neither listening to nor understanding what one said to him. In fact, why one cared for him at all, considering how he trampled roughshod over one, Aurea couldn't conceive. Just love, she supposed, whatever that apparently simple word with all its hidden implications might mean. If only one could stop the machinery for five minutes, and look around and take breath. But one couldn't; and time moved on so swiftly towards the day that was to end all, and still she was no nearer Valentine than she had been when they first met. A little more experience would have taught her that love brings one no nearer to people at all; but there would be plenty of time to discover this and a thousand other disillusionments when the waste of seas divided her way from his. It was curious that one still had no particular sense of wrong-doing; except that her childhood's conscience told her that mother and papa would not approve. Aurea had been a fairly innocent but quite deliberate, hypocrite to them. To her father she had said very little, and greatly feared that he knew too much. With her mother she had bluffed more brazenly, owned frankly to a love affair, and left her mother persuaded that she was exaggerating. What made it all the more difficult was her parents' attitude of quite friendly interest in Valentine, combined with her father's slightly condemnatory attitude toward her, as one who Led Men On. Of course, darling papa enjoyed thinking the worst of one so frightfully that it was on the whole worth behaving a little badly for the pleasure he got out of it, bless him.

The last week passed. Aurea and Valentine had one frenzied dinner, too painful to be repeated, and four frenzied lunches together. They also walked miserably about the National Gallery, the Tate Gallery, the British Museum and the Brompton Cemetery, holding hands whenever possible, and falling foul of each other whenever they opened their mouths, through sheer nervousness. They found the Brompton Cemetery, especially that remote part which marches with the railway, the most conducive to lovemaking, but even so, such events as funerals, and people bringing flowers to put in jam jars, were far too apt to intrude.

Fanny tried to arrange a farewell party for Aurea on the spur of the moment, but Arthur for once did not seem ready to support her.

"Why not a party?" said Fanny. "We ought to cheer Aurea up as she's leaving us. We might have Val and Ronnie, and make a night of it."

Arthur said he didn't feel like making a night. Why not, he said, ask Aurea to dine with them and go to a play. They might ask Val too, and then he and Fanny could go on and dance if they liked while he, Arthur, took Aurea home. Fanny agreed, and rang Valentine up.

"Come to dinner and a play tonight, Val."

"I'd love to, Fanny, but I'm not quite sure—"

"Never mind about not being sure. Aurea goes tomorrow and this is her party. You've got to come and chaperone me while she and Arthur say goodbye to each other. Come and have a cocktail first."

Mr. Ensor said after all perhaps he could manage it, and left Fanny thinking that he was coming on her account. But when she rang Aurea up, she found unexpected opposition. Mrs. Howard answered the telephone, and at first wouldn't hear of it.

"No, Fanny, this is Aurea's last night, and her father and I simply can't spare her. You and Arthur can look in on us after dinner and say goodbye."

But this wasn't in the least what Fanny meant, and she begged and prayed so prettily that Mrs. Howard began to relent. "I'll see Aurea when she comes in and let you know," was her last word, with which Fanny had to be content.

Aurea was lunching with Valentine. They were both so overwrought that the waiter benefited to the extent of two cocktails and most of Valentine's beer, while the pig-tub, or whatever is the city equivalent of that useful institution, probably received most of the lunch they had ordered, but could not eat.

"What are we to do about tonight?" said Aurea. "Mother and papa expect me to stay in, and I shall die."

"Couldn't they possibly do without you?" said Mr. Ensor. "Can't you dine with me? I'll bring you back early, truth and honor."

"Possibly I might, but I can't bear to think of hurting them. Oh, dear, how awful it all is. Look here, Valentine, I will ask mother when I get back, and ring you up. Would that do?"

"Darling," said Mr. Ensor. "Only I'll ring you up. It might be more convenient. At half-past three."

"Do you promise, Valentine?"

"Of course I promise. Nothing on earth shall stop me," said Valentine heroically, for which Aurea admired him very much.

So they walked hand in hand like idiots to the bus stop, and Aurea went home and Valentine went back to work. When Aurea got in, her mother was hovering about waiting for her.

"Darling," she said, "Fanny wants you to go to dinner there tonight. Of course, you must do what you like, but I know papa will be terribly disappointed."

"Oh, mother, I don't know. I can't bear to leave you both, but it will be so awful at home, if you know what I mean. Wouldn't going out be almost better? So as not to be alone?"

Aurea looked so white and drawn that her mother rather agreed, and suggested that she should dine at home and ask the Turners around afterwards. While Aurea was trying to think of a tactful way to suggest that she should spend the whole evening with Valentine, and not finding any, the telephone rang. Aurea plunged at it like a madwoman, and felt the earth reeling as Valentine's voice came through.

"Dear darling," said Mr. Ensor, who had a fine contempt for what the exchange might overhear, "Fanny has just rung me up to ask me to dine and go to a play and says you are coming. Wouldn't that be rather a solution? Then I could bring you back afterwards."

"Wait while I ask mother. Oh, mother, it is Valentine. Apparently, Fanny had made all her plans, and was taking us to a theater. It seems too bad to let her down now. Do you think papa would mind frightfully?"

Mrs. Howard noticed her daughter's unblushing use of the word "us," but made no comment. Her heart was wrung by the child's anxiety, though she knew Will would feel the desertion.

"What shall I say, mother? It will be all right to go, won't it? Yes, Valentine, hold on a minute. Mamma is weakening."

Mrs. Howard made a decision. "You go to the play, then," she said firmly, "but you must all dine here first. We'll say dinner at seven-fifteen, and then papa will see more of you."

"Oh, thank you, mother. Valentine, mother says we must all dine here at a quarter past seven, and then we can go to Fanny's play and arrange the rest later. Will that be all right?"

"I suppose it will have to be—but thank Mrs. Howard very much for asking me. Will you be telling Fanny?"

"Yes, we'll tell Fanny, and oh, Valentine, couldn't you come around a little earlier than the others?"

"Darling, I'd love to, but I have promised Fanny to go for a cocktail first, so I can't very well say no now, can I?"

"Oh, Valentine, my last night."

"I know, I know, darling. Do you think I don't feel that? But I did promise—you understand, don't you?"

"Very well."

"Goodbye then, darling. Bless you and bless you."

Aurea hung up the receiver, her joy suddenly darkened.

"Thank you very much, mother," she said dully. "It's very good of you. Valentine says thank you very much, and he will come to dinner at a quarter past seven. Will you tell Fanny or shall I?"

"I will tell Fanny. You had better go up and rest before you go out to tea."

Aurea trailed wearily upstairs, and Mrs. Howard applied herself to the telephone. She was not in a mood to stand Fanny's nonsense and the affair was quickly settled.

"Dinner here at seven-fifteen sharp, Fanny, and I want a few words with you alone, so come a little before seven if you can."

"All right, Mrs. Howard. Do you mind if we bring Val along with us?"

"Yes, do."

Mrs. Howard left the telephone and composed herself to thinking out plans for the evening. After the sight of Aurea's haggard face she had decided to be perfectly ruthless with everyone, even with Will, so that the child should have time to say goodbye to Mr. Ensor. It probably wasn't going to do anyone any good, but to refuse Aurea this last meeting would be like telling a condemned criminal that he couldn't have the sausage for breakfast which he had ordered for his last morning. The child couldn't be more nervous and unhappy than she was, and if having half an hour, or an hour, or even an hour and a half alone with Mr. Ensor would still the anxiety in her eyes, she should have it, even if it meant locking Will into his study, or drugging him. Evidently a good deal of diplomacy would be needed. Fanny was the key to the situation. She would, of course, want to take them to a dancing place, and then all come back in a taxi or two in the morning, dropping Aurea first. Or it was quite conceivable that she might take Mr. Ensor off herself, sending Aurea back in charge of Arthur. She knew Aurea would behave well whatever happened, but was determined to make things happen nicely for her. Will would be difficult, but something would probably happen to smooth her path where he was concerned, though it could hardly be expected that Providence would arrange for him to have another crashing cold at a few hours' notice. It was on Fanny that she must concentrate. Really, she would like to beat Fanny as the unconscious originator of all this trouble. If only Fanny hadn't asked Mr. Ensor down for a weekend, Aurea would have gone on placidly enjoying her life at home, and gone back to Canada with no more than her usual homesickness. Ned wasn't a bad husband, and later on he might manage to let her come with the children—send the boy to an English university, perhaps, if the Howards helped; and after all, what was money for if it wasn't to help one's only daughter and her children? But now all poor Aurea's chance of peace was wrecked because of a weekend. Oh, why couldn't men control themselves and be quiet? Aurea would never have fallen in love unless Mr. Ensor had taken the first steps, or if she had, she would have squashed and stifled it industriously. If only he had held his tongue, or goggled less abjectly, said Mrs. Howard angrily to herself, the child would never have opened the gates of her heart. She was far too trusting. Mr. Ensor was a very nice young man and couldn't have meant to do wrong, but he had taken Aurea by surprise, battered her suddenly into submission, and with the fatal generosity of the inexperienced she had given her heart and mind completely. If only he was good enough for her, thought the mother irritably. He can't really understand or appreciate my Aurea. He simply falls in love, Fanny says he is always doing it, and is determined to get what he wants. Her unusual gifts, her diffident charm, her childish trust are quite beyond his comprehension. I believe he really cares for her, but it isn't going to break his heart. Of course, it isn't going to break Aurea's heart either, because she is too strong, much stronger than Mr. Ensor, if he had the wits to see it, but she won't easily get over it. Then Mrs. Howard thought of Aurea alone for a week on the Atlantic, racked by seasickness and lost love, and her wrath rose high. "I wish Fanny and Mr. Ensor were boiled in a pot," she said aloud, viciously. It didn't occur to Mrs. Howard to consider how much those two young people were making her suffer herself; it was a mother's job to stand by and help, and any pain one received was all in the day's work.

Then it was teatime, and Mr. Howard came down from his study, and a dull friend came to tea and told them all about a cruise in the Mediterranean, and Mr. Howard suddenly rose to epigrammatic heights and said the only advantage of foreign travel was that it put you on an equality with other bores. Then he wondered if he had let himself go too far and hurt the dull friend, and Mrs. Howard wondered too. But the dull friend laughed heartily, and said that was so like Mr. Howard, and told them all about a bird sanctuary at her place in the country which she called Heinz, because she had seen fifty-seven varieties, and Mr. Howard had to have the joke explained to him, and was willfully dense and altogether trying. At last the dull friend went, and Mrs. Howard in the relief at her departure quite forgot to tell her husband about the evening's arrangements and went upstairs, leaving him comfortably established by the fire.

His thoughts very naturally fell upon his daughter's departure. Mr. Howard thought far more about Aurea than she imagined, and though he could be so excessively annoying and, for a clever man, really stupid, he had flashes of insight which paralyzed her. Ever since he had coupled her name and Valentine's she had looked on him with increased respect, mingled with irritation. Mr. Howard was quite unconscious of the effect he produced. He saw in his mind an Absolute Daughter, who was also Absolute Wife and Mother, and poor Aurea was tacitly expected to represent all three in their highest and most abstracted form. If he had admired her less he might have understood her more, for to be on a pedestal frightened Aurea, and she was torn between duty, which told her to go on standing there looking dull, and inclination, which told her to kick it down and show her papa how human she was. But this would have hurt the poor darling too much, so she had to go on letting him admire her, feeling altogether unadmirable.

It was quite inconceivable to Mr. Howard that his Aurea should be deeply in love with a man who wasn't her husband. He looked upon her relations with Valentine as a very foolish flirtation, which was luckily being stopped before it had got too conspicuous, or made Aurea lose her head. He would, and justifiably, have staked his life on his daughter's strength of principle, but what he did not understand was that she was almost killing herself for those principles. If he had realized the intensity of Aurea's feeling for Valentine, he would have been really shocked and almost disgusted. She was being silly and needed pulling up, he considered, and it would be his painful, though rather pleasurable duty, to speak to her for her good. If he had been able to formulate his thoughts about Valentine, it would have been found that he thought he was protecting that promising young man against a Rapacious Female, and sticking together as man with man against Femininity. What Valentine would have thought, we shall never know, for he never considered Mr. Howard at all except as a kind old gentleman, who was Aurea's father and was to be humored and respected. Luckily, neither of these gentlemen will ever see into the other's mind.

Mr. Howard must have been sitting alone for some time in the firelit room, when he was roused by the lights being turned on. It was his erring daughter who came up behind him, kissed the top of his head, and threw her hat and furs upon a chair. Mr. Howard had been prepared with several good openings for her improvement, but it did not somehow seem quite the moment for them.

"Where's mother?" said Aurea.

"Upstairs, I think," said her father. Then there was a silence while he considered. Finally he could think of nothing more tactful to say than, "Did you get your heavy luggage off?"

Aurea nearly laughed out loud in the middle of her grief and fatigue. It was so like darling papa to ask one that. She knew he only asked her because he couldn't express sympathy and was afraid of sitting silent, and she understood him well enough to try to continue on the safe lines he had laid down.

"Oh, yes, papa, that all went this morning. It is rather like burning one's boats, isn't it? And now I have to live in a suitcase till tomorrow."

"I dare say," said Mr. Howard, finding this conversation rather difficult, "you will manage all right for so short a time."

If this, Aurea reflected, was papa's idea of a comforting talk, she wished he would say right out how ghastly it was that she was going away. But if it made him feel safer to trample about unconsciously on her feelings, why, then, he should.

"I dare say I shan't," she answered gloomily and not too politely. "I hate living in suitcases. There seems to be room in a suitcase for everything except your shoes and evening dress and cloak and hair-brush and anything you really want."

This turned out to be a most unwise remark as it roused Mr. Howard's slumbering suspicions.

"But you won't want an evening dress tonight, will you? Aren't we alone?"

"Oh, no, papa. Didn't mother tell you we are going to a play?"

Mr. Howard could not afford to lose this opening. In a voice of far too patient resignation he said, "I thought, Aurea, you were spending your last evening at home."

Aurea nearly screamed. Of course this scene was bound to occur, but now it had come it was nearly more than one could bear. She thought her mother would have told papa about the plans for the evening, as indeed Mrs. Howard had fully intended to do and would have done, if the dull friend had not driven everything out of her head. Part of her blamed herself bitterly for deserting papa on the last evening; another part pointed out that they would only get on each other's nerves and be miserable if they spent the evening alone; yet another part regrettably murmured what a pity it was papa had to be so important about it, but she was ashamed of this murmur and stifled it. She couldn't prevent an answering tone of patience creeping into her own voice as she replied, "We are dining at home, papa, but we're going to a play afterwards."

"I," pronounced Mr. Howard, in a justly aggrieved voice, "am always the last person to know what is happening in this house. If you and your mother choose to tell me nothing, I am hardly to be blamed for my ignorance."

What is the correct answer to a father who expresses himself thus? Aurea would dearly have liked to say, "Oh, aren't you?" and flounce out of the room, banging the door. But that would startle and hurt papa, and then one would have to come back and say one was sorry, and be mortified, and feel more embarrassed than ever. Remember, said that first part of herself, how much papa loves you and how unhappy he really is at your going away, only he can't show it. But he needn't make a song about it, said that other part of her, very rudely and vulgarly, though not without some justification. Then she was overcome with remorse, and got up and kissed the top of her father's head again, saying plaintively:

"You don't mind, papa, do you. It is not so awful as sitting here all evening, pretending that tomorrow doesn't exist."

Mr. Howard was filled with a flood of tenderness for his wayward child, and nearly told her that whatever she did was right. But a perverse spirit entering into him at that moment caused him to make a speech of quite unnecessarily noble renunciation.

"Tomorrow," he said, "will come whether you pretend or not, but if it is going to make you any happier, my child, by all means go."

A more exacerbating remark could not well have been made. Aurea's first impulse was to say, "All right, then, I shan't," fly to the telephone, put everyone off, and sulk all evening. Her better self then put in a word of warning about people who cut off their noses to spite their faces. She must, she must see Valentine that night whatever happened, even at the risk of hurting her dear papa. She gulped down her resentment and thanked her father very much.

"It is darling of you," she said. "But I shall be full of remorse all evening for deserting you and mother."

"Don't add that to your unnecessary worries. Your mother and I shall have a quiet evening with some reading aloud, and be quite happy. I would like you to enjoy yourself."

A pang shot through Aurea as she thought of her parents' peaceful evening, taking it in turns to read themselves to sleep. So many such evenings when she was a girl and preferred to get away, and be out and about with her friends. So many such evenings, thought of with desperate longing, while she was away in Canada. So many such evenings to come when she had gone again. Even tomorrow evening, when she was at sea, her father and mother would be here in this room, by this fire, beside this lamp, reading, with aching hearts for their daughter each moment further from her true home. A hot flood of tears surged to her eyes at the thought of them so lonely, and herself so lonely. So many such evenings. But how many more? When one's parents were getting older, each parting held an unspoken fear. If either of them died, what would the other do alone by this fire, beside this lamp, without even a daughter to give what comfort she could. But there was no turning back. While the children were young she must be with them. Later perhaps—but what might later days bring? She must speak at all costs before the tears brimmed over, before her voice was past control.

"You and mother do have fun with your reading aloud," she said as cheerfully as possible. "It must be lovely to be a husband and wife that are happy together, and enjoying spending a quiet evening. What I have always wanted and can't have."

Mr. Howard felt a chill at his heart. Was the child even less happy than he feared? Very courageously he put a direct question.

"Is your marriage not a success, Aurea?"

This was almost worse than being questioned about Valentine. Aurea was so taken aback that her very strong instinct for telling the truth got the upperhand.

"Not exactly, papa," she said dully, and then burst out: "Oh, dear, oh, dear, everything one does seems to be wrong."

Mr. Howard would have given all the Roman excavations in the world to be able to thaw and take Aurea in his arms and comfort her, but he did not dare. She had so defended herself with a ninefold wall of reticences, turning aside questions, laughing at herself and everyone else, that he could not approach her. Nothing could scale the hill of glass on which she had established herself. His deep pity finding no outlet was checked, turned to self-consciousness, and had to wound what it most loved.

"I wouldn't go so far as to say that," he answered, trying to sound unconscious. "In any case, don't indulge in remorse and self-pity, Aurea. They are impure passions, and so do no one any good."

The slightly didactic flavor of this remark, more bracing than any sympathy, made Aurea pull herself together.

"All right, papa," she said, quite lightly, "I won't feel remorse. As for self-pity, I think it rather depends on how you feel. If you are quite well you don't bother to be sorry for yourself. If you are unwell—seasick, for instance" (or lovesick, Valentine, Valentine)—"you can do quite a lot of it. I expect I'll be full of self-pity on the voyage."

"We all hope not," said Mr. Howard, rather drily. He was thankful to be spared emotion, but not entirely satisfied with his daughter's flippancy. Her suffering tore at his heart, yet he was slightly offended that she could shake it off so easily. A peculiarity of fathers.

"How many of you are going to the theater?"

"Only Fanny and Arthur and ourselves, papa."

"But your mother and I aren't going, are we? I understood that we were staying at home. It is extraordinary how people can't stick to the simplest plan."

"Oh, no, papa, not you and mother. I meant Valentine and I."

If it hadn't been for Aurea's rash use of the word "ourselves", Mr. Howard might have left the matter alone. Now his proprietary feelings as a father were ruffled, and his original determination to speak roundly to his daughter returned in full force.

"I am concerned about you and Ensor, Aurea," he remarked portentously.

"Oh, papa," said Aurea, startled and again on the defensive.

"I don't want to seem harsh, Aurea, but it has pained me to see my daughter forgetting herself as you have done in the last few weeks."

"Oh, PAPA!" cried Aurea, with a large indignant voice to which no capitals can do justice. Indignant as she was, she was also a little afraid, and not too sure of her ground.

Mr. Howard, once launched, was beginning to enjoy himself thoroughly, and rolled majestically on, over his daughter's disclaiming outcries.

"Not, my dear, that I want to interfere with your friendships, but I don't think this one has done you any good. And I very much disapprove of night clubs."

It was very unfair of Mr. Howard to drag night clubs in, as he knew nothing about them except that he had once had lunch at one with Fanny. But his blood was up and the chase in view.

"You make it sound as if I were living in night clubs, papa," cried Aurea. "I've only been two or three times, and one must dine somewhere, and equally one must dance somewhere."

"Possibly, but they are a type of place with which I do not like my daughter to be associated."

Aurea was torn between fury at her papa's unexpected attack, and thankfulness that night clubs seemed to have ousted her misbehavior with Valentine from her father's mind. Praying that he would stick to this new scent, she continued to defend herself.

"But, papa, if you went to one you would see how harmless they are. If it's the Vampire you mean, I have only been there with Arthur, which is very respectable."

"Nevertheless, I repeat that I cannot approve of them, and it will pain me very much if you go to one again. The—Vampire—" said Mr. Howard with a slight hesitation in case the name should sear his lips, or evoke the devil, "is no place for a decent woman with a name to lose."

"But, papa, everyone goes there. Fanny does. The Vampire is quite full of propriety."

"I hear much about it which I do not like," said Mr. Howard in a sinister way.

"You really shouldn't listen to the scandal the bishops talk at your club, papa darling," said Aurea, amused and irritated.

This shot went nearer home than she knew, for Mr. Howard was basing his attack on night clubs on a conversation he had had with an old friend at the club that very day. When we say old friend, we do not mean that he and Mr. L. N. B. Porter, C.B.E., that permanent pillar of the Civil Service, had been nurtured on the self-same hill, nor frequented the same groves of Academy. Nor indeed had they ever met except on committees and boards of governors, and Mr. Howard had never so much as thought of asking Mrs. Howard to call on Mrs. L. N. B. Porter, nor contemplated an invitation to lunch or dinner. But gentlemen have great powers of self-deception, and if anyone had asked Mr. Howard for a character of Mr. Porter, he would without hesitation have described him as an old friend whom he knew very well. Mrs. Howard had never heard of him. Mr. Porter had a great-nephew who had recently become notorious in a rather scandalous drinking party, the members of which had sampled the Vampire among other night clubs, before finishing the evening at the great-nephew's flat in Battersea. There had been a splash in the evening papers, which described the great-nephew as a well-known west-end clubman, and several night clubs had slightly increased their membership in consequence. The great-nephew was now reaping what he had sown in the shape of a broken leg and collar-bone sustained, as the evening papers put it, through falling from an open window while endeavoring to obtain fresh air. Mr. Porter had much private information about what he called this defenestration, and was frightfully enjoying the horror of fellow members of his club to whom he imparted it.

"The wretched boy," said Mr. Porter to Mr. Howard, in a voice of compassionate blame which could have deceived nobody, but was the recognized and proper approach to injudicious gossip. He got such pleasure from this phrase that he pretended he had mislaid his eyeglasses, found them, and began again. "The wretched boy was literally pushed from the window, Howard, pushed, I say, by some young woman in the party. She was, I understand, trying to embrace him, and the unfortunate lad in trying to avoid her, fell from the first floor to the pavement. I have been to see him in hospital, but it is much to be feared," said Mr. Porter, with gloomy satisfaction, "that they will have to break his leg again and re-set it. All this is a terrible blow for his mother—poor Lydia, you know."

Mr. Howard did not know, but was far too cowardly to say so.

"A shocking business, Porter, a shocking business," he said, with much enjoyment. "From all I hear these night clubs are leading our young people to all kinds of excesses."

"Exactly what I say myself, Howard. It is incredible that such places should be tolerated," said Mr. Porter, who had once been taken to a night club by another great-nephew, not yet qualified for defenestration, and given a kipper and some light beer, and so to bed at eleven-forty-five.

They had then separated, Mr. Porter to visit the great-nephew, who had won the hearts of all his nurses and made them promise to say he was asleep whenever Old Man Porter called, and Mr. Howard to a meeting of the Library Committee, where he got in first with the story of "Porter's nephew—the wretched lad gives him much cause for anxiety, I fear," and thus obtained immense temporary popularity.

Home shots are rarely appreciated by the recipients. Mr. Howard stiffened slightly.

"I have my reasons, Aurea, and, as I say, I shall be much pained if you go to such places."

After all, it wasn't worth bothering about. How like papa suddenly to get up on his hind legs about night clubs, just when one was leaving.

"All right, papa," she said kindly. "But I haven't much chance of going to any more, have I?"

Mr. Howard melted.

"I knew you would understand, Aurea. I had only thought that perhaps you were going to one tonight."

"I don't think so, papa, but anyway I won't if you'd rather not. Not that anyone would notice one."

"Whether they notice you or not, my child, you must remember that you lower yourself by going to such places, and in lowering yourself you lower the dignity and honor of all women."

Upon this appalling speech he got up and gravely kissed her on the forehead, to her unspeakable horror. It was inconceivably embarrassing, and nearly broke down Aurea's patience.

"Really, papa," she expostulated, "I don't know what I've done for you to be so unkind to me. I can't help it if Valentine likes me, and it isn't as if we had done anything disgraceful. If people can't have lunch or dinner together with people without other people being angry with them, one might as well go to bed, or stay in Canada forever." She began to sniff ominously. Mr. Howard did not recognize this sign of an impending storm, and was moreover slightly indignant that his kiss of peace had not been better received. So he addressed himself again to his daughter's improvement.

"You have been in a very unsatisfactory and restless state ever since you met this young man, Aurea."

"When you say "young man", papa, it sounds as if he were fond of the cook, not of me. I only wish he were fond of the cook. No one would bother about whether she went to night clubs or not. I thought you liked Valentine, papa."

This unfortunately gave Mr. Howard another excellent opening.

"So I do, Aurea," he said. "And that is why I do not like to see my daughter running after him."

"Oh, papa! Running after him? I suppose you think he needs to be protected against me." She sniffed rather more loudly and rapidly, and began to dab her eyes with her handkerchief.

"Well," said Mr. Howard, who felt he had now done his duty and by no means wished to face the consequences, "perhaps I do, my dear. But don't cry about it," he added kindly and unhelpfully. "I must go now and write some letters before dinner. When you come back from the theater we will finish our talk."

Aurea made a face of disgusted resignation which her father could not see. As her sniffs increased in volume, Mr. Howard thought it best to leave the room before he was involved in a scene, so he got up, took a step towards Aurea, thought better of it, fidgeted with a book on a table, muttered something about the post, and escaped.

CHAPTER 8

Aurea, left alone, could not check the flow of her tears. To be accused of having run after Valentine was too unkind a cut. Could there be any justice in what papa had said? True, she had liked Valentine from the very first moment she saw him, but not in a falling in love sort of way. If he had never told her that he loved her, she could have gone on feeling sentimentally fond of him quite happily. It made one reflect on the appalling power which resides in words. Until Valentine, too eager, too uncontrolled, let loose the fatal word love, all was fairly well. With the loosing of that word, all had been ill. There was quite definitely some primitive magic in the word that suddenly blinded one to all real values, leaving one in a world whose days were trances, whose nights were dreams. Had she succumbed too easily to this word of power? Aurea had spent a good deal of time in torturing herself quite unnecessarily by wondering if Valentine thought less of her for having answered his declaration with her own. A woman with more intelligence would, she thought, have kept Valentine very charmingly at arm's length, and while confessing to some inclination for him, would have given always very much less than he did. While she, poor nincompoop, had stripped herself of every reticence from the first moment. It would have felt so ungenerous to hold back. When a gentleman, his eyes bulging out of his head, his tongue six sizes too large, his utterance that of intoxication, says he can think of nothing but you, is it kind or fair to withhold the fact that you can think of nothing but him? Possibly not, but it would, perhaps, thought Aurea, have been wiser.

Perhaps if I had been less forthcoming to Valentine he would have been kinder to me sometimes. Another instance of the power of words, this time to confuse and mislead. One has read that in some countries there are certain words and phrases only to be used by women. We also have our words which, used by a man or a woman, mean entirely different things. If a man asks a woman to be kind, hasn't the word one ultimate significance? If a woman asks a man to be kind to her, it usually means the beginning of muddles. She is asking for what to her seems reasonably her due in the way of consideration and attention; he is resenting what seem to him her unreasonable demands upon that precious but indefinable jewel, his complete freedom to be as selfish as he chooses. And how irritating a loving and exigent woman can be to a man, is what the female sex can barely understand. If Aurea had been less proud, she would have been the self-humiliating type that unavoidably rouses the sadistic instincts of any nice man; too ready to believe herself in the wrong, too ready to apologize for her lover's lapses, and be graciously forgiven for what he has done. But though her heart was very humble, it was held up by her pride. If Mr. Howard had known how very manfully she had subdued her many impulses to throw herself into Valentine's arms and see what would happen next; how often she had submitted with apparent cheerfulness to his thoughtlessness or selfishness rather than complain, he would perhaps have been a little less embarrassing about the honor of women. Aurea felt her cheeks burn as she thought of that revolting phrase. And what an evening it was going to be if it went on as it had begun. All one's clothes packed except one old rag of a frock, papa preaching to one, Fanny and Arthur coming to dinner and taking far too much interest in her, Valentine coming to dinner and unable to get her alone, and probably flirting with Fanny, the theater where Fanny would be sure to put her next to Arthur, the uncertainty of getting Valentine to herself afterwards, the prospect of papa sitting up for her to finish their talk, then tomorrow and the last of England. It was too, too dreadful, and she broke out into the most undignified crying.

Upon this Mrs. Howard, ready dressed for dinner, came in, and looked as if the last straw had been placed upon her back.

"What *is* the matter, Aurea? she asked, aghast at her daughter's appearance.

"Oh, mother, mother," sobbed Aurea, throwing reticence and dignity to the winds, "it's papa. He has been talking quite dreadfully about my making myself cheap and running after Valentine, and awful expressions about the honor of women. I do wish he wouldn't enjoy himself quite so much at my expense, and on my last night too."

Mrs. Howard would have laughed if Aurea hadn't looked so miserable, and been so obviously spoiling for hysteria.

"Darling, you mustn't cry so much," she said kindly, but not too kindly. "Papa didn't mean to be unkind. It's only because he is so anxious about you."

"Well, I wish to goodness he weren't," said Aurea, blowing her nose defiantly. "He seemed much more anxious about Valentine. Here am I, perfectly respectable, and behaving like a lady, and not even letting Valentine hold my hand in taxis, or at least not very often, and what do I get for it but papa telling me I am the Scarlet Woman."

She cried again more hopelessly than before, while her distracted mother hovered around begging her to be reasonable and stop crying.

"You'll look wretched all evening, Aurea, if you don't stop."

"Perhaps papa will be pleased if I do," sniffled Aurea. "Perhaps he would like me not to go to the theater, and not see Valentine again, and have a thoroughly miserable evening."

"You mustn't talk like that, Aurea," said Mrs. Howard rather sharply. "Pull yourself together. Papa has been very much worried about you, and so have I, and if we didn't trust you a great deal, one of us would have said something of the sort much earlier."

Aurea's sobs were dying down, and she made an effort to talk properly, but her feelings were still lacerated.

"It's all very well for papa," she said complainingly. "When he feels an attachment for an attractive female, he can be paternal and kiss her rather lingeringly on the forehead as if he were the Pope."

"Popes don't kiss people's foreheads, darling," said Mrs. Howard, relieved by her daughter's recovery. "And you mustn't make me laugh at papa."

"Yes, I know, mother, people kiss Pope's toes, which sounds like a piece of a chicken, but it's all the same. And you really don't mind laughing at papa. He is such a darling, but he is always so desperately right."

"Hush, Aurea."

"Well, only watch papa with Fanny tonight and see what there is to choose between us. And then just because I have an attachment for an attractive gentleman and have never kissed him at all, here is papa saying that we will finish our talk when I come back tonight, and I shall go quite mad if we do. I must have a chance of seeing Valentine alone before I go, mother. I must, I must."

"Aurea, you must be good. Papa does love you."

"I suppose he does," said Aurea a little sulkily. Then, making an effort, she added, "I'm sorry. I know he does, and I'm an ungrateful pig."

Mrs. Howard breathed a sigh of relief that the storm was over. Probably Will had not been very tactful with Aurea. It was a foolish moment to choose for scolding the child when she was worn out with late nights and emotion and the thought of parting. She considered quickly and said, "You shall see Mr. Ensor alone, Aurea, when you come back. I'll manage it somehow. I don't know if I'm doing right, but I suppose you know what you are about."

Aurea's pinched, tear-stained face became radiant.

"Oh, thank you, thank you, darling. Oh, mother, I'm so sorry if I'm not behaving well. I'm a horrible daughter, and do nothing but be beastly and upsetting, and you have to bear it all. I can't think how you can stand me." And she hugged her mother violently.

"I can always stand you," said Mrs. Howard, touched by Aurea's joy and gratitude. "That's what mothers are there for. Now run up quickly and dress. I believe I hear Fanny already. She's early."

"She would be too early tonight," said Aurea, hurriedly collecting her out-of-door clothes and bag. But she was too late to slip away unseen. Fanny, followed by Arthur and Valentine, met her in the doorway. There was a hubbub of greetings, one look into Valentine's eyes, and she escaped, calling that she would be down in a moment.

While the others passed on to greet Mrs. Howard, Aurea lingered for a moment in the half open door to gaze sentimentally upon the back of Valentine's head, but no one noticed her presence, as they all had their backs to her.

Mrs. Howard said how do you do to her guests.

"I'm afraid we're frightfully early," said Fanny; "but better too early than too late, and don't bother about us; we can amuse ourselves. We brought Val along with us because he's always late."

"I hadn't noticed that you were a late person, Mr. Ensor," said Mrs. Howard pleasantly. "A rather particularly punctual person, I should have said."

"He is never punctual, Mrs. Howard, unless he's in love," said Fanny. "I've seen him through about twenty love affairs, so I ought to know."

"Fanny, you are nothing if not tactless," said Valentine. "Mrs. Howard please don't believe a word she says. I have wasted so much time waiting for Fanny that I have learnt never to be punctual where she is concerned."

The door was suddenly closed. No one noticed, because Fanny, ever prompt to resent an insult, had turned on Valentine.

"Ungrateful viper," she hissed, so far as one can hiss a sentence without an "s" in it, "drinking all my good cocktails and bringing me here to insult me. Oh—Arthur—did you bring the tickets?"

"Did you give them to me?" said Arthur.

"Don't try to put me off with evasions. Find them and let me see them, or we shall arrive at the theater, and have to go to the pit because we can't run to four more stalls."

Assisted by Fanny, Arthur began to rummage in various pockets. His wife's running comments made a cover under which Valentine had a chance to speak apart with Mrs. Howard.

"Is anything wrong with Aurea tonight?" he asked anxiously. "She looks as if she had been crying."

"She is upset and overwrought. We all are with her going tomorrow. Don't take any notice. She will be all right when she comes down. Don't tire her and don't keep her up late."

"Not supper after the play?"

Mrs. Howard put her hand on his arm. "I'd be so glad," she said earnestly, "if you'll bring her straight home. She can't stand much more."

Valentine felt sorry for her. "If I can get rid of Fanny and Arthur I'll bring her straight back myself," he promised. "May I come in and say goodby?"

"Don't be too long, will you?"she begged.

"Goodby is soon said."

"I have known it take hours and hours," said Mrs. Howard sharply. "But I have trusted you—a great deal more than was fair to you perhaps—and I appeal to you about this."

"I'll be good," said Valentine, touched by her anxiety. "I only want to tell Aurea— "

But what he wanted, Mrs. Howard was never to know, for at that moment Fanny emitted a high screech.

"And there they were in my bag the whole time," she exclaimed indignantly. "Why didn't you say so, Arthur?"

"I asked you if you had given them to me," said Arthur dispassionately.

"A sensible question to ask when I had them!"

"But you would insist," said Arthur calmly, "that you had given them to me."

Fanny nearly burst with rage. "Let me never hear of tickets again," she cried furiously.

Valentine thought it time to interfere.

"You'd better let me have the tickets, Arthur," said he. "Fanny trusts me."

"Oh, no, I don't," said Fanny viciously. "Who upset the incubator? Who was going to dine with me on Tuesday four weeks ago and threw me over—who—oh, Arthur!"

Arthur was talking to Mrs. Howard and did not hear.

"ARTHUR!" his wife repeated in stentorian tones. "Forgive me, Mrs. Howard, but I want Arthur to go down and see if the car is locked."

"But you locked it yourself, Fanny, didn't you? Don't you remember giving me the key?"

"Am I always to be met with evasions?" said Fanny, appealing to the company generally. "If you have the key you probably didn't lock the car and I certainly didn't. Here, Val, I don't trust you, but you have some sense. Go down with Arthur and see if it is locked and tell me in which pocket he has the key when you come back."

"All right," said Valentine agreeably. "You don't mind, Mrs. Howard?"

You'll find Will somewhere about downstairs," said Mrs. Howard to Arthur. "Do tell him it's nearly time to dress for dinner. He has probably forgotten that we are dining early."

Arthur and Valentine went downstairs together. Mrs. Howard brought Fanny over to the fire and they sat down.

"How are the children, Fanny?" she began.

"Very well, thank you. The holidays begin soon, but I suppose I'll survive them somehow."

"Aren't they going to your mother-in-law?" said Mrs. Howard innocently.

Fanny looked suspiciously at her, and then roared with laughter.

"Quite right," she admitted, "but I thought I'd get a little free sympathy. What's the matter with Aurea? She's been crying."

Mrs. Howard mentally wrung Fanny's neck. "She is very upset, poor, poor child," she said sadly.

"Who has been upsetting her? If it's a gentleman friend, let me see him and I'll get my claws into him, that's all," said Fanny truculently.

"Fanny, don't be absurd, and I must say a little vulgar with your gentlemen friends. It is very upsetting for poor Aurea that she is leaving us tomorrow, and then all the packing and fuss. I rather hoped she would stay at home tonight, but perhaps it's a better plan to pass the time away at a play. So please try to be a little considerate, Fanny."

Fanny for once had the grace to look slightly abashed and said meekly: "I am so sorry, Mrs. Howard. I do talk without thinking."

"You think too much, Fanny, and then you talk, and then the mischief is done," said Mrs. Howard severely.

"I'm really sorry," said Fanny, a little frightened. "Please forgive me. What can I do to make up?"

"Well, Fanny, you are very good at arranging things. Can you see that Mr. Ensor gets a taxi after the play, and brings Aurea straight home? If you go on to dance, she'll be absolutely done up."

"We'll all bring her home," said Fanny.

"No, dear, don't do that. If you all come here you'll stay on and talk, and she won't go to bed and have a good night. Let Mr. Ensor take her home, and then he can go back and join you if you want to dance. He won't want to stay here long." And may Heaven forgive me for telling such a lie," she added to herself.

At any other time Fanny might have suspected Mrs. Howard's motive, but after the affairs of the tickets and the key she was still fuming with rage against Arthur, and here was a chance to annoy him. He would naturally expect to escort Aurea while his wife went with Val. Very well, then, he should stay with his wife and be deprived of his last chance of philandering. Fanny's temper must have been severely tried before she took such harsh measures against her Arthur, but he had been very trying and absent-minded all evening, and the key was only the last of a series of grievances which Fanny had been nursing.

So she responded eagerly, "Of course I will. It may take some doing, as Val always wants to dance, but I'll see them into a taxi, and I'll give the driver the address myself, and I'll follow them in another taxi, and if Val tries any dirty work on me I'll have a real row with him in the street. What fun!"

Mrs. Howard congratulated herself on having managed things well so far, but did not want Fanny to spoil them by overacting her part.

"I don't think you need go quite as far as that," she said. "But if you'll just see that they start in our direction, I shall be very grateful, dear. You needn't be a sleuth."

Just then Mr. Howard peered around the door.

"I was writing some letters," he said, "but I heard Fanny was here so I came upstairs. How are you, my dear?"

He kissed Fanny on the forehead. Fanny regretably winked at Mrs.

Howard, who nearly spoilt the idyll by laughing, as she remembered Aurea's charge against her father.

"Quite well, Mr. Howard," said Fanny piously.

"That's right. Now come and tell me about the children."

"If you don't mind, Will, I have a letter to finish," said Mrs. Howard. "You won't disturb me. But don't be too long, because we are dining early and you haven't dressed yet."

"Very well, very well," said Mr. Howard, rather impatiently, as his wife sat down at her writing table.

"The children are quite well, thank you," said Fanny. "We shall be having them home for the holidays soon. They are going to Arthur's mother for most of the time. I should love to have them, but I'm so highly strung that I can't stand them for long. The very thought of the darlings makes me look at wreck."

"You look delightful," said Mr. Howard.

"That's because they are still at school. I am so much better when they are away, though, of course, it's very sad. I am much fatter than I was. I haven't lost any rings since you gave me the new one."

"That's right," said Mr. Howard, gratified.

"Will you have lunch with me one day?" continued Fanny. "I really feel I owe you a lunch for the one you gave me when we got the ring."

"With pleasure."

"All right, then. What about Friday, and I'll take you to the Vampire again."

"That will be delightful, my dear."

"And then I'll see if Mrs. Howard can come too." said Fanny pleasantly. She watched Mr. Howard's face, where politeness and loyalty struggled with truthfulness, with some amusement.

"I think," said he, glancing a little nervously at his wife, "that Mary would hardly care for the Vampire. It might be better for us just to lunch there together, and we will ask her another day to some place she would like better. Then after lunch we might go to the exhibition of Obscure and Justly Neglected Copyists of the Early Eighteenth Century in Old Burlington Street. I hear it has points of interest."

"That would be lovely," said Fanny, quite determined that as far as she was concerned the copyists should remain in their Just Neglect.

By this time Aurea had changed into the rag, which looked perfectly adequate. Fanny's remark about Valentine's twenty love affairs had not improved her spirits. It was only too obvious that as Valentine had been married for some years, she could not possibly be his first and only love. Nor was it reasonable to expect that he should have had such a prophetic vision of her charm that he went about with his eyes shut until she burst upon his view. No, one must look at things sensibly and realize that Valentine had loved perhaps not twenty people, but at any rate a great many, and that it was no dishonor to one's own attractions that, by a mere accident of time, one happened to come late on the list. Frankly, it was Fanny's way of putting it that jarred. Fanny, who would assume proprietary airs about Valentine; whom one couldn't put in her place because one wasn't going to betray one's own secret. Fanny, who had everything she wanted and avoided everything she didn't want. Fanny who, when Aurea was far away and forgotten, would be lunching with Valentine and dancing with him, and probably flirting with him. For the moment she almost hated Fanny.

When she came down she met Arthur outside the drawing-room door. He looked a little paler and more somber than usual, she thought, but perhaps that was only because she felt pale and somber herself. In any case she forgot about it as she entered the drawing-room.

"Hello, love, how are you?" said Fanny.

"How are you, Fanny dear?"

"Was the car locked, Arthur?" said his wife.

"Yes," said Arthur shortly, "it was, and the key is in my pocket, so now you know."

"And where is Val?" continued the insufferable Fanny. "Doing something he oughtn't to, I'll be bound."

"Ringing someone up downstairs," said Arthur.

"He would be. He hasn't a telephone at his rooms, Mrs. Howard, and his conversations are all too private for his club or his office, so he uses other people's telephones."

Aurea couldn't help saying, "You seem to know a lot about it, Fanny."

"And why not?" said Fanny, staring at her. "What that man owes me in twopences for all the telephoning he does at my house would pay the drink bill for six months. And if you try to ring him up at his bank he never knows who you are because he has so many charming friends with refined voices like one's own."

Aurea, sick with alarm, and off her guard for a moment, said, "But I thought he didn't like one to ring him up at his office."

Fanny looked at her searchingly, and appeared to Aurea to read to the bottom of her soul and not find it worth reading.

"Oh, you did, did you?" she returned. "Val keeps his friends in very watertight compartments, and what the heart doesn't see the eye doesn't grieve, or words to that effect."

Mrs. Howard, who had finished her letter and joined the others, came to her child's rescue by saying "Fanny!" in a reproving voice.

"Sorry," said Fanny, collapsing, "I forgot."

"What's the time?" asked Mrs. Howard.

"Nearly seven," said Arthur.

"Will," said Mrs. Howard, "you ought to go and dress. Fanny, do you want to come with me?"

"Thank you, Mrs. Howard, I'll come to your room and remove the traces of emotion with a powder puff. Besides, I've something amusing to tell you."

They went out together, laughing. Mr. Howard looked suspicious, and said he would go and finish his letters.

"But, papa darling, you'll be late for dinner," said Aurea.

"Plenty of time, my dear, plenty of time. You and your mother do *fuss* so."

Aurea and Arthur exchanged smiles as Mr. Howard left the room with offended dignity.

"Come and be quiet for a moment, Arthur," she said. "Everyone is on the jump tonight."

"Cigarette?"

"No, thanks, I still don't smoke."

"Sorry. Do you mind if I do?"

"Of course not. Why this politeness? Sit down here and be peaceful. I need it."

"I'm sorry it's your last night," said Arthur presently.

"Oh, so am I. No need to rub it in."

"Sorry."

After another short pause Arthur continued, "We haven't seen much of you."

"There hasn't been much time, has there? But I have one heavenly weekend to thank you for. It was perfect."

"I'm glad it was perfect," said Arthur, in a carefully controlled voice. "You were perfect too."

"A momentary suspicion flashed through Aurea's mind. Arthur couldn't conceivably be going to be silly, could he? She decided that he couldn't, and it was only her nerves that were jumpy.

"That's very sweet of you, Arthur," she said kindly.

"True, that's all."

And conversation languished again. Certainly Arthur was heavy going. But it was far better for people to be remote and taciturn than to shock and terrify one as Arthur did, when he said, "Aurea, there isn't much time, and I want to tell you that I think I have guessed."

Aurea's heart appeared to perform a series of violent gymnastic exercises, winding up with the high jump, which it missed. How could he have guessed? She had never said anything. There had been that evening at the Vampire when Valentine was dancing with that horrible Mounsey girl, and she had told Arthur she was unhappy, but there might be a thousand reasons for unhappiness, and surely the fact that she was leaving her parents was quite enough. Hadn't he asked her, though, whether her unhappiness had anything to do with the weekend at Waterside? Oh, heavens, was it possible that she had betrayed herself and Valentine? It never occurred to her for a moment that Valentine could have given her secret away, and in this she did him no less than justice.

"Guessed what?" she said feebly, and was conscious of a flaming face. But perhaps by artificial light one's blushes didn't show so much.

"About your unhappiness, my dear."

"Oh, I don't think you do. It's all rather complicated. I couldn't possibly explain it."

"Let *me* explain," said Arthur in a voice of deep manly emotion for which Aurea could willingly have choked him.

"You?" she said. "But you don't know what it is."

Arthur was just beginning to enjoy himself. He had made up his mind to speak to Aurea before she left, but there had been no opportunity. Now his chance had come, and he was determined to use it. He would never have dreamt that his love would care for him still, if she hadn't almost told him so at the Vampire in so many words. It was a miracle, of course, but one just had to accept miracles and do one's best to live up to them. She was goddess and child. The goddess had stooped to him, but the child was afraid to reach out her hand. He had debated long with himself whether he should remain a worshipper on his knees, or touch the image and bring her to life. Of his own powers to bring her to life he had no doubt. He knew quite well that he had no business to make or receive vows of affection with Aurea, but his feelings had got the better of him and, for the moment, he thought as little of Fanny as Aurea had been thinking of Ned. Like Valentine, and indeed like most of his sex, he was a bad gardener, and could not resist pulling up his plants to look at the roots.

Accordingly he answered, "I think I do. And you mustn't mind my having guessed. It's all quite all right, and not your fault. These things just happen to one and it can't be helped."

This was surely clear enough. Now the goddess would put her warm hand in his, and be a woman.

Aurea was horrified. It was surely clear enough. Arthur had seen the feeling between Valentine and herself, and was trying to tell her tactfully. If he had seen it, who else might not know? Had she and Valentine been burrowing their heads in the sand in vain for all those weeks? Did everyone who saw them together say, "Ha ha, those people are in love?"

"Oh, Arthur," she exclaimed piteously, "if you know, then other people must. How awful!"

Arthur would help her. He was an old and trusted friend and wouldn't let things go any further. He was only telling her as a warning to be careful, and a hint that he would screen and shield her. But his next words were a thunderbolt.

"I don't think so, Aurea. But I shall tell Fanny, of course."

Arthur felt too noble for words as he said this. In one breath he was having the blessed relief of avowing a pent-up passion, and at the same time securing absolution from his wife in advance. With a rare flight of imagination he could see himself, when Aurea had gone, telling Fanny that he had cared for Aurea more than a little, and she, poor girl, for him. Fanny would probably lecture him vigorously, but it was, after all, she who had more or less schemed for him and Aurea to revive a dead flame, and she couldn't be resentful if her own plans worked so well. Then he would take Fanny to her favorite dancing place, and they would eat and drink and dance and go home together, and the incident would be closed.

Aurea could only express her stupefaction in the questioning, word "Fanny?"

"Naturally," said Arthur, "I shall tell her, though I expect she will hardly be surprised. But she will absolutely understand. She is wonderfully broad minded."

Aurea's horror may better be imagined than described. Arthur would tell Fanny that she, Aurea, loved Valentine Ensor? Oh, it was outrageous, impossible. Fanny was the worst gossip in London. No malice, but an insatiable appetite for snapping up news, and great generosity in broadcasting it again. What was Arthur thinking of? But she mustn't be too indignant. She must show tact, diplomacy and finesse—however one did these things—and perhaps he would take a less serious view.

"But how could you think of telling her, Arthur?" she said. "I mean I am terribly fond of Fanny and she has been a perfect dear to me, but—excuse me, Arthur—she does talk."

"Oh, yes," said Arthur, "Fanny does talk, but you needn't worry about that. In a matter that touches herself she is very discreet."

Because, he argued to himself, Fanny won't be so anxious to tell all her friends that I have been in love with another woman. She boasts about her own affairs, but she would hardly boast about mine. Or yet, perhaps, would she? A slight chill struck to his heart as he reflected that his Fanny would sacrifice almost anything to make a good story. Would it really be wiser not to tell her? He thought it would.

A chill also struck to Aurea's heart. If her and Valentine's affection was a matter that touched Fanny personally, that meant that her worst fears were confirmed. Fanny did care for Valentine and now was her chance with Aurea out of England. With her mocking tongue she would make all her circle laugh about Valentine's last little affair. Sooner than be ridiculed by her, Valentine would return to his old allegiance, and she would be forgotten for evermore. Quite desperate she looked from side to side.

"Oh, Arthur, this is dreadful. If Fanny knows, I shall die."

Arthur felt very sorry for the goddess, now a frightened child, and tried to reassure her.

"Perhaps I had better not tell her then," he said magnificently. "Of course she had probably guessed, but then she only likes new gossip, and this is so old."

Old enough, twenty years old, and Fanny must be tired by now of laughing at him for his calf-love.

"Old?" said Aurea, in utter bewilderment, "Old? But how could it be old? I've only been in England a few weeks."

Could Fanny have got it into her head that she had lost her heart to Valentine twenty years ago, as she had, just a little, lost it then to Arthur? The idea was too preposterous. Arthur didn't help her confusion by adding: "I don't mean this time only. I mean long ago as well."

He was, he felt, getting on nicely, and managing it all with infinite tact.

"I shall go mad," said Aurea resignedly. "What has long ago to do with it?"

Now was the moment. She understands so well what you mean, but dares not confess it. One touch more and she is yours.

"Only," he said, and found to his annoyance that his voice was so husky that he had to cough violently and start again, "only that I cared for you so much when we were both young—"

"Oh—Arthur—" gasped his unhappy idol, upon whom the whole hideous misunderstanding was just beginning to dawn.

"—and in a sense I've never stopped, and I think it has been the same with you."

Relief, mortification, fury, surged in Aurea's mind. Fool that she had been to think that Arthur was talking about her and Valentine—as if men ever talked about any man but themselves. Fool that she had been not to see whither Arthur's approaches led. What a horrible muddle he was landing her in. Fool that Arthur was, to think that she had any tender feeling for him; fool, if loving her hadn't sharpened his wits enough to see that her eyes and heart were only for his friend.

"You mean," said Aurea, slowly and looking him full in the face, determined to get it right this time, "You mean, that is why I'm unhappy at leaving England?"

"I do."

"Oh, my God," said Aurea.

Aurea began to register nobility again. "I hate to think of your being unhappy," he said with revolting tenderness, though Aurea blamed herself for feeling revolted, "but I can't help being proud that you care so much."

"And do you think Fanny knows all this?"

Arthur was a little annoyed at Aurea's want of tact in harping on his wife. It would have been far more becoming in her, he thought, to lay her head on his shoulder with a sigh, like a dove coming home to roost, if that is what they do.

"Oh, yes," he said, "she must have some idea. But she would approve." (The idea of being *approved* by Fanny!) "She likes me to have my friends separately sometimes, because it gives her a chance to amuse herself with hers—with Val for one."

It is almost impossible ever to feel the same towards a man who has exhibited the fatuousness of a successful lover—unless, of course, the lady burns with an equal flame. In these few moments Arthur had succeeded in destroying all Aurea's long cherished romance about him. He was too old a friend for her to dislike him, but never again could she feel safe as she used to do. Whenever they met again, next year, or after twenty years, she would be on the defensive. She would say goodby tonight to a dear lover, whose embrace she would never know. Was not this hard enough, without at the same time an eternal barrier being placed by Arthur's folly between her and one of her oldest friends? And Valentine. What did Arthur mean by saying that Fanny liked to amuse herself with him?

"Oh, hell, oh, hell," she said plaintively, getting up and walking about.

Arthur looked surprised. This was hardly the result he had anticipated. The goddess had not melted, and indeed seemed more remote than ever.

Aurea began to laugh. "Fanny—and Valentine—and you—and I. Oh, it's too funny," she said, in a loud hard voice, unlike her own. "I'll have to laugh."

"Hold on, Aurea," said Arthur anxiously.

"You are such a dear," said Aurea, in her hard, breathless voice. "And I'm so wretched—and it's all so upside-down and wrong—and it's so amusing."

In proof of the amusement she laughed again very uncontrolledly.

Arthur now understood. It was her exquisite sense of right and wrong that was shocked. What a brute he had been to try her so cruelly. He must reassure her at all costs. Poor child, how earnestly she took it all, how unmodern she was.

"Not really wrong, Aurea," said he kindly and patronizingly. "You are doing nothing wrong in still caring for a very old friend, who cares very much for you."

His conception of what she meant by wrong set her wildly laughing again, so wildly that Arthur seized her arm to stop her wild-beast perambulation of the room.

"Stop!" he said.

"I can't stop. I can't help laughing. I didn't mean that kind of wrong. I meant it's such a mistake—so funny."

"Aurea, do stop, please," pleaded Arthur, quite distracted by what he had evoked. "They'll be coming back in a minute."

Aurea struggled with her hysteria and wiped her eyes, while Arthur patted her back. Voices were heard approaching. To Arthur's everlasting astonishment, she put her arms around his neck, hugged him violently, and was at arms' length again before he knew what had happened.

"You're a dear," she said, "and I won't ever forget your kindness."

When Mr. Howard and Valentine came in, they only found a gentleman lighting a cigarette, and a lady powdering her face in what appeared to be a curiously dark corner for the toilet.

"Where is your mother, Aurea?" asked Mr. Howard.

"With Fanny in her room, I think," said Aurea. "You really must hurry, darling. It's almost dinner time."

"Don't *fuss*, Aurea," said Mr. Howard. "There's plenty of time. I have asked for dinner to be at half-past, as you are all so late. I found Ensor telephoning in the hall. It's cold there, so I brought him up to use the drawing-room telephone. There you are, Ensor; never mind us, you won't disturb us."

Valentine looked a little sheepish. "Thank you so much, sir," he said, "but I'd finished, really. It was rather impertinent to use your telephone. I hope you didn't mind."

"Not at all, not at all. Finish your talk up here, by all means."

"Yes, say anything you like, Valentine," said Aurea, in a clear voice. "We shan't listen."

Valentine was conscious of a strange inimical note in Aurea's voice. "I'd finished," he said. "Really."

"All I can say is," remarked Arthur, "it's not like you, Val. You usually have such a passion for the telephone. When you ring Fanny up, it goes on for hours and hours. And if she rings you up at the bank, it's worse."

"But it wasn't Fanny I was telephoning to," said Valentine, puzzled and impatient, "so it's all over now."

"And in any case, Arthur," said Aurea, turning away from Valentine, "I don't think it's particularly interesting to know which of Valentine's friends he was talking to."

"You would have a long list to choose from," said Arthur.

"Some people," Aurea continued in the same impersonal voice, "don't like to be rung up at their offices. I suppose they are afraid of their friends getting on the same line. It might be awkward."

"That's what I'm always telling Fanny," said that lady's husband. "She'll get into trouble over it some day."

"It's all right for Fanny," said Aurea in her natural voice, "she doesn't—"

"Doesn't what, dear?" asked her father, "I do wish you young people would finish your sentences."

"Oh, nothing, papa."

"But you are quite right, Aurea," her father continued. "Office telephones shouldn't be used for private conversation. I never allowed it in my department."

"My chief doesn't allow it either, sir, though some of it does go on," said Valentine, who was still at a loss. "But Arthur exaggerates."

Aurea walked up to Valentine and looked at him, her eyes blazing with all the concentrated hatred that can be felt for a person whom you hopelessly, and past all right or wrong, worship and adore.

"Then I suppose," she said, "Fanny was exaggerating too."

"What on earth is the matter?" asked Valentine, surprised at the introduction of Fanny's name.

"Nothing," said Aurea. "I'm not worth considering." She turned away, leaving Valentine half angry, half amused. Evidently that devil Fanny had been up to some of her tricks. He must get Aurea alone and put things right.

Mr. Howard had quite forgotten about dinner again, and was asking Arthur about the new car.

"She's running splendidly, sir," said Arthur, who adored his cars. "I wish you'd let me take you out one day when Aurea has gone, and Mrs. Howard."

Mr. Howard said he would like it very much when the weather was warmer. Arthur explained the glories of a new electric cushion he had bought for warming people in the car. You could sit on it, or have it on your lap, or under your feet. Mr. Howard said that sounded very comforting, and made the proposed drive far more inviting.

"Would you like me to get it, sir?" said Arthur eagerly. "I brought it into the hall because I thought it might interest you."

Valentine said he had noticed that Arthur had a new back tire on tonight, and he might bring that up too.

"That was quite unnecessary, Valentine," said Aurea coldly. "Arthur, dear, we should love to see your warming pan or whatever it is."

Arthur was pleased and flattered, and offered to get it at once.

"Don't trouble," said Mr. Howard. "I have to go down for a moment, and you can show me the cushion in the study. It is warmer than the hall."

"Oh, papa," interrupted Aurea, "you really *must* get dressed. You know we are going to a play, and we don't want to be late."

Mr. Howard glared at his only daughter. "I told you not to fuss," he said. "You know quite well I only take a few minutes. Come on, Arthur."

"Coming, Aurea?" said Arthur, who was enchanted by her kind interest.

"Too cold, Arthur. I send it my blessing, and hope it will keep you warm when I've gone."

"What about you, Val?" said the proud owner.

"No, thanks; I'll stay up here."

"All right," said Arthur, and followed Mr. Howard downstairs.

Aurea was alone with Valentine, and wished she wasn't. It was all too difficult. Proof upon proof all day of how little she was wanted, of how many other women had claims on his attention. If only she could hit him, or somehow hurt him badly. Failing that, it would be better to leave him.

"I think I'll go and see it too," she said politely, and was opening the door when Valentine called, "Aurea."

"What?" she asked, not troubling to look at him.

"Please don't go down."

"And why not?"

"Please shut the door and come back."

Aurea shrugged her shoulders very rudely, shut the door, and stood before him in the attitude of Circassian slave before Pasha.

"Please sit down," he said.

"No, thank you."

"May I smoke?"

"Was that all you wanted me for?"

"No. Sit down."

Much to Aurea's surprise she sat down at once.

"Why were you angry with me about the telephone?" he asked.

"Angry? I wasn't angry."

"Then why did you pretend to be angry?"

"Pretend? I didn't pretend," said Aurea illogically. "I *was* angry."

"Why?"

"You haven't any right to ask me all these questions. You are behaving as if I were in the wrong, and not you."

"That isn't the point," said Valentine, with maddening patience. "It isn't fair to be angry with me because I was telephoning for five minutes in your father's house."

"Oh, you can put anything so that it sounds right," said Aurea wearily. "But you're not right. If you want to know I was unhappy because—"

"Because?"

"Well, I was so sad," said Aurea in a more gentle voice but without looking at him, "that Fanny and other people could talk to you for hours on the telephone, and I'm not allowed to."

Valentine felt rather guilty, but had no intention of admitting it.

"But, Aurea," he said, "isn't it rather because I am anxious for you that I have asked you not to ring me up?"

"Anxious for me?" said she, looking at him for the first time, "I don't understand."

"It's so difficult to talk plainly to you," said Valentine slowly. "You're so sensitive. I mean—with Fanny and other friends there isn't any question of its being in any way—I don't know how to say it without hurting you."

Aurea was only too eager for any excuse by which she could honorably emerge from her sulks, but at the mention of Fanny her face set.

"What you mean, I suppose," she said, deliberately picking her words to wound, "is that you are a little afraid of my being in any way compromised—and a good deal afraid of my compromising you with any other woman who might happen to overhear."

If a hen suddenly ran at one and tried to knock one down, one would feel rather as Valentine did at this moment. There was enough truth in what Aurea had said to make him incapable of any utterance but a very indignant "Aurea!"

"I suppose," she continued recklessly, "you have been laughing at me for supposing I am the only woman in your thoughts."

"I didn't laugh at you. By heaven, I never have. Who has been putting melodramatic ideas into your head about other women?"

"F—," Aurea began, altering it hurriedly and lamely to, "Nobody. And anyway, I shan't tell you." But hope was beginning to spring again.

"Then," said Valentine, "I shall draw my own conclusions. You darling half-wit, can I possibly ever make you understand anything?"

Aurea's heart warmed to this expression of affection, but she only replied, "Probably not if I'm a half-wit."

"Well, that is what you are where any kind of worldly wisdom is concerned."

"It's not my fault," said Aurea, raising sad eyes to him.

"I know it's not," said Valentine, sitting down near her, "and I wouldn't for the world have you different in any other way. But I'm not sure that it's not your misfortune. Do you honestly think I could ever love anyone in the way I love you?"

"Yes. I wouldn't blame you, because it's all I deserve for the way I'm behaving, but it sadly seems to me that it is so."

Her acceptance of the fact, without any rancour, smote Valentine.

"Dear half-wit," he said, taking her hand, "you are right in a manner of speaking—"

"I knew it," said Aurea hopelessly, but leaving the unresponsive hand where it lay.

"—but," he continued, "hopelessly wrong. I do love people rather easily, and my kind of life makes it easy to love. One is unattached, one is useful for dances, dinners, all kinds of fun. There are many more women than men in this bit of civilization and one is rather flattered by charmers who pursue one, and if charmers throw themselves at one's head, it's a little difficult not to respond—and I'm very human, my dear, I'm afraid."

Aurea possessed to the full the very feminine characteristic of total inability to talk generally. Whatever was said she had to wrench around to some personal application.

"*I* never threw myself at your head," she said.

"Good God, do you think I meant that?" said Valentine, really horrified that she should have so misunderstood him. "I know you didn't."

"I only couldn't help loving you," she said, always following her single thought.

"You poor child."

"I like you to call me that."

"It's the way I think of you. And, Aurea, I would be as ashamed of hurting you deliberately as if you were really a child, but I can't suddenly alter my whole life because of you."

"I suppose not," said Aurea, on whom all the unkindness in the world seemed to be falling in heavy waves. "But I don't understand."

"And I don't think you ever will—but it's of no great importance. Whatever you may think of me, you can't help loving me—you said so yourself. And as for me, however much I love you—and it's a man's love, Aurea, and goes a good deal deeper than you may think—I care for other women, and shall care for yet others."

Aurea withdrew her hand quickly. "You might as well hit me in the face as talk to me like that," she said.

"Hush, hush. Listen for a moment," said Valentine, taking her hand again, straightening and bending her fingers one by one as he spoke, as if the mechanical action helped him to formulate his thoughts. "Whatever other women I care for—and if I know myself as I think I do, it is inevitable that this should happen—I shall always come back to the thought of you. A cold kind of comfort, you'll say, but it means this, that you, whatever you are, the essence of you, whatever it may be, your dearness, your loveliness, your trust, your ridiculous inexperience which I adore—all have made such a place for themselves in my heart that something of you will be with me forever. Do you remember what the doctors said about Henry King, whose chief defect was chewing little bits of string?"

"'There is no cure for this disease.'"

"Good girl. I'm glad you know your classics so well. Yes, for me there will never be any cure for loving you. And, believe it or not, my dear, as you may choose, the thought of these few weeks, in spite of all the pain and misery of them, will always be very safe in a most sacred corner of my heart which no one else will ever see. I know that to love you is hopeless, so I won't let it spoil my life, any more than you are going to let it spoil yours, but it may be some comfort to know that something of each of us belongs to the other forever."

Such gentle peace descended on Aurea's tired heart and mind that she wanted never to move or speak again. Only to breathe her lover's name, "Valentine," on the lightest of sighs. He, finding no answer to this, and always explaining to himself that to take her in his arms and squash her flat was the one thing he must not do, sought safety in saying "Aurea," in gentle mockery of her tones. And there they might have sat, mutely enchained, till dinner was ready, had not Aurea, unable to escape her own self-tormenting spirit, suddenly asked:

"But what about your wife?"

"My wife?"

"I mean, the wife you are going to have."

"You know more about her than I do. This is some of Fanny's devilry, I suppose."

"I don't know," said Aurea doubtfully. "It was a Mr. Graham who mentioned her."

"Graham? Not Ronnie Graham. What the devil did he have to say about it?"

"Only that you were going to marry a person called Mounsey with pots of money," said Aurea in a cheerful voice, adding with a good deal of vehemence for so detached an onlooker, "and I hate her."

"Darling half-wit," began her lover, but Aurea continued with some acerbity, "You are bound to marry again, of course, and that will be a certain cure. Oh, how I hope that Mounsey creature is a wayward strong-willed hussy who will lead you such a life, and bully you, and break your spirit, and make you fetch and carry, and laugh at you, and bring you up properly."

"Isn't this rather fierce?" said Valentine. "Besides, there has never been any question of my marrying anybody; truth and honor."

But Aurea was in full cry after her idea and paid no attention. "And I hope," she went on, working herself up, "that she won't let you use the telephone ever, and that she'll pull the skin off over your head if you don't pay her perfect attention. And then you'll wish you had been nicer to me."

Valentine resented this criticism. He wondered exactly what meaning she attached to the word nice. If by not being nice she meant that one had tried to hold oneself in check in every way, not seeing her as often as one might because one knew that any failure of self-control would frighten and repel her; then, and not otherwise, she was justified. "I couldn't have been much nicer, Aurea," he said. "It has been difficult enough, more difficult than you know. And you aren't an easy person to deal with."

"You don't deal with me much," said Aurea, getting up. "You walk over me like a steam-roller. Fanny was right."

This maddening iteration of Fanny. What immeasurable mischief she must have done in his poor Aurea's mind.

"Right about what?" he asked with rising irritation.

"About the telephone."

"Oh, my God," said Valentine, getting up in his turn and walking up and down the room angrily. "You aren't still thinking about that telephone? I'd like to wring Fanny's neck."

These words were a little comforting, but Aurea was so sick at heart with love and fatigue and the inevitable march of time towards the end of everything, that she perversely replied:

"Never mind. I'll be gone soon and you'll be free."

Two furious people stopped in their meaningless pacing, and met face to face.

"Aurea," almost shouted Valentine indignantly, "this unfairness—"

Nothing was left for them but a blow or an embrace, but they were spared the necessity of a choice by the opening of the door, and the appearance of Mr. Howard.

"Are Fanny and your mother down?" said he mildly, not appearing to notice the strained atmosphere.

"No, papa," said Aurea. "Oh, goodness, papa, you aren't dressed yet."

"Never mind," said Mr. Howard quite sharply and disappeared.

The lovers then went on where they had left off, as if Mr. Howard had never existed. Love and hatred, violent, indistinguishable, were hurtling about the room. A blow or a caress would have been the same, but one's training made both impossible. Intense longing, thwarted for so many days and nights, was almost repulsion. One touch would have dispelled all these heavy dreams, but, rigid, neither dared to move a step. Only bitter words could pass between them, flashing harmfully from pole to pole, gathering evil power.

"Be reasonable, Aurea," said Valentine harshly.

"Reasonable?" cried Aurea in a high peacock screech. "Why should I be? Why," said she again, coming a step nearer with arms rigid by her sides and clenched fists, "why should I be? Why are you to do just as you like, and I do all the suffering?"

"Stop it," said Valentine quite brutally. "Stop it at once, I tell you."

Aurea hated and defied him. "I won't," she said. "How dare you order me about? I've stood it long enough. I'll say what I like, where I like, when I like, and you can kill me if you like." She then considerably weakened her effect by adding, "And I'm a married woman, so there."

Again they stood silent, thought and feeling suspended, unable to extricate themselves from the circle of their passions. Again the door opened, but this time it was Mrs. Howard, who came in calling, "Will, Will." She looked about and saw her daughter and her daughter's friend standing amicably on the hearthrug. "Oh, Mr. Ensor,' she said, "have you seen Will? I can't find him downstairs."

"He was in here just now, looking for you and Fanny," said the well-mannered Mr. Ensor. "He went out again a moment ago."

"Just see if he is there, will you," said Mrs. Howard, unsuspicious of storm in the air.

Valenine opened the door, and evidently caught sight of Mr. Howard for he called out, "Is that you, sir? Mrs. Howard is looking for you."

"Do you want me, my dear?" asked Mr. Howard, coming back into the room.

"Yes, Will dear, only to say do get dressed. You are keeping everyone waiting, and we've put dinner off once, and these young people have to get to their play. I've asked you three or four times already." It was unlike Mrs. Howard to nag, but she had had a trying evening.

Mr. Howard took off his glasses with annoying and calculated deliberation, polished them, and put them on again. "I know, Mary," said he, "and I was just on my way to dress if you hadn't called me. Now you will make me late, but so be it."

He went out; a just man, persecuted, misunderstood. Mrs. Howard made a face of mock despair to Aurea and followed him, to see that he didn't mislay himself again.

Aurea sat down inelegantly with a flop.

"We can't even quarrel in peace," she said piteously. So that, thank heaven, they both had to laugh quite naturally, and felt much better.

"Bad luck, isn't it?" said Valentine. "Just when you were spoiling for a quarrel."

"I'm not," said Aurea, scenting recriminations. Then she caught Valentine's eye and had to laugh again. "Oh, well, perhaps I am," said she handsomely, "but you are, too, and I don't intend to indulge your whims."

"Bless you, child," said he and was just going to kiss her hand, when what he mentally described as the blasted door opened again and he had to say damn and drop it. It was Mr. Howard and Fanny, in very good spirits.

"And where is Arthur?" asked his wife.

Valentine saw that Aurea wasn't fit to face Fanny, so he stood up, screening her and prepared to skirmish with Fanny.

"He took Mr. Howard down to show him a new way of warming the car."

"And used up half the battery, I'll be bound," said the ignorant Fanny. "You're not looking very cheerful, Val."

"It must be the effect of seeing you again," said the gallent Mr. Ensor.

"Effect of the telephone, if you ask me," said Fanny scornfully. "Which of them was it you were throwing over."

"Would you like to know?" said Valentine, really terrified that Aurea might take Fanny seriously, and begin to mistrust him again. But his heart leapt as he felt the slightest touch on his hand. He didn't dare to respond under Fanny's eagle eye, but he felt safe and comforted.

"Not a bit," cried Fanny, "so long as you don't throw *me* over for next week."

"What are we going to do?" asked Valentine conversationally. By all means let Fanny drivel on so long as it gave Aurea time to recover.

"Embassy, I think, and I have a fat cousin coming from the country who will do nicely for Arthur."

"Why drag Arthur in?"

Fanny made large innocent eyes. "Oh, my dear, I must. If I were seen going about alone with a gentleman of your reputation, where would mine be?"

Here Aurea suddenly entered the lists on Valentine's side. "I didn't know you had a reputation, Fanny,' she said carelessly.

Fanny stared. "Bless your heart, I have several. I keep a special one for you."

This was rather rude, and meant to be so. Fanny wanted to hint to

Valentine that Aurea was rather too proper and babyish for his serious attentions. Aurea felt this. She wasn't going to mind for herself, but it was going to make Valentine uncomfortable, and this she would not stand. If she chose to hurt Valentine herself, that was one matter, and anyway, it hurt her far more than it hurt him; if Fanny tried to touch him, that was another, and the mother hen in her began to fluffle up its feathers.

Before she could answer, Arthur came in, to be greeted by his wife with, "Oh, here you are. Where have you been?"

"Downstairs," said Arthur. He was already suffering considerable remorse for having upset Aurea so much, and longing to make it up to her in some way. If only there were a dragon or a drunken man in the drawing-room, that one could fight on her behalf. He realized, with great discomfort, that he had been quite thoughtless and unkind. It was far better for the goddess to stay where she was. If she had come to life it would all have been extraordinarily inconvenient. Now she would always be for him a thing exquisite and apart. And he would always know—though in this he was perfectly incorrect—that the goddess would have loved him if she had dared, that she would always think tenderly of him from her starry sphere; and that there was now no need for Fanny to know anything. How very much annoyed Aurea would have been if she had been able to see his thoughts.

It is unfortunate that the backwash of our holier and deeper emotions often has no other visible token than a very bad temper, and a tendency to quarrel with everything that is not connected with the adored object. How often have we not emerged from a theater, blinking and fuddled by poetry, beauty, romance, only to fall straight into an ignominious row with a taxi-driver or a waiter from whom our higher feelings are hidden. Just so was Arthur, emerging from his dream, like an infuriated owl, and this was not the moment to cross his path. He will return to his Fanny unscathed, but let his Fanny beware how she treads for this one evening.

Valentine was asking Mrs. Howard if he might call on her later. "I wouldn't like to lose sight of you altogether," he said, "after you have been so kind to me."

"Why, of course. Will has always wanted to hear about those excavations. We are hoping to get to Rome ourselves perhaps in the autumn. I suppose you won't be there?"

"I'm afraid not," said Valentine, his words nearly drowned by the booming of the Howards" rather frightening gong.

Mrs. Howard became agitated. "We really won't wait much longer for Will, or you young people will be late for the play. Aurea, do you think your father is dressing?"

"I think so, mother."

Mrs. Howard began to fiddle with the fire. She and her husband, an outwardly united couple, liked to take every opportunity afforded by one another's absence to arrange a fire as it really should be arranged.

Fanny, looking around for trouble, cast a proprietary eye on her husband. It was quite long enough since she had seen him for her to want him to account for the way he had spent his time.

"Arthur," she said, so suddenly that her husband jumped, "what were you and Aurea talking about while I was out of the room? She looks quite pale."

Before Arthur could collect his wits, Aurea had rushed to the breach, sword in hand. In a very clear voice she said, "We were talking about old days, Fanny—when Arthur and I were young—before either of us was married."

"How romantic," said Fanny, looking curious.

"It was romantic," said Aurea, still alarmingly distinct. "And that's why I'm looking pale. It was even more romantic, Fanny, than you can understand."

So saying, she went over to her mother who, quite unnecessarily wrestling with a log, had not noticed the battle, and offered her help. It is always doubtful whether Fanny could feel a rebuff, for all her superficial quickness of wits. "It seems to have upset her, anyway," she remarked hopefully to the two gentlemen. "Arthur, what were you saying to her?"

Arthur, still in a dream of sentiment, penetrated with gratitude to the goddess who had so unexpectedly left her machine to come to his assistance, was for an instant quite seriously angry with his Fanny. "For once in your life, Fanny," he said coldly, "will you mind your own business?"

He went over to the fire, and began to hinder Mrs. Howard and Aurea in their work of reconstruction.

Fanny looked blankly about her. "Ill-mannered churl," she remarked, not without heat. Then, slipping her arm through Valentine's, she said, "Val, you are a gentleman. What was it all about? Or," she added, struck by a sudden thought, and fixing her piercing gaze on him, "was it you that upset Aurea?"

"My dear Fanny," said Valentine very courteously, extricating himself at the same time from her arm, "I am glad you think I am a gentleman, and I should always wish to be mistaken for one, but, if I may presume upon an acquaintance of many years' standing, I quite agree with Arthur's last remark."

He went over to the piano and turned over some music. Fanny, aghast, stood by herself in the middle of the room. She could not have kept silent long, but an end was put to this unbearable situation by Mr. Howard who, standing framed in the open door, said in an accusing voice to the world in general, "The gong went some minutes ago." So they all went down to dinner.

CHAPTER 9

Reading aloud has occasioned more displays of temper than perhaps any other diversion, except croquet. Some are born to read aloud, or to be read aloud to; others are not. The gulf is fixed. The scorn of natural readers for bad readers is deep; but no less profound, and possibly less snobbish, is the scorn of bad readers for people who are affected enough to read clearly and distinctly. The contempt which is felt by people who don't like being read aloud to for people who are dull and tame-spirited enough to enjoy it, is only equaled, or excelled, by the despising attitude of people who like to be read to while they paint, or work, or even sit comfortably doing nothing after dinner, for those who get restive and bored. The two cannot be reconciled. In one way the anti-reading-aloud camp is the more united, for it desires neither to read, nor to be read aloud to; whereas the pro-reading-aloud supporters may be divided into those who prefer to read and those who had rather be read to. To us, as pro-reading-alouders, the most maddening experience possible is to be read to by a bad reader; one who hesitates, who cannot catch the drift of a sentence before he has finished it, who drops his voice at the end of a sentence, who ignores or misuses punctuation, who mumbles, who sounds all the while ashamed of what he is doing, who hurries through a hateful task, who reads as though he had laid a wager to make himself unintelligible, who, in short, exhibits what we should call qualities of ill-educated oafishness.

Not such were Mr. and Mrs. Howard. Both had been brought up

on reading aloud, and both exercised the humane art frequently. Sometimes Mr. Howard, laying aside his pipe, would read to Mrs. Howard, while she sewed, until her eyes softly closed. Sometimes Mrs. Howard, laying aside her sewing, would read aloud to Mr. Howard till he sank into a peaceful slumber. Sometimes again, Mr. Howard would read himself into a coma, nodding himself asleep as the book fell from his nerveless hand. Or again, Mrs. Howard, taking the book from her husband, would read more and more slowly, till sheer rubbish issued from her lips and her voice trailed away into nothingness. And there were occasions when both were to be found asleep, reader and read-to, lulled by the sound. For a time the Howards had dined once in each alternate week with two old friends, who in their turn would dine with the Howards in the intervening week, for the express purpose of reading aloud after dinner. Aurea always said, and apparently no one was able to contradict it, that if she happened to assist at one of these readings there would be four people asleep by the end of the evening.

At any rate, reading aloud was a long established pastime in the Howard family, and Mr. and Mrs. Howard had a kind of secret mental score against each other for falling asleep in an active or passive capacity.

On the evening which we have been describing Mr. Howard was reading aloud after the theater party had gone off, while Mrs. Howard reclined on the sofa. This attitude, conducive to repose, gave Mr. Howard an unfair advantage. From time to time he looked cautiously over his spectacles to see if his wife was still awake. When her closed eyes and peaceful breathing announced that Mr. Howard had scored again, he looked at her with some triumph, and repeated the last sentence he had been reading in a loud and patient voice. Mrs. Howard gave a slight start and came awake suddenly.

"Asleep as usual, Mary," said Mr. Howard carelessly.

But Mrs. Howard unfairly took the wind out of his sails by remarking, "It is such a rest, dear, to go to sleep while you read. Don't you find the same when I am reading?"

"No," answered her husband indignantly. "I don't sleep during your reading, Mary."

"Perhaps you are on the lookout for my mistakes, and that keeps you awake."

"You don't make mistakes, dear," said Mr. Howard, feeling that the victor could afford to be generous.

"But you do go to sleep," said his wife with female injustice. "And what's more, you know you go to sleep yourself while you are reading aloud."

"I think not," said Mr. Howard shortly.

"Sorry, Will, but you do," said she sitting upright. "What's the time?'

"Nearly eleven."

"Time for bed," said Mrs. Howard, in an offhand way, hoping to catch her husband unawares. To her annoyance he replied, "But Aurea hasn't come in yet."

"She might be late, dear. I don't think we'll sit up."

"I shall sit up, Mary. It is her last night." Mrs. Howard's heart sank. She knew her Will so well. If he wanted to see Aurea alone, he was capable of sitting on in the drawing-room till Mr. Ensor was forced to leave. It would never even occur to him that he might more tactfully go and sit in his warm study for a bit. She tried persuasion.

"That's exactly why I didn't want to sit up," she said. "She is so tired, and she will want to go straight to bed, poor child."

Then Mr. Howard made one of his more annoying descents from his heights.

"Is Ensor bringing her home?" he asked. Mrs. Howard could have bitten him with great pleasure. She had fondly hoped that, having unburdened his mind about Mr. Ensor, he would now leave his daughter alone. She said in an unconcerned way that she supposed so. Mr. Howard took off his glasses, folded them up, and put them away. He then relighted his pipe and said, "Mary, I am much concerned."

"What about, Will?"

"About Aurea and Ensor."

Mrs. Howard gnashed her teeth inwardly, if this is physically possible. Will was in that mood when he would have more joy over one sinner that didn't repent than his family could possibly bear. And such a very mild, milk-and-water sinner, too. With a blank expression, she asked her husband why he was concerned. Mr. Howard, after a slight hesitation, said, very conclusively and comprehensively, that he did not approve.

"But, Will dear, there is nothing particular to approve or disapprove."

Mr. Howard, in the manner of an Inquisitor handing over a relapsed heretic to the secular arm, said that Aurea was not behaving well. Mrs. Howard again gnashed her teeth in silence, and also foamed invisibly at the mouth.

"Dear Will," she said, "I think Aurea is behaving as well as she possibly can."

Mr. Howard, hurt at his wife's want of concurrence, said that of course no one regarded his wishes or opinions in the matter.

"But they do. Aurea does. We all do. You must make allowances."

If Mr. Howard secretly knew that he was being unreasonable, he had no intention of admitting it. His conscience told him that if he had wanted to make a protest he should have made it a good deal earlier, instead of waiting till Aurea's last day at home. His common sense also told him that he would have done far better to let well alone, but his unhappy urge to create mental discomfort was too strong. There was some inherited twist in his mind which gave him vague discomfort if other people were enjoying themselves in their own way. To him the gods of unhappiness and ill-luck appeared to need frequent propitiation, and they could best be served by making oneself and everyone else unhappy now, in case they were in any event going to be unhappy later, which sounds illogical, but to self-tormentors is full of sound sense. So all he said was, "No, Mary. There are such things as right and wrong, and I don't like to feel ashamed of my own daughter."

"Will, you are too unreasonable. Why on earth should you feel ashamed?"

This was a difficult question to answer. There really was no reason at all, so he was reduced to saying, "It isn't what I should have expected."

This was more than Mrs. Howard could bear. "Well, Will," she replied rather sharply, "I have never noticed that things did happen particularly as one expected, and I certainly don't know what it was you were expecting, but if it included such a darling attractive creature as my Aurea going through life without anyone taking any notice of her, it's high time you expected something else."

Mr. Howard was so taken aback by this onslaught that he pulled out his glasses and put them on, with a vague idea of sheltering behind them.

"My dear," he expostulated.

"You must realize," continued she, in the same unpleasant way, "that young women now are rather different from what I was as a young woman."

"I should hope so," said Mr. Howard fervently, and then wondered if that was what he meant.

"Kindly meant, doubtless," said his wife. "And even I was not without admirers."

"Of course, my dear, of course. But this, you must admit, is different."

"Different?" said she pugnaciously. "I don't know that it is. The only difference I can see is that I had plenty of swains and flirted with them all, because I loved you so much that I felt quite safe." As her husband made a gesture of dissent she added hastily, "Oh, yes I did, Will, and you had to put up with it, and very nicely you did it. But poor Aurea doesn't flirt—she often doesn't realize that people are attracted by her and that puts them off—and when she does care for anyone it's rather cataclysmic. Of course, I wish as heartily as anyone that they had never met, but there it is and can't be helped, and most unfortunately there isn't any one like you that she can care for all the time."

She looked so pretty as she exulted in her own early married life and defended Aurea's, that her husband nearly dropped the subject of Aurea's shortcomings altogether. It would have been better for him if he had. Mrs. Howard adored her husband and her daughter, but when it came to the eternal battle between men and women, she was solidly with her own sex in public, however she might turn against it in private. If Mr. Howard cannot leave Aurea alone, he may find that war is carried into his own country. Mary, Aurea and Fanny will be rather a formidable opposition. He would have been wiser to lay down his arms and go on reading aloud, but his evil spirit impelled him to say, "But, Mary, you are defending Aurea! Justifying her in her most regrettable folly!"

"Oh, Will, do stop being a blind and idiotic bat. What do you think other young women do? And to herself she made a vow of no quarter to the persecutor.

"Other young women?" inquired Mr. Howard, offended. "What have they have to do with Aurea?"

"Only that nine out of ten of her friends would have gone much further than she has, and cared much less. Look at Fanny."

This was a declaration of war. But Mr. Howard, although conscious of a slight sinking, pretended to be quite unconscious of it, and merely questioned coldly, "Fanny?"

"Yes, Fanny. A puss and a minx if ever there was one, but just because she makes a habit of flirting, no one minds. Neither age nor sex are sacred to her. She would make eyes at me, only she knows it's no good, and as for the eyes she makes at you—"

Here she paused. "Perhaps, perhaps," murmured Mr. Howard, gratified.

"—and as for the way you encourage her to go on—"

She paused again. Mr. Howard, rather less gratified and distinctly anxious, protested, "My dear, a most unfounded accusation."

"Not at all," said his wife coldly. "It's most charming in you, Will, with your good looks and becoming gray hair, to kiss young women paternally on the forehead and hold their hands for a long time when you say how do you do; but when it comes to buying rings for them—"

Here she made a dramatic stop. Mr. Howard was appalled. Never in all their married life had his Mary flown at him so callously, so ferociously. Undoubtedly he had danced Platonic minuets with more than one lady from time to time, but Mary had always laughed and approved. Even when he wrote poetry to them she approved. It had been a slight mortification to him that his flames had always made great friends with Mary, even going so far as to ask her opinion of the poetry, instead of making a delightful mystery of the whole affair. And now Fanny—. He couldn't quite remember how he stood in the matter of Fanny. Had he told Mary about the wedding ring himself, or had Fanny, so artless and unsuspecting, let it drop? Aurea was completely wiped out of his mind. His only thought at the moment was to exonerate himself from Mary's so unfounded, so monstrous, so unfortunately well substantiated accusation.

"My dear," he began wildly, "poor Fanny had lost her wedding ring—probably left it somewhere while she was washing her hands—"

"I have yet to meet the woman who troubles to take off her wedding ring while she washes her hands," interrupted his wife with horrid judicial impartiality. "A diamond or a ruby ring, yes; a wedding ring, no. But go on."

She assumed a patient expression, infinitely exasperating to a wronged man.

"Or perhaps she wasn't washing," he said weakly. "She may just have taken it off for fun, but there she was, poor child" (Mrs. Howard moved her lips in the form of the words "child, indeed," with an unpleasantly sarcastic expression of which her husband judged it more prudent to take no notice), "without a ring; and it would have been so awkward for her to go and buy a new one, so I said I'd buy it for her."

"I should very much like," said Mrs. Howard with icy politeness, "to see Fanny looking awkward. What about you, Will? Didn't you feel awkward?"

"Oh, no," said he, feeling on certain ground this time. "Fanny came with me."

At this, to his mingled relief and indignation, Mrs. Howard burst out laughing and became herself again. He looked anxiously at her over his glasses, and said he was glad she was amused.

"Bless your heart, darling Will," said his wife affectionately, "of course I'm amused—and so was Fanny."

"Did Fanny tell you, then?" asked Mr. Howard, a thousand horrid doubts thronging into his mind.

"Of course she did, and about the lunch afterwards."

"I think," said poor Mr. Howard, inclined to cry with mortification, "that Fanny might treat me with a little more respect."

His wife, having effectually trailed red herrings across Aurea's track, now hastened to pour balm into her husband's wounds.

"So she should, Will," she said with feeling. "And it was very sweet of you to get her a ring."

"Then you aren't hurt?" said Mr. Howard, perking up.

"Hurt? Of course not. I think it was rather darling of you to," but observing a slightly fatuous expression stealing over his face, she amended her sentence sharply to "be so easily taken in." Mr. Howard's face fell, but taking no notice she went on, "And you must remember that Aurea is really grown-up, and not accountable to us for what she does; and you must make as much allowance for her as you do for Fanny—and rather more, because she is your own daughter."

"Well, well, dear, we won't talk about it anymore now. Shall I go on reading?"

Mrs. Howard was satisfied with her success; besides, her heart smote her for cruelty to deserving husbands, so she accepted his offer gratefully. Mr. Howard took up his book again and began to read. Gradually his voice got slower and slower, and the words more and more confused, till at last the book fell on his lap, and he remained fast asleep.

It would be idle to pretend that Fanny's theater party was being a success, though luckily she never discovered it. With Mrs. Howard's injunction strong in her mind, she watched over Aurea like a duenna watching over an heiress, especially setting herself to complete Arthur's punishment by separating him from Aurea as much as possible. To this end she sent Aurea first into her seat and followed her, telling Valentine to come on her other side. Arthur was thus left in the outside seat. "I put you there on purpose," said Fanny, leaning across Valentine, "because I knew you and Val would want to make nuisances of yourselves going out between the acts and now you won't either of you walk over my legs." As the curtain was just going up, Arthur was unable to expostulate, but during the next interval he took a subtle revenge by buying a very large expensive box of chocolates done up in transparent paper and orange ribbon, and giving it to Fanny. Well did he know what his Fanny's feelings were on the subject of people who eat chocolate in theaters, and the social standing of husbands who so disgrace their wives in public. Fanny had to say "Thank you," but she said it as ungraciously as possible, and tried to push the box under the seat. In this she was foiled by Valentine who, seeing no chance of talking to Aurea and a good deal of chance of annoying Fanny, insisted on undoing the ribbon and passing the box around. By passing it across Fanny to Aurea, he was able to touch Aurea's fingers for a moment, but he was obliged to get any further pleasure he required by watching Fanny's ill-concealed attempts to do away with the offending box.

"All packing and shavings as usual," she commented ungratefully. "For the Lord's sake put the thing away, Val, or take it home and give it to your landlady."

"How sweet of you, Fanny, but I couldn't bear to take it." And he placed the box affectionately on her lap. "You must keep them for the boys, whenever you next have them at home."

Fanny gave him a withering look which, owing to the lights being dimmed down at that moment, entirely failed in its effect. After a short but unseemly scuffle with Valentine, she was obliged to sit nursing the box in sulky fury.

During the second interval both the men fled from her wrath, and she was left to pour her complaints into Aurea's inattentive ear.

"I've never known Arthur so trying as he has been today," she exploded. "Cross and sulky at breakfast, cross and sulky before dinner, a perfect fool about the tickets, and now positively rude and insulting. What was he saying to you before dinner, Aurea? No one would tell me. Not that it matters, because I'll get it out of him later. Anyway, I am going to pay him back afterwards. He has some idea of taking you home, but whether you'd like it or not, Aurea, I am not going to allow it. Val shall take you home, and then he can come and join Arthur and me at the Vampire, for if Arthur thinks that he can get out of supper and dancing just by being fouly rude and unpleasant, that is where he trips over the mat. Of course, darling, we'd love it if you came on to supper, too, but as a matter of fact, I promised your mother I'd send you home early because of the Last Night in the Old Home and all, though if you ask me, I should say keep away from the old home as long as possible; you'll feel ten times worse there than if you came with us, but, still, if your mother says so, so it must be. Here, you take the chocolates, blast them. I must go and say a word to Ronnie Graham, who has been trying not to see me for the last five minutes."

Thrusting the box into Aurea's hands she hurried across the gangway to where Mr. Graham was enjoying himself with a pink young woman, quite unconscious of Fanny's presence.

"Hi, Ronnie," said she, so loudly that most of the remaining inhabitants of the stalls looked around, "what did you mean by telling me such a whacking lie?"

Mr. Graham looked up, startled and speechless.

"About Val," continued Fanny severely. "The Mounsey girl's engagement was in *The Times* today. I'll never forgive you for misleading me like that."

Mr. Graham sat with his mouth open, while Fanny walked majestically away, hastening her pace, however, as she saw Val and Arthur returning. But she was too late; Arthur had slipped in beside Aurea. Fanny followed him and tried to change places, but the third act was just beginning, and Arthur was able to ignore her protests.

As the play ended Arthur said to Aurea, "I am going to take you home, Aurea. I won't stay long, but I must see you for a few moments."

"I thought you were going on to supper," said Aurea, surprised.

"Yes, but I'll easily get back to Fanny and Val in time. It will be all right." And with a conquering air he herded her up the passage towards the exit. Valentine, who possessed both luck and skill in dealing with porters and commissionaires, had already secured a taxi, and was standing by its door.

"You and Val had better go on to the Vampire, Fanny. I'll take Aurea home," said Arthur, heading Aurea into the taxi.

But he spoke too soon. Neither Valentine nor Fanny had the faintest intention of letting this high-handed abduction take place.

"Oh, we had, had we?" said Fanny in a voice which had the effect of making everyone in the neighborhood turn around and stare. "Well, let me tell you, Arthur, we hadn't; and the sooner you understand it the better."

A commissionaire's voice was heard saying that if the gentleman wanted to get into the taxi to look sharp about it as there was a whole line of them waiting. Valentine thanked the commissionaire, tipped him, and got into the taxi, stumbling over something as he did so.

"Oh, it's Arthur's chocolates," cried Aurea.

"Then we won't deprive him of them," said Valentine, and picking up the box he leaned out of the window and called Arthur loudly. Arthur, who was still arguing with Fanny, looked around, and saw his taxi slowly drawing away from the curb, with Valentine's face at the window. Tearing himself from Fanny's grasp, he ran along by the side of the cab.

"Hi, Valentine," he shouted. "It's my taxi."

"Sorry, it's mine now, but I thought you'd want these back," said Valentine, shoving the chocolates into Arthur's arms. The taxi made a grinding noise with its gears and drove rapidly off. Arthur turned, and found Fanny beside him.

"Well," she said tartly, "have you any explanation of your conduct, leaving me alone here, the butt of a gaping crowd?"

"Valentine has taken Aurea home," said Arthur blankly.

"Well, and why not? I told him to. And now you take me to the Vampire. What's that you're carrying?"

"Chocolates," said Arthur feebly.

"Ah-h," shrieked his wife, "are you bent on making me a laughing stock? Chocolates, indeed. This is the crowning mercy, I don't think. Blast you, Arthur Turner, will you never learn sense?" So saying she snatched the box and threw it into the road, where it burst, and all the remaining contents were ground to pieces. Then, pushing aside our old friend Mr. L. N. B. Porter, C.B.E., who had just secured a taxi for his widowed sister-in-law, mother of the defenestrated nephew, on whose account the sister-in-law was spending a few days in London, Fanny hustled Arthur into the cab, got in after him, and slammed the door. She then put her head out of the window and yelled, "Vampire," which confirmed Mr. Porter in his views of London night life.

So Fanny and Arthur drive out of the story in their taxi. Fanny will quickly forget. Indeed, Aurea has already become a ghost in her memory, for Fanny does not live in the past. She liked Aurea well enough while she could see her, and could admire quite generously a kind of charm and beauty which she herself did not possess. But, Aurea being gone, or as good as gone, she has dismissed her from her mind. Also, Aurea had proved distinctly disappointing as a flirtation for Arthur. Vanna had been right in calling her a little dull and cold, and obviously Arthur shared that opinion now. It was a shame that Aurea hadn't been more amusing and given Arthur a run for his money. Poor Arthur. She must find someone more forthcoming for him. Perhaps there would be friends at the Vampire for him to play with, while she danced with Val. But there Fanny is wrong. Long, long may she sit, partaking of beer and kippers—a nauseating mixture affected by her set at the moment—before she sees Valentine's tall form coming down the steps of the dancing room. He will not be there that night, and when she rings him up tomorrow to expostulate he will be inaccessible, well defended by the competent female voice. Nor will he be seen at Fanny's house for a week or more. By the time he reappears, Aurea will have vanished as completely from Fanny's quicksilver mind as if she had never existed, and Valentine will be troubled by no questions about her. Life goes on, and those who are absent or forgotten, sunk without trace. Fanny will continue her career of amusing herself and secretly adoring her Arthur, and nothing will change or upset her.

Arthur will forget, too, if not quite so soon. Just for the moment he is feeling bereaved, but it will not last. Fanny is always there, his adored incalculable Fanny, who by the end of the evening will be so furious at Valentine's unexplained absence, that she will forget the affairs of the tickets and the key, and be her most charming self to her husband. If he ever had any serious ideas of telling Fanny about his very mild lapse, that idea has taken wings and flown away before the first of the Vampire cocktails. Arthur will think of Aurea vaguely from time to time as a dear creature, who cared for him more than she should; so mercifully have circumstances and his own fatuity blinded him to what was really happening. As he will never know what Aurea thinks of him, he will be none the worse. She had so hoped for kindness and understanding from him, but that was all of a piece with the rest of her folly. He has shattered her romantic feeling for him, and never again will she feel safe, or at her ease. When they will meet again cannot be told; but it matters little, now that the harm has been done.

So we will leave Arthur and Fanny at the Vampire. They can well take of themselves, for though each is capable of devoted self-sacrifice for the other, neither is truly kind at heart where anyone else is concerned. Nothing will ever hurt either of them very deeply, and as it is their choice to be like that, we need feel little concern for them.

Meanwhile Valentine, rather pleased by his Parthian shot at Arthur, and Aurea, greatly relieved by her rescue, were driving towards the Howards' house. If they had hoped to have a few minutes alone, they were disappointed to see a gleam of light from the drawing-room window. Valentine suggested that Mr. and Mrs. Howard might have gone to bed and left the light on, but Aurea could hold out no such hopes.

"You don't know mother and papa," she said. "They are probably both asleep with reading aloud. The only thing to do is come up, and hope they'll go to bed soon."

They tiptoed upstairs. Aurea opened the door. There was her dear papa, fast asleep in his chair, but her mother was wide awake. Mrs. Howard beckoned to them to come in quietly and sit down. Then she got up and went conspiratorially to the mantelpiece, moved a glass of flowers so that it hid the face of the clock, and sat down again. The lovers were a little perplexed but waited patiently. All her dispositions being completed, she dropped a book. Mr. Howard started, sat up with suspicious alertness, and looked around madly.

"I must have been asleep," said Mrs. Howard, lying brazenly.

"I told you you always go to sleep, Mary," said her husband, much gratified by this proof of weakness.

"So I never heard those young people come in," continued Mrs. Howard, imperiling her immortal soul. "How long have they been here, Will?"

Mr. Howard looked at the clock, but it was hidden by the flowers, so he determined to bluff, and said ten minutes or so.

"What a shame," said his wife. "You must forgive us, Mr. Ensor. And I had no idea it was so late. Come along, Will dear, you can finish reading to me another time when I'm not quite so sleepy."

Mr. Howard, still blinking with sleep, and confused by this frontal attack, did not attempt to resist. With an apology to Valentine he said good night. Aurea felt remorseful, and clung tightly to her father as she kissed him good night for the last time.

So Mr. Howard goes up to bed and out of the story. He will miss Aurea more than anyone guesses, mutely, his heart knows how. All he has to ask is that she may come back again before it is too late. If fate is kind he may see her again and find her gentler and more loving than she has been in these few difficult weeks. He would not ask even this reward for all his deep and tender affection, for he is a man who gives much and expects little, finding his joy in the giving. But if he sees his daughter again, there will be nothing wanting to his content.

"Come and see me before you go to bed, darling," said Mrs. Howard to Aurea. "Good night, Mr. Ensor. And," she added, all her mother's anxiety in her eyes and voice, "don't be too long in saying goodbye."

"I'll be good," said Valentine, and she left them alone.

How should one conduct a parting scene? Aurea, one of whose weaknesses was to rehearse events that never happened, had been arranging what she was to say for days and days. It was to be a fine piece of heroics in which she was to establish an eternal claim upon Valentine; renounce him forever; receive his vows of perpetual celibacy for her sake; bless his union with that odious Mounsey girl and offer to be godmother to their first child (this master-stroke gave her much pleasure and had been repeatedly elaborated in her mind); give and receive a dying kiss; and say goodbye with averted head, and no hand-clasp. In fact, a fine range of possibilities.

"May I smoke?" asked Valentine.

"Of course. But I can't see the cigarettes anywhere."

"Don't bother. I've got some."

"Sit down, then, and be comfortable for a few minutes."

"I mustn't stay long, Aurea."

This was not a promising beginning. What was the proper riposte? Should she encourage him to go, saying she could not love him, dear, so much, loved she not honor more? which would be very noble. Or should she combine a nobility with a moment's pleasure, and saying in a broken voice, "You are right. Goodbye, my dear," print a burning but chaste kiss on his neatly brushed hair, and fly from the room? Then of course, there would be the bother of having to wait about upstairs till one heard him leaving, and then come down and turn the lights out in the drawing-room and hall, otherwise mother and papa would be annoyed. Besides the front door was difficult to shut without slamming, and it would be so undignified to hear Valentine banging away at it when one could easily run down and shut it for him, and so begin the business of parting all over again. Or had one the courage to throw everything to the winds, fling oneself into his arms, and burrow one's face against his shoulder? That would be worth any amount of subsequent pricks of conscience, only—if one gave way even so little, mightn't he feel justified in taking what to him would seem so very little more? To burrow one's head was safe and comfortable, but gentlemen didn't seem to know where to stop, and if someone a great deal stronger than you were suddenly felt like not standing any more nonsense, and kissed you full on the lips, fiercely, possessively, what would happen? Would there be any response in you, or would blind terror, uncontrollable, strike one to dumb madness? Man-shy had been Arthur's word for her, and a true word. What kind of love is it, she had tormented herself by asking again and again, that consumes one's whole being and yet fears a touch? And she had reluctantly come to the conclusion that it was a poor selfish kind of love, not at all good enough for Valentine. Love, like most experiences in life, goes by the first lessons. Aurea had been badly taught, and that was the beginning and the end. It was her misfortune more than her fault, and now nothing could alter it. Bewildered and exhausted she said the first thing that came into her mind, and of course the wrong thing. In a voice that presaged storm, she answered him, "You have never stayed very long, have you?"

"As long as I could."

"Yes. As long as you could. As long as you wanted to."

"What do you mean?" asked Valentine, as his voice also fell insensibly into the intonations of a quarrel.

"You have just fitted me in when it suited you—every time."

"That's unfair."

"No, it isn't. You know it's always been like that. When I ask you to come here you are always engaged, or you come on from something else, or you go on to something else. I have to take when you want to come—always on your terms, not on mine—always restlessness—always an eye on the clock—no peace—never any time to talk."

"Aurea, what is the matter?"

"Only the unfairness of it all," said she, feeling herself sinking deeper and deeper into the mire of misunderstanding, and too tired and confused to pull herself out.

"But, dear darling," expostulated her lover, "you know it isn't that I don't want to see you all the time—you must know that. Only one doesn't happen always to be free, and one can't break engagements—one owes something to one's friends. One must be fair to them."

"Oh, fair," said Aurea contemptuously. "You have been fair to everyone but me. You knew I had only a few weeks in England and would soon be out of your way. You knew you were safe with me—that I am too proud to make demands on you—and you've taken every advantage of it. Any friend who could offer you an amusing party with drinks; anyone who wanted you to dine and dance; anyone who was more approachable than I am, I suppose; you can be fair to them. But when it is someone who only has the misfortune to love you, with nothing to give, then you are cruelly unfair. You are just spoilt, Valentine, utterly spoilt."

Most of this, allowing for an angry woman's exaggeration, was too true to be comfortable. Therefore Valentine began to find it difficult to keep his temper steady. "If I took you seriously, Aurea, I'd be hurt," he said, taking himself seriously enough. But this didn't impress Aurea.

"It would do you good if you *were* hurt," said she, giving rein to her exasperated nerves. "You are far too afraid of being hurt. You are always thinking of protecting yourself and keeping yourself safe. You have some ridiculous idea that someone is somehow trying to attack your liberty, your freedom. Though what your freedom is except that you think you ought to be free to do what you like, and everyone else wait on your pleasure, I don't know."

True enough. When Valentine had, with pains, smoothed his dancing floor and laid dead hopes and faith beneath it, something good in him had been buried there as well. Where he would once have walked recklessly on the high hills, welcoming whatever he met, he now picked his road along the plain, choosing the more trodden ways, avoiding the stream that might wet his feet, the hedge that might have thorns to tear and hold, the paths that led to windblown slopes where one might need to put out one's strength. It was all very pleasant, and so long as one remembered to forget, all was well. Then this entrancing creature had crossed his path, herself bound for who knows what rocky heights, what lonely upland pools; certainly to no calm or happy journey's end. Like an untried youth he had left the dancing floor to follow her, careless if her steps, hastening as his pursued, might lead her to harm. But not for long. Her paths were too steep for him; the upland wind blew too keenly from the land of lost desires. Better to forget again, to forsake the hills and tread the level floor to which his feet were accustomed. If she could not understand, it was not his fault, it was hers—entirely hers.

"I won't stand much more," he said. "You are utterly unreasonable and wrong."

"I'm not, I'm not. I never asked you to love me. I was unhappy enough before, but it was dull, quiet unhappiness. And then you were there, and I suppose you were just spoiling for a fresh affair, and I happened to be handy, and I was enough of a romantic fool to think your love was a rare heavenly thing and not the nine days' wonder that it is. . . ." As Valentine, furious, tried to expostulate, she scornfully amended her words to ". . . oh, well, the four weeks' wonder, we'll say, if you are feeling very accurate. I suppose I have only myself to blame. If a person who is respectably married so far forgets herself as to fall hopelessly in love, she deserves all she gets. And I have got all I deserve—and from you. That's rather funny, isn't it?"

In the slums one has clouted a woman over the head, or strangled her, before she gets as far as this. In a drawing-room things are much less simple. Probably the best thing one could do would be to take up one's hat, like Mr. Frog, and wish them good night, but then it isn't so easy to leave a lady without a word, and anyway one's hat and coat and scarf and umbrella are in the hall, and one can't leave without them. Mr. Frog had only to pick up his opera hat and leap through the window, upsetting the flower pots; but to go downstairs, collect one's belongings, return to the drawing-room, and jump out of a first floor window with area railings below, would be foolish, and probably get one into trouble with the police. Also, how could one leave her, whatever she said? She was too dear.

"Aurea, you'll say something in a moment that you are sorry for, or you'll make me say something I'm sorry for."

"I'd *like* to say something I'm sorry for," responded his idol with equal ferocity. "I've done nothing but control myself and behave like a lady ever since I met you, and I'm sick of it."

Valentine's anger melted. If self-control was torment to Aurea, that at least he could understand.

"Don't, child, don't. Oh, don't you think I have to control myself too? Don't you believe that I'd have made far more opportunities for seeing you, only it's all I can bear to be in the same room with you and not even touch your hand, while you are so lovely, and always so cool and far-off."

"Cool and far-off? Valentine, are you deaf and blind? Idiot!"

Unbelievable that Valentine could think of her as cool and remote. How could she ever explain to him how utterly mistaken he was? If one held him for an instant, warm in one's arms, could he ever be mistaken again? But her thoughts shuddered away from the dear delusion. Nothing in the world will ever explain one human being to another, and the more you explain, the worse the misunderstanding. Better to allow oneself to be misunderstood passively than to make matters worse by speech or action. Valentine could not guess how slight the barrier was that she had placed between them, nor of what childish materials it was made. Part of it was her almost morbid feeling of right and wrong, an idea, inherited from her father, that happiness was dangerous and wrong, and should not be enjoyed in the present, lest some dark destiny held unhappiness in store. The rest was her anxiety for what her father and mother might think, and a grim determination not to make them unhappy; or at least not any unhappier than she knew she had made them already. If she had strength enough to hide her wounds from them till she had gone, they would grieve the less. Probably Valentine would laugh at her if he knew, and perhaps it was funny, if one came to consider it, to think of one's parents' feelings more than one's husband's, in this particular case. But when people were far away you could put them at the back of your mind, unless you loved them very much. Ned also would laugh at the whole thing, Aurea thought, and call her a little silly, which, indeed, she regretfully admitted she was. And if he and Valentine met, she had an uneasy feeling that they might find grown-up things to talk about and get on quite well, and she would be left out of it. But there was no chance of their meeting. Sometimes she almost wished there were. It would be very embarrassing, no doubt, but would also clear up the situation. A woman like Fanny, who had a resident husband, was provided with a safe background, and could do pretty well anything she liked. If she went too far, Arthur would assert himself, or she would suddenly lose courage and run back to him, shrieking for the support that she could rely on. Fanny was rather like a rude child who yells and throws stones at passers-by, and if they attempt to remonstrate, dashes back into its front garden and screams for its mother, who will take its part; and the more odious the child, the more she will support it and attack its helpless victims. But Aurea had no front garden to run to. If Ned had been in England with her, she might conceivably have let herself go much further with Valentine, thrusting the responsibility of her waywardness upon her husband's shoulders. As he was many hundreds of miles away, she had to shoulder the responsibility herself, and she didn't think she had made a very good job of it. The sensible thing to do, she supposed, would be to have one's fling while one's husband wasn't there, and then say nothing about it. Then conscience came cranking in, and said one ought to behave much better when Ned wasn't there than when he was, because of loyalty. Oh, what a word that was. What a man's word. Something to break one's heart over quite unnecessarily. What actually did it mean? Was it loyalty to Ned that made her keep Valentine at arms' length, or only cowardice? If people were Great Lovers, like Selleeney, thought Aurea, they certainly wouldn't worry about loyalty; nor would they gibber at the mere thought of a lover's kiss. And at the thought of Selleeney she couldn't help giggling, so that Valentine, whom she had just called an idiot, was considerably surprised, and asked her what she was laughing at.

"Cellini," said Aurea weakly. "I was thinking that if he was a typical World's Great Lover, you and I don't seem to come up to the standard."

"I don't go about banging people's cups into art goblets, if that's what you mean."

"I know you don't, darling. Nor do you ride a thousand miles on a white bus horse to see me, with all the Popes at your heels. You only ask me not to telephone, and go about featuring self-control till I could burst. It had been bad enough having to behave like a lady all this time, and I sometimes think it has been a great mistake for you to behave like a gentleman."

"But, dear darling, I have only tried to do as you asked," said the

Great Lover, rather bewildered. "You said we were to be a lady and gentleman going to a party, and if that made you happy I was willing to let it be like that; and I hoped it was all right."

Aurea glared at him. "I've often wanted to shake you, Valentine Ensor, and now I'd like to hit you. In fact, I would hit you now if it weren't so unladylike."

"Do, if you like," said Valentine affectionately.

"I can't. I daren't touch you."

"I wouldn't hit back."

"Oh, it's not that," she said scornfully. "Idiot! Great half-wit!"

Bewildered at every turn by his idol's changing moods, Valentine could only say "Aurea!" in the voice of a nurse admonishing a child for bad behavior at meals.

"Yes, great half-wit!" continued the adored one, working herself up to a frenzy. "Senseless mole."

So demented was her appearance, and so far had the conversation wandered from the orthodox paths of leave-taking in polite society, that Valentine offered to be a mole or anything else she liked, if only she would calm down and explain. "What do you mean, Aurea? What is it?"

Aurea's rage suddenly fell from her like a cloak. She looked into the fire, always her refuge when in distress. Valentine saw her face grow clouded and remote. She said quietly, "Only Love."

Her somber voice fell heavily on the air. As if she had dropped the word of Love into a still dark water, waves of silence rippled outwards and filled the room. Valentine felt that he had spent his whole life in this hushed stillness, and dared not speak. No sound but the little noises of the fire, till Aurea spoke again, never raising her eyes from the heart of the fire, never raising or changing the tone of her lifeless voice.

"You say it is hard for you to be in the same room with me and not touch me. May I point out to you, Mr. Ensor, that what is sauce for the goose is sauce for the gander—at least the other way around if you take my meaning. May I draw your attention to the fact that I can't be near you without shaking from head to foot and becoming a gibbering idiot. Oh, I hide it quite nicely, but there it is. Do you know why I never danced with you? Not because I was too tired, as I always said, but because I daren't, I daren't. I couldn't be so near to you and keep my senses, and you may thank me for sparing you; how very little you would have enjoyed having a lady faint all over you at the Vampire. If you took my hand in a taxi—which I must say with your charming sex seems to be more a matter of routine than anything else—what do you think it cost me to take it away, or let it be unresponsive in yours? Do you think it hasn't torn me to be so cool—never to respond, never once to lift my face to yours? Valentine, it's not that I want to live in sin with you, because the very idea makes me perfectly sick—and I must say it would be a forward thing to do, considering that you've never asked me, and what's more no one would be more embarrassed than yourself if such a thing were suggested—it's not that. I don't know what it is. But it has nearly killed me."

Women, in Valentine's experience, were very fond of being sorry for themselves. They appeared to think that they could endear themselves by complaining of husbands, parents, friends, life. But it was precisely at that moment that one began to stand aloof, ready to retreat quickly at any further menace from their possessive minds. No woman could be content to know that she was loved. She expected so much besides. What she needed was not so much a lover, as a mirror in which she might see a flattering reflection of all her emotions. One was expected to guarantee a permanence of affection impossible to give; to sympathize with small or imaginary troubles; to be a receptacle for every kind of outpouring by word or letter. And then, invariably, there came the moment when they enjoyed the artistry of their own emotions so much that they began to cry, and instead of the charmer one had so happily pursued, one found a damp, pulpy, complaining female, who expected an arm around her waist, or a shoulder to cry on. Not that one had any objection to lending an arm or a shoulder; it was a not unpleasant occupation for one's idler moments; but they appeared to find implications in these moments beyond what one could consider. Then a promising friendship, flirtation, whatever one liked to call it, was spoilt. Luckily there was always another to compensate, and no one was badly hurt, so one took things as they came.

And now there was Aurea, who was just different enough to make one feel less self-confident than usual. She had seemed at first to have no idea of self-defense. As far as an avowal of mutual attraction was concerned, she had met him halfway. They had crossed swords and thrown them down. But then, without withdrawing anything of her open love and devotion, she had set herself apart, a remote loving spirit. Valentine, not naturally diffident, had found himself suddenly paralyzed with shyness before her. When your most ardent avowals are met with blank terror, or quite genuinely misunderstood, it cramps your style considerably.

But he couldn't help being amused, in the middle of all this turmoil and stress, by her efforts to be fair-minded about it. She seemed to have covered the whole ground in her ill-considered statement, besides suddenly producing an unexpected kind of courage. A wild fluttering kind, like the thrush caught in the strawberry net who pecks your finger savagely. Her frank acceptance of the whole question of "living in sin" rather took his breath away. He imagined that she must get all her ideas from books, and was now desperately trying to bring common sense to bear upon them. Wherever she might have found her ideas, they were, for her case, extremely sound. "Living in sin"—the words had nothing to do with her at all. She had known at once what Valentine would have liked to ignore: that nothing of lovers' passion would ever be possible between them. She was so entirely dominated by her mind that her senses would never be allowed to take their way. If she could once be carried off her feet, she would, he believed, have been capable of self-abandonment, and shown him a side of herself which, even in dreams he had hardly dared to suspect. But he was not capable—and without conceit he believed no other man was capable—of penetrating her defenses. Fear and unhappiness, of a kind which he could guess only too well, had forced her away into herself—in no other way was her horror of physical contact explainable. Here, looking out from her fortress with frightened eyes, she had built up a rule of conduct for herself, and by heaven she had kept to it. He had seen her so shaken, so drowned by love, that she could hardly stand or speak, yet able to resist. It had not been the easiest part of his task to watch her controlled suffering and do nothing, when one cruel-kind gesture from him might have set her free. Again and again he had been on the point of using his strength against her, but the risk was too great. He had seen apprehension so often in her eyes, that he dreaded doing anything that might frighten her from him irrevocably. If, on the other hand, she could forget herself in his arms and relax for a moment, what then? She had a husband, who appeared to be a perfectly decent sort of fellow, except that he made demands which he had every right to make: if she could not bear them it was hellish, but not his business at all. And she had children, and it was perfectly clear that she would do nothing which could in any way imperil her position with regard to them. So what would one gain by breaking down barriers? One had to look at things practically, whatever kind of groan it wrenched from one's spirit. She was bound by circumstances more firmly than if she had been in a castle with moats and dungeons and boiling oil.

As for what she had said about the embarrassment which any idea of living in sin would cause him, he had to confess to himself, while finding the phrase laughable and very Aurea-ish, that any more fervid response from his idol would have been excessively awkward. It was all very well for heroes of novels to ask ladies to come in a compromising way to their rooms: but when your rooms consisted of a bed-sitting room, even though large and airy, the whole affair was hedged around with difficulties. The question of ways and means and times, would bulk so large that love would simply have to slip in where it could, effectually quenching romance. Selleeney would have made light of these difficulties, but then Selleeney was a Great Lover, and Valentine had to face the fact that he wasn't up to the Selleeney standard. The most he could hope was that he had behaved as much like a gentleman as was possible under the circumstances.

The pressing need of the moment was to comfort Aurea, who had exhausted herself by her apologia, and looked like death. But all he could find to say was, "Don't, darling, don't, I can't bear it."

As usual, so Aurea reflected, Valentine had failed her. It was perfectly true that if you tried to lean against a man, first he bended and then he broke, even without being necessarily false. One always had to take up the woman's burden, and let him do the leaning. She gave Valentine a searching look which made him feel slightly guilty, and said:

"No, I dare say you can't. And, as usual, you will have to be spared. Oh, well, men have died before now and worms have eaten them, but not for love—Shakespeare,' she added parenthetically, seeing Valentine's look of blank bewilderment. "I'm sorry I let loose."

"At least, Aurea, give me credit for some kindness, some consideration. I could so easily have held you against your will so many times."

"No, you wouldn't; you would have been afraid of compromising yourself," snapped Aurea, annoyed by his nobility.

"You couldn't have stopped me," continued the conquering male, disregarding this unkind cut.

"No," said Aurea slowly, "practically speaking, I couldn't. But you see, my dear, there wasn't any need. You just wouldn't have done it. You see I do give you credit for some kindness—though it's always possible that I might, madly, have preferred cruelty."

Valentine got up and walked about to help his feelings. She was right. He had behaved so much like a gentleman that there was nothing at all to show for it. Except that, and this comforted him a little, there would be nothing ugly to remember when she had gone; neither of them would have any cause for self-reproach. Though here he did not take into account Aurea's conscience, which was apt to surge so inopportunely. His own did not surge.

"Sit down, Valentine," said Aurea, with sudden energy. "I've stopped ramping now, and you can just go on having a good opinion of yourself. Oh, I'm so tired." But she didn't make any room on the sofa, which she was somehow contriving to fill by herself.

"Talking doesn't help much, does it," said he, ruefully. "Let me stay near you for a few moments, and then I must keep my promise to your mother and go. You look so worn out, and you will need all your strength for tomorrow."

"Always tactful. Do you think we might talk about something else?"

"Like a lady and gentleman at a party?"

"Rather like that," she said, doing her best to smile. And then there was a pause.

"You'll write to me, Aurea, won't you?" said he at last.

"I promise you," said she, "that I'll answer every letter you write to me."

"Thank you, darling. But you won't mind if I don't write regularly? You know how bad I am about letters, and if I don't write it won't mean that I'm not thinking of you. You do understand, don't you?"

"Yes, my dear, I understand. I must take what I can get,' said she, not unkindly.

And that, probably, is the last word about letters. To Aurea, as to many a fair and unexpressive she, letters are self-expression, and therefore almost life itself. All that she could never say she will pour out, quite unabashed, on paper. Everything that happens to her she will put into words mentally, as part of an eternal letter to Valentine, even if it is never written. To write to him often, and at great length, will in some measure satisfy her hunger to give. But that is the only satisfaction she will ever get.

As for Valentine, he will always be glad to get a letter from Aurea, but he won't trouble to read it very closely. Her outpourings may become a little wearing in time, and it is not his habit to include things that bore him in his plan of life. Whether he is conscious of it or not, he is in a very strong position. Aurea writes to him because she must—because it is the only kind of contact she can have with him, however illusory. If he does not write to her she will be too proud to beg for letters, and will pretend to herself that she never expected them, though this will not prevent her hopes from rising and falling with pitiful regularity. If a woman wrote the *Odyssey* (which one does not in the least believe), it would be just as easy to prove that a woman wrote the *Book of Proverbs*. "Hope deferred maketh the heart sick," is text enough to go upon. It is astonishing how the human heart can be lifted to empyrean heights and dropped, to lie stunned and bleeding on earth, and all by so small a thing as an envelope with a piece of paper in it. One knew that it was silly to expect Valentine to write often, because he had his work and so many friends and charmers, and one would never wish to be a bore; but if only he understood. That, perhaps, is exactly what he doesn't want to do. He is far from unkind at heart, but he has very little of that sensitive imagination which fills Aurea's life with baseless dreams: and the happier he. From time to time he will write to Aurea, full of his own plans and interests, never answering her questions, nor making reference to anything she has written; hurriedly, without consideration. She, poor half-wit, will try to read into these letters all that is not there, and then, fatally bound to her obsessing idea, will comfort herself with imagining the letters that she would like to have had, that she would have written in Valentine's place. A pretty literary exercise, but not helpful to happiness or a sane outlook. Sometimes she will shrink as from white-hot steel, wondering if she has made an impossible and abject fool of herself, an object of boredom and scorn to her lover. The one thing she will never know, the one thing that might have comforted her, is that, even against his will, she is part of Valentine's being forever; whether he writes or not, whatever years and distances are between them, whatever charmers may sway his facile heart. Sometimes, when he is least thinking of her, there will come upon him a feeling of most bitter loss, and that is her hour, unknown to her. This ignorance, and her own reproaches, are punishment enough; and to her that punishment will be so heavy that we might almost be a little sorry for her.

Valentine appeared to think that the subject had been exhausted.

"And I'll see you again before too long," he said. "You are sure to be back again to see your people."

"I hope I will. But it won't be the same for us, Valentine. Never again the same."

Silence fell once more. Valentine knew that he must break the circling charm and make an end.

"Aurea dear, I must go."

"I suppose you must," said she wearily. They both got up. Aurea was far past pretending, past any staging of imaginary scenes. Her one present preoccupation was to get Valentine out of the house without any further explanations or delays; but there he was, between her and the door. His attempt at taking leave had not altered his position.

Valentine was almost as much at his wits' end as Aurea. It was unbearable to leave her, and even more to leave her looking so worn out and broken, but go he must; when to his astonishment Aurea came up to him, and said in a perfectly flat, uninterested voice:

"You can put your arms around me if you like, Valentine, for a moment."

The ardent swain was too much taken aback to respond with immediate fervor, so his idol added, with a hint of impatience:

"I suppose it's got to come sooner or later, so we might as well get it over. I'm here."

This sacrificial attitude seemed to Valentine, in his present state of mind, more touching than foolish. He was just going to carry out the idol's instructions, when she looked up, and said anxiously:

"Don't frighten me—it would be cruelty to children—and I can't stand much more."

Very obediently Valentine took his silly romantic love in his arms. She was quite unhelpful, and might have been a lay figure except that, as her head at last came into its proper position on Valentine's shoulder, she quickly turned it away. Valentine guessed, quite correctly, that this was a sop to conscience, because, though it is wrong to let a gentleman put his arms around you, it mitigates the guilt to avert your face so that he shall not kiss you. It was hard work to hold the beloved half-wit so close and appear to remain unmoved, but if she wanted it, it should be done. It was only for a moment of perfume, of warmth, of forgetfulness; a moment while the whispering of the fire was the only sound that broke the night's stillness. Then, Aurea making a movement to release herself, there was nothing for it but to let her go, and watch her anxiously, as she moved clumsily, unseeingly, towards the door. So clumsily, that Valentine just had time to get her into a large chair, where she lay quite still.

What does one do after midnight, in a practically unknown house, with an unconscious female on one's hands? Her parents had long since gone to bed, and he didn't particularly want to disturb them. Looking around, he saw whisky and soda on a table at the far end of the room, so he filled a glass with lavish splashings, and knelt down by Aurea.

"Could you hold this, darling, and drink a little?" he said.

Obediently Aurea lifted her hand, but it fell again. She was trying to speak, but all Valentine could hear was the sighing of his own name. It was all disturbing and embarrassing to the last degree, and Valentine felt the whole responsibility upon him.

"Aurea, darling, can you hear me?" he said again. "Could you drink some whisky if I helped you?"

He was about to hold the glass to her lips, which might have proved a restorative in the sense that cold water trickling down one's front restores one; for no one can drink tidily when another person is holding the glass. But she shook her head, and pushing him gently away, managed to get up.

"I'm sorry, Valentine," she said in her own voice. "I couldn't help it. And you must admit it wouldn't have looked well at a night club." And she laughed.

Valentine was taking himself far too seriously to join in this ill-timed mirth. "I can't leave you like this," he said. "It's not safe. You might hurt yourself. What can I do? I can't take you to your own room for obvious reasons. May I find Mrs. Howard? Where is her room?"

"No—please," cried Aurea, laying a detaining hand on his arm. "I'll be all right as soon as you are gone. Truth and honor I will," she added, seeing his worried expression. "It's only loving you so much. I don't seem quite equal to it."

"Then I had better go."

"Yes, better go. I have nothing more to give you."

"My dear, I wouldn't ask it."

Aurea lifted his hand and bent her head over it, murmuring, "I'm not good enough, not worthy." And though she meant it, it is to be feared that she was enjoying herself in a way, as she said it.

"You? Good God, child," said Valentine with some vigor, "don't be a fool."

"That sounds more normal," said Aurea, loosening his hand. "Oh, please go. But, oh, please, please don't forget me."

"Darling, I couldn't. I'll never, never forget."

"I love you to say that," said Aurea meditatively, "even if it's what you say to all the charmers."

"Must you always laugh at me?"

"Always. It's the only way. Be happy and be good. Goodbye."

She had opened the drawing room door, and standing by it, gave Valentine her hand.

"I'm afraid you'll faint again," said he. "Can't I find your mother?"

Aurea was leaning against the wall, quite still, hardly able to speak. "No, no. Only go. I'll be all right when you are gone. Oh, Valentine, Valentine."

Valentine kissed her averted face and left the room quickly and quietly, shutting the door behind him. And so he too goes out of the story. He will do very well with Fanny, who does not require courage or unselfishness in her friends, and can well look after herself. It is just a pity that anyone so foolish as Aurea ever had the ill-luck to meet him.

CHAPTER 10

Mrs. Howard had been lying awake for what seemed to her hours and hours. She wondered what was going on in the drawing room behind the closed door, directly beneath her room, but no sound came to enlighten her. Once or twice, overcome by anxiety, she got up and opened her door to listen, but beyond an occasional murmur there was nothing to hear. Wild visions floated through her mind of Aurea clasped in Valentine's arms; Aurea deciding to elope, packing a bag, and stealing downstairs to her lover. So strong did this last obsession become; that she rather shamefacedly went to Aurea's room and knocked at the door. No one answered, for no one was there; the light turned on showed only a room strewn with the drift of final packing, which made Mrs. Howard's heart sink. What if Aurea had eloped already, without even a bag? How could she bear it? What would Will say? Would Aurea come back to them? Would Mr. Ensor's bank let him keep his job? Quite irrelevantly she remembered how Aurea had once discussed mothers with Fanny. Fanny had boasted that her mother, dead some years ago, would have sheltered her and believed in her, even if she had, with her own eyes, seen her kill Arthur and all the children. Aurea, not to be outdone, had countered with the statement that her mother would receive her with open arms if she suddenly came home in rags, with illegitimate triplets. Mrs. Howard laughed at the thought of it and felt comforted. Just then she heard the drawing-room door open, and the sound of two voices. Conscience-stricken she fled back to bed and lay there till the front door closed, waiting for Aurea to look in on her. As Aurea delayed her coming, Mrs. Howard's fear of elopement began to surge again, unreasonably she knew, but at that hour of the morning no fear is too unreasonable to seem perfectly probable. At last she could bear it no longer. She put on a dressing gown and went downstairs. The drawing-room door was open, and her daughter was wandering about, putting the glasses back on the tray and the chairs into their usual places. She looked quite normal, and Mrs. Howard felt a pang of relief.

"Aurea," she said softly, because Will must not be disturbed.

"Yes, mother," answered Aurea, continuing her task.

"Has Mr. Ensor gone?"

"Yes, mother."

"He went so quietly I didn't hear him," said Mrs. Howard, trying to find an excuse for her interference, "and I just came down to see where you were," she added, with a sense of sounding imbecile. What if Aurea suddenly realized that her mother had been suspecting her of an elopement?

"Yes, he went very quietly," said Aurea, pushing the heavy sofa back against the wall.

Her toneless voice and abstracted manner made her mother's fears return.

"It's all right, isn't it, darling?" said she, hating herself for interfering, but so anxious for her daughter that she couldn't help it.

Aurea stood up and looked at the fire once more. Once more she spoke straight into the dying flames.

"Yes, quite all right. I love him more than I have ever loved anyone in my life."

Mrs. Howard sat down and looked at her aghast. It had come to this. My poor, poor child, was her thought; and again, I never guessed how deep it was. And again she thought, poor Mr. Ensor to have to leave my darling Aurea like this. Aurea felt sorry for her mother, even through the web of dull grief that held her fast.

"Don't worry, darling," she said in her light, clear voice. "I haven't even kissed him, and he only kissed the top of my head, which doesn't count."

"My darling."

"Of course we'll always be friends, but the word doesn't mean so much just now, when I love him so much."

Only a shattering emotion could make Aurea speak of herself like that. Hardly ever since she grew up had she spoken so directly to her mother, who understood by that, more than by anything else, how much her daughter was suffering.

"And I was so afraid of your being hurt," she exclaimed piteously, as if asking Aurea forgiveness for something.

"Hurt?" said Aurea, as if surprised. "But I've never been anything else, mother. I've never had a moment's happiness out of it and never shall—though that, of course," she added cheerfully, "serves one right for misplacing one's affections."

"Is there nothing I can do, darling," said her mother, almost timidly.

"Nothing, thank you, mother dear. I am too ill."

"Ill, darling? You didn't tell me that. What is it?"

"I am ill," said Aurea slowly, "of an illness which I haven't the strength to get well of." When this had sunk into her mother's mind, she continued fiercely, "And even if I had the strength, I haven't the will. And if I could have the will, I wouldn't."

Mrs. Howard had nothing to say.

"And now, as I am so very tired," said Aurea conversationally, "and have all my packing to finish, I think I had better go to bed, and having a clear conscience I expect to sleep well, so good night, darling, and don't worry."

"Good night, my pet. I'll try not to."

At the door Aurea paused to say, "I shan't be seeing Valentine again. If he telephones before I go, I'm not there. But when I have gone will you ring him up, mother, and give him my love, and say I'll never forget him."

Mrs. Howard looked up with a stricken face. "Oh, Aurea, my child," was all she could say.

Aurea came back and hugged her mother tightly. Then she went upstairs to bed. Her story has no end. Only, in time, she will be able to look back steadfastly on those few weeks, acknowledge her own folly without blenching, and laugh not unkindly, at her own pitiful inexperience. What she will think of Valentine by then is another question; but compassion will never be wanting.

Mrs. Howard sat for some time in silence. The fire had died down, and she felt chilly. She got up and looked around the room. Some cushions were lying in huddled disorder on the sofa. Mechanically she shook them up and laid them in their proper places.

"Oh, why didn't I guess and understand?" she said aloud. "But what could I have done? It's hard work being a mother."

She sighed deeply and, turning out the lights, went slowly upstairs. Outside her bedroom she paused in the darkness to listen, but there was no sound.

COLOPHON

This book is being reissued as part of Moyer Bell's *Angela Thirkell Series*. Readers may join the Thirkell Circle for free to receive notices of new titles in the series and to receive a newsletter, bookmarks, posters and more. Simply send in the enclosed card or write to the address below.

The text of this book was set in Caslon, a typeface designed by William Caslon I (1692-1766). This face designed in 1725 has gone through many incarnations. It was the mainstay of British printers for over one hundred years and remains very popular today. The version used here is Adobe Caslon. The display faces are Adobe Caslon Outline, Calligraphic 421, and Adobe Caslon.

Composed by Alabama Book Composition, Deatsville, Alabama.

The book was printed by
Data Reproductions, Rochester Hills, Michigan
on acid free paper.

Moyer Bell
Kymbolde Way
Wakefield, RI 02879